THE ENEMY STALKS

THE ENEMY STALKS

Betty Sullivan La Pierre

ISBN 1-59109-204-3

THE ENEMY STALKS

To my husband, Don who supported me fully while writing this book. Acknowlegement: I want to thank my publisher, Chuck McNeal of E-Pub2000 for giving me a chance to publish my work and for creating a great cover. Thanks to my critique group, WWS for their patience as they agonized over rewrite after rewrite: Robert Warren, for the man's point of view. Leila Anne Pina for her expertise of the English language. Selma Rubler for her fixing up those sentences that didn't sound right. Sue Edwards for making the plot work. I couldn't have done it without you all. God Bless.

CHAPTER ONE

Dirk Henderson punched the intercom on his desk. "Krubes, hold my calls."

"Yes sir."

Assuring himself privacy, he locked the office door from the inside, then paced the room. His fists clenched, he stopped at his desk and glanced down at the black and white photograph of a man releasing a hawk. "You bastard! The Agency tried to convince everyone you were dead, but I didn't buy it. That beard and long hair don't fool me. I'd recognize you with a sack over your head." A cynical chuckle escaped his lips. "How about that eye-patch? Is it for real, Casey?" he sneered.

Dirk's face turned crimson, clashing with his mop of thick red hair. "How the hell did that idiot miss you at such close range? They ought to call you Catman. You got more than nine lives and always land on your goddamn feet!"

He yanked out the desk chair, sat down and rummaged through the drawers for the voice changer. Placing it over the receiver, he keyed in a number and drummed his fingers on his thigh. When a male voice answered, he leaned forward, resting his elbows on the desk. "Interested in a heavy job? You'll have only one chance. I'll leave instructions at the usual place."

He dropped the phone back on the cradle and flopped back in his chair. A muscle twitched in his neck while his fingers formed a pyramid atop his chest. After a few moments, he picked up the photo and flipped it with his finger. "Well, Hawk Man, as you now call yourself, your bird-lovin' days are numbered."

Hawkman, chewing on a toothpick, leaned against the fender of his truck and folded his arms across his chest. His gaze stretched out over the flat piece of land, surrounded by tree covered hills. It soothed his soul. He inhaled deeply and smelled the clean crisp air that penetrated his lungs. Not many places left like this, he thought, savoring every inch of the open space.

The noise of chopper blades suddenly broke the silence and he cocked his head toward the distinct sound. Searching the horizon, he caught a glimpse of an unmarked helicopter passing high over Copco Lake. He spit out the toothpick, hooked his thumbs into the front pockets of his Levis and strolled down the dirt road watching the aircraft. Strange, he thought. Why this area? What's going on?

Stopping, with legs apart, he rocked back and forth on the heels of his cowboy boots while watching the chopper disappear over a distant hill, memories flooding his mind. A few he'd just as soon forget. But, over years of Agency service many of the experiences jolted his adrenalin. After the injury that forced him to wear an eye patch, the Agency denied him field work but offered him a desk job which he couldn't accept, so he took the disability retirement. Now, he missed the challenges.

He stared at the ground, sliding the toe of his boot back and forth in the dirt making half circles. Once he gets his life in order, he'll start a private investigation business. Well, one of these days soon. Maybe that would bring some excitement back into his life. He kicked a rock, and sent it skipping across the dirt road.

He exhaled loudly, pushed his cowboy hat back on his head, then plodded back to the pick-up where he reached through the open window and dragged out a long leather glove. Pulling it over his arm up to his elbow, he scanned the sky and let out a long, loud whistle that resonated through the air.

A few minutes later, he heard the falcon's cry. A smile etched his lips as he watched the hawk circle high above his head. God only knew how many times he'd given that bird a chance to go back to the wild, but he'd always chosen to return. He held the gloved arm high. "Come on boy."

The majestic bird set his wings, then gracefully soared downward, landing lightly on the outstretched arm. Hawkman spoke in soft cooing tones while walking back to the truck. Inside the cab, he placed the falcon on a portable perch where he fluffed his wings and settled for the ride home. Leaving a trail of dust behind, Hawkman headed for his cabin on the south side of Copco Lake.

⊹⊹⊹⊹⊹

Later, that same afternoon, on the north shore of the lake, Jennifer Morgan a young widow, sat on her dock fishing. Suddenly, a frightened cry from above made her glance up. She shaded her eyes from the glare of the sun and leaped from her chair when she recognized the strip of leather hanging from the osprey's leg. "Ossy, what are you doing loose? Hawkman said you needed at least six weeks to heal that cracked wing."

She'd rescued the half-drowned hawk from the lake several weeks earlier and rushed him to Hawkman, the man who'd earned the reputation for healing injured wild birds. He'd assured her the osprey would be well in about six weeks and that he'd care for him at his place. The last time she'd visited Ossy, he sat tethered to a perch inside Hawkman's cabin with his wing immobilized by a sling. He needed at least two more weeks for full recovery, so how'd he get loose? His strange cries bothered her. Something's wrong, she thought.

Jennifer reeled in her fishing line, dropped the rod on the dock table and jumped into her boat tied at the side of the dock. She steered the Mysterious Lady into the narrow channel near the bridge where the Klamath River dumps into Copco Lake.

The osprey immediately flew down and dipped above the helm as if leading the way. She followed him to Hawkman's dock, where he circled overhead, squawking as she tied up the boat. His strange behavior made her uneasy. Had Hawkman left the injured birds alone and some predatory animal got into the house? She glanced about the boat looking for some sort of weapon and picked up one of the oars, but decided that would be too awkward, so she opened her tackle box. The leather-sheathed filet knife happened to be the only thing in her gear that would serve the purpose, so she slipped it into her pocket and stepped onto the wooden dock. A feeling of dread shivered through her body, making her breath catch in her throat as she raced up the crooked dirt path toward Hawkman's A-frame cabin. When she twisted around the corner of the porch to reach the steps, she stopped abruptly. Her screams rent the air.

Hawkman lay crumbled on the stairs, his face and head were covered in blood. One arm was stretched out in front of him with a gun dangling from his fingers. She dropped to her knees beside him.

Not quite sure what to do, she gently shook his shoulder. "Hawkman, say something." Her heart lurched when he didn't respond. Then his eye lids and lips moved slightly. She put her ear close to his mouth, barely hearing his whisper. "Get help. Hurry"

She let out a long breath and sat back on her haunches. "Thank God you're alive." Scanning his bearded face, she gently pushed the blood soaked long hair off his forehead and came to the conclusion that the superficial wound to the scalp had caused the bleeding on his head and face. But that injury alone wouldn't have caused his apparent weakness. Maybe he'd been beaten up and had internal injuries. She quickly stepped over his body to go call for help when she noticed the puddle of blood near his right hip.

Yanking the fillet knife from its sheath, she sliced the leg of his jeans from the hem up until she exposed a bloody gaping hole in his thigh. Here's the real problem, she thought, reaching inside the door and grabbing a dish towel off the kitchen counter. She hastily folded it into a square and pressed it against the bubbling wound.

Hawkman suddenly raised his head and in a hoarse voice rasped, "Get help. Radio . . ." Then he dropped into unconsciousness, his head falling back against the wooden plank porch with a thud.

Jennifer struggled against Hawkman's large bulky frame as she pulled his belt through the loops of his jeans. When she finally got it free, she lashed it snugly around his thigh to hold the towel against the oozing puncture. She wiped her bloody hands down the legs of her jeans before racing into the house to the radio. Flipping on the transmitter, she tuned it to the emergency channel and grabbed the microphone. Her voice shook. "Need ambulance. Hawkman's been shot. South side of lake, his place."

When Fire Chief Ruskin acknowledged the message, Jennifer dropped the mike and hurried back to Hawkman's side. She knelt beside his body and gripped his shoulders, her mouth close to his ear. "Help is coming."

Panic filled her as his head lolled from side to side without any response. "Don't you dare die on me." Tears welled in her eyes as she cradled his head. "Oh God, please don't let him die."

When he moaned, she laughed in relief and brushed the tears from her cheeks. She laid his head down gently, then checked the make-shift bandage on his thigh, making sure it wasn't too tight. When the sound of the Fire Station siren reverberated through the hills and across the lake, she raised her head. A comforting sound. Help is coming. When the ambulance finally pulled into the driveway, she waved frantically. "Over here. Hurry."

Within minutes, the men had Hawkman strapped securely on a gurney, rolling him out to the waiting vehicle. Jennifer ran alongside, intending to go to the hospital, then Hawkman raised his head and looked at her with glazed eyes. "Take care of the birds."

She stepped back and watched the paramedics load him into the back of the ambulance. One of the men, his hand on the door, glanced in her direction. She hesitated for a moment, then shook her head. He slammed the door and the vehicle sped off toward Yreka, leaving her standing alone.

She watched them disappear around the bend of the road as the haunting sound of the siren faded. Suddenly, several police cars screeched to a halt in front of the house, jarring her back to her senses. Uniformed men swarmed over the area within minutes.

In a state of shock, Jennifer wandered through the yard before coming to a standstill behind the yellow security tape that the police had quickly strung around Hawkman's cabin. She was staring at the open front door when suddenly an arm slipped around her shoulders. Startled, she jumped and gasped in relief. "Amelia. I'm so glad to see you."

Amelia and her husband, Jake, had not only befriended Jennifer when she moved to the lake, but were the store owners and volunteers of the fire department. They had a two-way radio in the Copco Lake store so they could be abreast of all the happenings within the small lake community.

"I came as soon as I heard the message."

Jennifer clung to her hand, grateful for the presence of this motherly woman.

A team of officers marched out of the house and headed for a nearby stand of pine trees. Frowning, Jennifer watched them wondering what they were doing. Then she stiffened when she realized they were examining another body.

"Oh my God." She grabbed Amelia's arm. "There's someone else out there. I had no idea." Then she heard one of the technicians call for the coroner's wagon. "Oh no," she whispered, closing her eyes and covering her mouth.

At that moment, a rugged faced man in a dark rumpled suit, his tie knot hanging mid way down his chest approached her.

"Excuse me, I'm Detective Williams. Are you the lady who called for help?"

Pushing loose wisps of hair behind her ears, she looked him in the eye. "Yes. I'm Jennifer Morgan"

He took a small paper pad from his pocket. "I need to ask you some questions?"

Amelia stepped back out of the way.

"Are you a relation to the victim?

"Which one?"

He raised a brow. "Did you know both men?"

I know Hawkman. But, I didn't see the body of the other man, so I can't answer that."

'What's Hawkman's real name?"

"Tom Casey."

Williams jotted it down, then glanced at her again. "Were you present when the shooting occurred?"

Jennifer gnawed her lip. "No." She deliberated whether to tell him how the osprey's strange behavior led her here. It sounded ridiculous, but the detective looked like an understanding person, so she told him. He took a few notes then stuck the pad into his pocket.

"Thank you Ms. Morgan." He walked away and joined a group of officers collected near the house.

Jennifer turned on her heel, stepped over the yellow tape and marched toward the front door. Those poor ailing birds were probably frantic with fear by now.

Detective Williams, noticing her movement, ran toward the house and headed her off. "Ma'am, you can't go in there. We'll call if we need anything further from you. You're free to go home."

Amelia stepped up and grasped Jennifer by the arm. "Honey, let's go."

Pulling away, she shoved past the officer. "Not until I get the birds."

"We'll come back and get them later," Amelia urged.

Ignoring her plea, Jennifer proceeded up the porch stairs.

Williams placed his arm across the door, blocking her passage. "I said, you can't go in there."

She narrowed her hazel eyes and glared at him. "Hawkman asked me to take care of the sick birds and that's what I'm going to do." She gestured toward the scurrying police and technicians "They're not used to all this commotion. It's frightening and upsetting. I won't leave without them."

The detective let out a long breath and dropped his arm. "Okay, but don't touch anything else." He escorted her inside and watched her take a large leather glove off a table and pull it over her hand.

Her jaw set, she moved slowly toward the falcon sitting on a perch in the corner of the room. What if he won't get on my arm, she thought, feeling the warm sweat beads forming on her forehead. She began cooing in a soft voice. "Come on Pretty Boy, I'm taking you home with me." Gently, she brushed the gloved hand against the bird's talons, but her heart dropped after several attempts when the bird shied from her. She glanced at Amelia in despair. I'll try one more time, she thought, then smiled in triumph when the falcon stepped on her arm, squawking and flapping his wings. "Good boy," she said, releasing the tether.

Williams scratched his head when she walked past him speaking softly to the hawk.

"It's okay Pretty Boy, I'"m not going to drop you. I'm taking you home with me where you'll be safe until Hawkman returns." Before leaving the cabin, she turned to Amelia. "My boat's at Hawkman's dock, so I'll drive it back. Do you think you could bring the other hawk and the perches?" Then she grimaced at the falcon on her arm. "I hope he likes the ride and stays put."

Amelia called one of the officers nearby to help. After they finished putting the perches and the remaining hawk into her car, she drove to Jennifer's house. She pulled into the drive at the same time Jennifer came around the corner, the falcon still on her arm.

"Thank goodness, he didn't fight you on the way over. That beak of his could have torn holes out of you." Amelia rested her hands on her ample hips. "You know that falcon is about as big as you are. Let me get these perches set up inside before your arm gives out completely."

Jennifer instructed Amelia to cover the carpet in front of the fireplace with a sheet and set up the perches on each end. Relieved to unload the heavy hawk, Jennifer tethered both birds to their respective thrones and rubbed her arm. "He is heavier than he looks, my arm is throbbing."

"That, I can see," Amelia said, setting the water tins on the counter. "Is there anything else you'd like me to do."

"No. Thank you so much. I'm going to shower and head for the hospital."

Amelia left and Jennifer filled the water troughs and attached them to the perches, then undressed in the laundry room, throwing her blood smeared clothes into a cold water soak. After cleaning up, she drove into Yreka.

Jennifer tapped her foot impatiently as she stood behind another couple at the hospital receptionist's desk. When they finally departed, she stepped up to the counter and spoke with urgency. "What's Hawkman's room number?"

The woman looked puzzled. "Who?"

Jennifer rubbed her hand across her forehead and shook her head. "I'm sorry. I'm not thinking straight. Tom Casey's room."

The receptionist smiled and glanced through the records. "He's still in the surgery recovery room, but doing fine. Check back with me in an hour and I'll be able to tell you his room number."

Hunger pangs rippled through Jennifer's stomach. A good way to pass the time, she thought; find the cafeteria and have a bite to eat. She picked up someone's left-over newspaper but couldn't concentrate on the print. The quick sandwich felt like a heavy rock in her stomach as she hurried back to the receptionist's desk. Hawkman still hadn't been moved out of recovery, so she paced while the minutes dragged.

Finally, Jennifer got the information and entered Hawkman's room. She stood quietly by his bedside, fidgeting with the strap on her purse for several minutes before he finally stirred. He struggled to open his eyes, trying to focus on her face, but winced at the light. "Is my eye-patch around?" he mumbled.

She had wondered about the condition of that eye and was gratified that it looked normal. Finding the black patch in the table beside his bed, she helped him maneuver it around his bandaged head. He settled back on the pillow and drifted off to sleep. Satisfied that his condition wasn't critical and he seemed comfortable, she slipped out of the room.

❖❖❖❖❖

The next day, when she entered the hospital room, Hawkman greeted her with a smile. She sat down on the chair next to his bed. "You certainly look better than you did last night."

"My head and leg hurt like hell, but my mind's clear." He grinned slightly, then shifted his position, wincing when he moved his leg. "Ah, that's better. So were you able to get the birds out of the house?"

"Yes. I took them to my place because of all the commotion around yours."

When he didn't meet her gaze, she sensed immediately that he didn't want to dwell on the incident, so she changed the subject. "I'm worried about Ossy. Did you know he's out flying around with that tether hanging from his leg? What if he gets tangled in the tree branches?"

Hawkman waved his hand, dismissing her fears. "That osprey's fine. I always say six weeks for recovery as a precautionary measure, but he's young and strong. That wing's healed. And as far as the tether goes, it's a soft leather that he'll nip off in no time with that sharp beak."

"Well, that's a load off my mind." She noticed Hawkman seemed uncomfortable and his gaze shifted to the other patient in the room. "Is there anything you need?"

"Yeah. As a matter of fact, how about a ride home in the morning."

She frowned. "They're releasing you? Isn't that a little soon?"

"I wanted to leave today, but the doctor insisted I wait until tomorrow because of the head injury." Again, he glanced around the room, not meeting her stare. "Hospitals are not my favorite place."

Tomorrow she'd question him in the privacy of the car about the shooting; today, she'd keep the conversation light. "You know, if it hadn't been for Ossy, you might have bled to death. Who would have believed a bird could sense that a man's in danger."

Hawkman nodded. "Sometimes animals surprise you."

Jennifer grinned. "That's true." She rose, feeling she'd been there long enough. "Well, I better get going. What time should I come?"

"Somewhere between ten and eleven o'clock."

On the drive home, she pondered the shooting, knowing Hawkman had purposely avoided the topic. Maybe he'd never tell her and she'd read about the sordid story in the newspaper. She let out an audible sigh as she turned onto the bridge going over the Klamath River, then stopped at the cluster of mailboxes which were only a half block from her house.

When she opened the front door, the falcon greeted her by flapping his wings and letting out a loud squawk. She dropped the stack of mail onto the kitchen counter and strolled toward him, cocking her head. "Pretty Boy, are you trying to tell me you're hungry and want to go hunting?"

She pulled back her long brown hair, securing it at the nape of her neck. When she picked up the leather glove and the falcon hood, which prevented the hawk from getting distracted, he immediately settled down in what appeared to be anticipation. This time, he stepped onto her arm the first time she brushed the glove against his talons and even let her slip the hood over his head. She released the tether from the perch and headed for the door.

By the time she reached the end of the driveway, she had to stop and catch her breath. She rested her arm on the fence for a few moments. "I'm going to have to get in better shape if I'm going to carry you around, Pretty Boy. You're heavy." The hawk moved his hooded head back and forth as if he understood her every word. It thrilled her that he no longer acted frightened. Wanting to make sure he continued to do so, she adjusted her arm and continued talking to him as she marched away from the houses.

When she reached the wooded area bordering the hills, she cautiously removed the hood and held her arm upward as she'd seen Hawkman do many times. The bird flapped his wings and lifted skyward, circling in graceful flight before disappearing toward the south.

Jennifer sat down on a large boulder nearby, rubbing her shoulder and flexing her trembling arm. She planned to do some exercises to make it stronger. After an hour, she pushed loose strands of hair out of her eyes and anxiously searched the sky. Where is that bird?

Then, from somewhere behind her, she heard the hawk's cry. She whirled around and spotted him flying high overhead. Relieved, she quickly pulled on the leather glove and held up her arm. "Come on, Pretty Boy. I'm waiting."

What a beautiful sight, the thought, watching the bird glide down and gently land on her arm. Walking back toward the house and trying not to think of the pain in her shoulder, she let her thoughts wander. Who shot Hawkman and why? Who was the dead man under the pines? It dawned on her that she knew very little about Hawkman and it made her nervous to find this secretive man so intriguing.

CHAPTER TWO

Hawkman sat on the edge of the hospital bed, his face distorted by anger. "I can walk out of here under my own steam."

The nurse glared at him with disapproval. "Sir, it's the hospital's policy that we wheel you out." She tossed her head and whirled the chair around on its rear wheels, pushing it rapidly toward the door.

Then he spotted Jennifer stepping out of the way of the charging nurse. "Bring that damn wheel chair back," he yelled.

Her jaw set, the nurse returned. He slid off the bed, refusing her help and flopped into the chair, grumbling loudly. "You win."

On the drive home, Jennifer remained quiet and withdrawn. He sensed she wondered why all this had happened. He twisted around in the seat and faced her. "I know you're curious about the gun battle. And you'll find it hard to believe that I can't explain it. All I know is that some guy came after me."

She gave him a quizzical sideways glance. "Why?"

He shook his head and stared out the window. "I'm not sure, but I guarantee I'm going to find out."

When they reached his cabin, Jennifer followed as he limped inside on his crutches. "Can I fix you a bite to eat?"

"No thanks. I ate breakfast. Can't say I enjoyed it that much, but it filled me up."

After she left, he flopped down on the couch and stared into space. Before leaving the hospital, he'd called Bill Broadwell, his old boss at the Agency, and told him what had happened. Broadwell feared that Hawkman's old nemesis had found him. The Agency offered to protect him if he'd go underground.

Not wanting to be obligated to them anymore, Hawkman refused the offer and informed Bill he'd flush the culprit out on his own. If this stemmed back to the time Sylvia died, then he had another worry, Jennifer Morgan. She'd be vulnerable to anyone who came after him. Maybe he could persuade her to leave the area for awhile.

Picking up the crutches from the floor, he swung his six foot two frame onto his good leg and hobbled to the window that overlooked the lake. He stared out across the water toward Jennifer's place. How could he convince her, without explaining why it would be safer, that she go away for awhile?

⋅⊤⋅⊁⋅⊤⋅⊁⋅⊤⋅⊁⋅⊤⋅⊁⋅⊤⋅⊁⋅⊤⋅⊁⋅⊤⋅⊁⋅⊤⋅⊁⋅→

After a restless night, Jennifer arose before the sun peeked over the surrounding hills. She brushed her hair into a pony tail, tied the sash of her robe around her small waist and went into the kitchen. She poured herself a cup of coffee from the automatic maker then strolled out on the deck, loving the quiet solitude of the morning. There wasn't one ripple on the lake's surface as the sun's rays danced across the water reflecting a picture of the trees surrounding the shoreline. Across the channel, Ossy sat like a king on his tree branch, waiting for his first chance to dive for a meal.

The sight delighted her and she mocked the osprey's whistle, then waited for him to twist his head in her direction before she called to him. "I haven't forgotten you, Ossy. I promise to catch you some fish today."

The majestic hawk cocked his head back and forth, then let loose with a response before spreading his wings and gracefully diving toward the water. Jennifer noticed the leather strip had disappeared from the bird's leg. Hawkman was right.

She watched the bird soar just above the water, drop his talons down like a plane's landing gear and skim them along the surface, leaving a spray in his wake. Puzzled, she leaned over the railing and studied the bird's antics. "What in the world are you doing?" she asked aloud.

The osprey lifted up, shook the water from his wings, circled, then repeated the procedure.

Jennifer reared her head back and laughed. "Now I get it. You're cleaning your talons."

She leaned against the porch post enjoying the bird's maneuvers until he returned to his perch, fluffed his feathers and stretched his wings to dry in the warm sunlight. Ambling back into the house, she stopped in front of the falcon's perch. "Good morning, Pretty Boy."

Then her attention drifted to the other hawk brought from the cabin. Although he appeared healthy, she didn't know the reason Hawkman had him in captivity. She studied the bird and ran a finger over the crown of his head while sipping her coffee. Rotating his head, the hawk watched her every move. Not as aggressive as the falcon, he actually tolerated her petting. "We need to find a name for you."

She stood back and observed him. "Since you're so rusty-red, let's call you 'Ruddy'. And it wouldn't surprise me a bit if you weren't ready to be freed." She hated the thought of it, but knew it would be best for him to return to the wild as soon as possible. "I better speak to Hawkman about you."

A noise from the side yard distracted her and she peeked out the dining room drapes. A man unloading firewood from a truck was stacking it onto pallets in her side yard. Setting her coffee cup down, she hurried through the laundry room, out the side door and leaned over the wrought iron bannister that surrounded the small porch. "Excuse me, sir, what are you doing?"

The man glanced up from his work and smiled. "Morning ma'am. I'm delivering your firewood. Is this where you wanted it stacked?"

"Oh, yes, that's fine," she stammered, feeling foolish that she'd completely forgotten she'd ordered a cord of oak. Since her husband's death, it had taken her awhile to get used to all the responsibilities of a home. And ordering firewood is something one did long before the winter hit.

Mid-morning, she glanced out the living room window and noticed Ossy still on his branch across the channel. She studied the two hawks on their perches in her living room. "If I go fishing, will you two behave yourselves while I'm on the dock?" When Ruddy nodded in return, she laughed.

Her arms loaded with fishing gear, she'd no more stepped out the sliding glass door onto the deck when the phone rang. "Darn." She quickly slipped back inside, banging the fishing rod against the facing, as she hurried to answer. "Hello." She frowned when greeted only by the sound of heavy breathing. "Who's there?"

The line went dead. Shrugging, she hung up figuring it must have been a wrong number.

Jennifer's dock, a sixteen by sixteen foot structure, made of the latest materials and flotation devices, gleamed of newness. Thank goodness, she'd no longer have to worry about the otters and muskrats making nests underneath, scaring away the fish. She'd adorned the new structure with a heavy round wooden table, fitted with a huge umbrella that sheltered her from the sun's rays. Four brightly painted red wooden chairs circled the table. Proud of her neat dock, she smiled as she baited her hook, concentrating on that big trout she'd seen leap out of the water more than once this past week.

After several casts, her disappointment grew, as the only thing she could catch were the small yellow perch. Most she threw back, but the ones that swallowed the hook and would die, she dropped into a bucket beside her. Periodically, she'd whistle her signal to Ossy and throw one of the small fish out into the water. She loved watching the hawk lift from his branch, soar down in front of her and clasp the prey in his talons. He'd return to his branch or fly off to an unknown place to eat his meal. But he always returned.

‹·⫶·⫶·⫶·⫶·⫶·›

The dock swayed with Hawkman's weight as he stepped onto the wooden gang plank. Jennifer glanced around and came to her feet. Surprise and concern showing on her face.

"What are you doing out so soon?" she asked.

He stopped, balancing himself on his crutches. "I figured I owed you a better explanation of what happened. Is this a good time to talk?"

"Sure." She reeled in her line and moved toward him, laying a hand on his arm. "But let's go up to the house where you'll be more comfortable."

He glanced down where she'd touched him, shocked at the feeling that had surged through his body. Something he hadn't experienced since Sylvia. For an instant, he froze in his tracks and watched her walk up the gang plank. He'd come to the lake to be alone and sort out his future plans. He didn't intend to get involved with anyone.

Giving himself a few moments to gain his composure, he followed awkwardly, hopping up the stairs leading to the back deck. Jennifer hung her fishing pole on the rod rack outside the door, then went inside tossing her jacket on the back of the leather couch. "Want some coffee?"

"Sounds great." Hawkman made his way into the living room where the falcon flapped his wings and squawked a greeting of recognition. "Hey there, boy. Looks like you're being treated like a king." He sat on the raised, river-rock hearth of the huge fireplace and grimaced when he stretched out his leg.

Jennifer waited for him to get comfortable before handing him a steaming mug. She sat on the couch facing him. "How are the injuries?"

"Head's healing great, as you can see, no bandage. The bullet just grazed my scalp, but the leg hurts like hell," he said, lifting it into a better position.

"I thought I saw a little pained reaction."

Uncomfortable, not knowing how to start, he sat in silence for a few moments, his large hands wrapped tightly around the cup. "Everything happened so damn fast that day, I'm not sure where to begin." He set the mug down beside him and clenched his hands together, wondering what questions were running through her mind.

"Why not start at the beginning?"

He nodded. "I'd just come home from taking the falcon for a hunt and fixed myself a sandwich at the kitchen table. Suddenly, this big guy kicked open my front door and aimed a gun at my head. I shoved the table into him and dove behind the couch, but not fast enough. That's when I caught the hit in the leg. I returned fire and he fled out the door. But I managed to make it to the porch before he got out of range. I fired and thought I hit him, but he fired back." He pointed at his head. "That's when I got this. Knocked me for a loop."

Jennifer, listening intently, pulling her jeans-clad legs up onto the couch and clasping her cup with both hands. "Yes, go on."

He took a deep breath. "I figured with the heavy bleeding from my leg, I'd better do something fast before I passed out. I tried to make it to the radio, but just got inside the door, where I grabbed the osprey's perch for support, but instead fell backwards, taking the perch with me. I managed to untie his tether from the the rail, but not from his leg. Little did I realize he'd be my salvation." He put a hand on his uninjured thigh and shook his head. "That's when I must have passed out, because I don't remember much after that."

She stared at him. "Why is someone trying to kill you? There has to be a reason."

He sighed. "I figured you'd ask that question. Guess it's time you knew more about me."

Leaning forward, she furrowed her brow. "What do you mean?"

"I used to work for the Agency and the job took me into some very explosive situations. I speak several foreign languages fluently, which allowed me to penetrate organizations of other countries. Over the years I supplied a lot of inside information to our government."

She gasped, her eyes wide. "So, you were a spy?"

He nodded. "Yes. My cover somehow got blown on my last assignment and the Agency brought me back to the States. They think we had an internal leak within my department. However, after a few months, things returned to normal and I thought it had pretty much blown over." His expression turned grave. He grabbed a crutch from the floor and limped to the window overlooking the lake, his back toward Jennifer. Staring out over the water, his mind drifted to those ominous days. "That is, until one morning my wife Sylvia took my car to run some errands, because hers was in the shop. I watched her leave. Half a block from the house, the car exploded. She was pregnant with our first child."

Jennifer covered her face with her hands. "Oh my God," she whispered.

He swallowed hard to dislodge the lump forming in his throat. "I vowed to find the creeps responsible and make them pay." He looked at her with an expression of deadly intent. "I found them all, except one, the leader. I promised over Sylvia's grave to find that bastard, but it looks like he's found me first."

⊹⊱⚓⊰⊹⊱⚓⊰⊹⊱⚓⊰⊹⊱⚓⊰⊹

The tone of his voice made a chill slither down Jennifer's spine. And from the look on his face, she knew he wouldn't hesitate to kill the ones responsible for the death of his wife and unborn child.

He pointed at the black eye patch. "I acquired this injury in a scuffle with one of the scum. The Agency wouldn't allow me to work in the field anymore, so I retired. I came to Copco Lake in hopes of starting my life over as a private investigator." He turned back toward the window.

Jennifer glanced at his back, her voice low. "Did you kill the leader the other day?"

Hawkman twisted his head around. "Hell no. Just another flunky hired by him." He leaned on the crutch, his hands clenched into tight fists. "But it's just as well I put the guy out of his misery, because his boss would have killed him sooner or later."

Jennifer winced and clutched the front of her blouse. "Why?"

"Because he failed in his mission to kill me."

Startled at his explanation, she stiffened, dropping her feet from the couch to the floor. "You mean he'd kill his own men just because they failed to get you?"

He hobbled back to the hearth and looked at her with a cold and calculated stare. "Yes. Men like him have no conscience and kill for much less. That's why I think you're in danger."

Jennifer leaped off the couch and pointed a finger at her own chest. "Me? Why am I in danger?"

"If this bastard has spotted you hanging around me, he'll use you. It's too dangerous for you to stay here."

She folded her arms and crossed the room. "I don't believe it. This is all too far-fetched. Sounds like some spy movie."

Hawkman limped toward her and grabbed her arm. "Let me tell you how far-fetched it is. When my old boss asks me to go underground with the Agency's protection, things are mighty damned dangerous." He dropped his hand from her arm and his voice fell to a pleading tone. "All I'm suggesting is that you leave the area for a little while, until I can flush the creep out and end this."

"I'll think about it." Jennifer walked over to Ruddy's perch and quickly changed the subject. "I don't know what ailed Ruddy when you took him in, but he definitely seems healthy now. You might want to think about setting him free."

Hawkman threw up his hands in surrender and in faltering steps moved toward the hawk. He looked deep into Jennifer's hazel eyes. "We're not done with this. I want you to think about it seriously and make a decision quickly. There's not much time." He then turned his attention to the hawk and stroked his head. "You've done a good job with him. I'll take these birds home today and get them out of your way."

She put a hand on her hip. "You're not ready to take that falcon out to hunt. I've been taking him out and I can handle it. You just leave them here until you're more stable on your feet."

His face lit up with surprise. "You've taken him hunting?"

Laughing, she glanced at the falcon with pride. "Yes, but he sure worried me. He stayed gone for over an hour. I thought Pretty Boy had left forever."

Hawkman threw back his head and guffawed, "Pretty Boy! You've given him a name." Then he pointed at the bird. "You think that falcon is pretty?"

She straightened, feeling her face grow hot. "Yes. I've called him that ever since he's been here."

"Hey, no wonder he's so content. He's hunted and been christened with a name. Before I know it, he'll be walking and talking."

Jennifer turned away. An awkward silence filled the room.

"Hey, I'm only teasing. I think it's great you've gone to all that trouble. But are you sure you want to do it for a few more days?"

"I'm positive. I've enjoyed both Pretty Boy and Ruddy."

He snickered good naturally. "Ruddy?" Shaking his head, he moved over in front of the hawk. "Well, Ruddy, guess we better free you before you become too dependent on humans like your cousin, Pretty Boy."

Jennifer reached over and stroked the hawk's head for the last time. "I'll miss him. I'd have tamed him in no time, but he's better off in the wild."

Hawkman dropped the crutch and whispered to the hawk while

undoing the tether. Ruddy nodded his head up and down. He gently took the bird into his hands and limped out the front door. Jennifer grabbed both crutches before following him, worried that he might trip or fall, tearing open his wound.

Stopping in the middle of the driveway, Hawkman spoke softly while slipping his hands down the bird's back. Once the wings were released, the hawk flapped frantically and he gently tossed him skyward. "Take care, Ruddy ole' boy." He put his fists on his hips and watched the hawk soar high into the sky until he appeared but a speck.

Jennifer noticed Hawkman's features soften. He obviously took great pleasure in setting the hawk free. When she finally pulled her gaze away from him and glanced up into the sky, Ruddy had disappeared. After a few quiet moments, she handed Hawkman the crutches.

He took a deep breath and his expression turned serious. "I hate to belabor the subject, but I can't emphasize the danger you're in and you need to leave the area while I deal with this situation. Make your decision quickly."

She set her jaw firmly and answered emphatically. "I told you I'd think about it."

He said goodbye and she could tell by the way he opened the truck door that his patience had grown thin. She heard the phone ringing, waved as he backed out of the driveway and dashed into the house.

⟨⁑⟩•⟨⁑⟩•⟨⁑⟩•⟨⁑⟩•⟨⁑⟩

Hoping he wouldn't sound anxious, John took several deep breaths while waiting for Jennifer to answer.

"Hello," she said, sounding winded.

"Jennifer, John Alexander here. Where you'd run from, the back forty?"

"Almost," she laughed. "What a surprise to hear from you twice in one month."

"I thought about how nice it would be to go fishing and take a look at the old homestead again. I've really missed my Copco Lake visits since the death of my parents." He cleared his throat. "Been catching anything?"

"The fishing's not too good right now, but we're not without excitement."

"What would disturb the peace and quiet of Copco Lake?"

"A shooting."

"Oh! Anyone I know?"

"Someone took some pot shots at Hawkman and wounded him in the head and leg, but he's okay. He killed the assailant."

A short silence followed, then John cleared his throat again. "I see. Take that as a warning, Jennifer."

"What do you mean?" She sounded puzzled.

"He's made a lot of enemies through the years. Maybe you should stay away from him."

"You know Hawkman personally?"

John closed his eyes and squeezed the bridge of his nose between his fingers, knowing he'd said too much. "I met him years ago when he worked for my father. He's always been trouble."

"John. . ."

"Gotta go. Another call coming in."

He hung up, relieved. Thank God they didn't kill him. Mopping his brow with his handkerchief, he leaned back in his chair and recalled the day Jennifer told him about taking the almost drowned osprey to a man called Hawkman. The vision of Jim Anderson had appeared in his mind. Jim had studied birds in college and after graduation entered the Agency. He'd prompted her for the description of the large, muscular man with an eye-patch. He'd heard about Jim's eye injury through the grapevine. It wasn't long after that, Jim suddenly dropped out of sight. The Agency claimed he'd been killed on a mission, but it all fit the picture. Being the son of an agent himself, John knew how they worked. Jim had been given a new identity: Tom Casey.

He clenched his hands together on the top of his desk. His stomach burned with guilt when he thought about how he'd revealed Jim's whereabouts to that bastard on the phone. But he had no choice when the son-of-bitch threatened his family. These men were cold-blooded killers and meant business. He couldn't take the chance.

Now he wondered how involved Jennifer might be. Were she and Jim just friends, or more? If she got in their way, they'd waste her, just like they did Sylvia. God, he didn't even want to think about it. He wiped his face again with his hanky. She could be in real danger and end up a pawn in a deadly game.

CHAPTER THREE

Hawkman's leg hurt like hell, so he pulled close to the mailbox at the end of his driveway and stretched his arm out the truck window to grab his mail. He immediately noticed the letter from Bill Broadwell. Pulling out his 'Buck Boot Knife', he slit the envelope's edge.

Bill had spoken with the higher-ups in the Agency. Since Hawkman still worked for them when the leak in his department occurred along with Sylvia's assassination, they felt responsible, agreeing he should now go underground where they could protect him.

He crumbled the paper in his fist and slammed his hand against the steering wheel. "No, I'll find that bastard on my own," he hissed.

A nerve twitched in his jaw as he stared out the windshield. He had to convince Jennifer to leave the lake.

The next morning he drove to Jennifer's house and spotted her at the wood stack struggling with a big piece of oak firewood. He intercepted her as fast as his injured leg would allow and took the huge piece of wood from her arms.

She dusted off her hands as she followed him inside. "It's cold this morning and I thought a nice cozy fire and a cup of hot chocolate would kill the chill."

The room soon filled with warmth. Hawkman shed his jacket and stood silently warming his back in front of the fireplace. He wondered how he'd broach the subject of her leaving, since she'd done such a good job of soft pedaling his concerns yesterday.

Jennifer emerged from the kitchen carrying two steaming mugs. She stood beside him as he took a deep draw of the hot chocolate. Feeling his insides warm, he set the cup on the hearth and cleared his throat. "I received a letter from the Agency yesterday." He watched for her reaction, but saw none. If she felt anything, she did a damn good job of hiding it.

"Oh. And what do they want?"

"They're pushing hard for me to go underground."

She turned and stared into the fire. "Are you?"

He shook his head. "No. Have you thought about what I suggested?"

"Yes, and I've decided not to leave."

Frustrated, he picked up the mug and drained it. "Jennifer, you don't seem to understand. Whoever's out there will use you to get to me. Just like they did Sylvia."

With a flip of her hand, she brushed his concern away. "They're after you, not me. And I'm really sorry about Sylvia. But it sounds like her death was accidental. Whoever planted the bomb meant for you to drive away in that car, not her. I appreciate your concern, but I'm staying put."

He glared at her and brushed his hand across his beard. "Anyone ever tell you that you're a stubborn woman?"

Jennifer remained silent, her hazel eyes locked with his. He blew out his breath and pointed a finger at her. "Then you're going to follow my instructions."

Putting a hand on her hip, she lifted a brow. "Oh?"

Somehow he had to convince her how quickly this dangerous situation had escalated. "You have to stay alert to everything going on around you. Beware of strange cars, new people, anything that strikes you as peculiar or unusual. If you see anything that leaves a question in your mind, call me immediately. Do you understand?"

Her expression questioned him, but she answered. "Yes, of course."

Hoping he sounded more controlled than he felt, he continued. "It might make the difference between life or death."

She looked surprised, but didn't comment. He could see that

she had no idea of the dark cloud of danger encroaching upon both their lives. Glancing at his watch, he limped toward the front door. "I'm going into town. Need anything?"

Jennifer followed him. "No, thanks."

When they stepped into the yard, the loud honking of a flock of Canadian geese overhead made them both glance upward.

She shaded her eyes. "Aren't they beautiful flying in that almost perfect "V" formation? But good grief, listen to that racket. No wonder they're called 'honkers'."

Hawkman looked down at this lovely woman, knowing her innocent life had just become endangered. "You've definitely mastered topic changing." He stepped toward his truck. "Yes, they're beautiful and they're good eating. When the hunting season starts next week, hopefully I'll bag one."

He climbed into the 4X4 and rolled down the window. "Just remember what I said. Keep your eyes and ears open. And for God's sake, be careful."

"Don't worry." She waved as he backed out of the driveway.

He drove away with a heavy heart. She'd made up her mind and he saw no way of changing it, short of kidnapping her.

Trying to ease the tension and worry within his mind, he decided to think about something else. He'd get ready for the goose season. What fishing did for Jennifer, hunting did for him. So over the next few days, he prepared.

He chewed on a toothpick while sitting at the kitchen table, cleaning the goose gun. Seemed like after he'd quit smoking, he never got over that urge of having something in his mouth.

After putting the final shine on the long barrel, he placed the gun in the closet, then went outside. First, he scanned the area for intruders before he pulled the scull boat from the storage shed and placed it upside down on the lawn. Wetting it down with the hose, he scrubbed the hull with a stiff brush. Focused on his task, he looked up in surprise to see Jennifer, her purse flung over her shoulder, strolling across the lawn toward him. Her long brown hair lifting like strands of silk in the breeze.

She stopped a few feet away from the spraying water. "Hi. You look mighty busy."

He shut off the water nozzle and dried his hands on his jeans. "Just getting ready for goose hunting."

She tapped the hull with the toe of her shoe. "What kind of a boat is this? It's different from anything I've ever seen."

Relieved that she didn't seem upset any more, he was more than happy to explain. He reached down and flipped it over. "It's a scull boat."

Bending over, she peered inside the shallow craft. "How do you get it to move? Do you use a special motor?"

Hawkman pointed to different areas within the boat. "You lie down in the bottom and push these pedals with your feet. That creates the energy that propels you across the water. See those peek holes? You look through them to see where you're going. It's called sculling."

She grinned and wrinkled her lightly freckled nose. "Well, it's certainly an odd looking thing."

Suddenly, a twig snapped behind Hawkman. He jerked his head around and inspected the tree lined area, relieved to see a squirrel jumping from one branch to another. Turning his attention back to Jennifer, he continued his lesson. "The hunter dresses in camouflage matching the color of the boat. He lies down in the bottom and pulls the cap or cover over him. He hopes the flock of geese will mistake him for a floating log." He pretended to lift a shotgun and line up the sight. "And when he's about thirty yards from the flock. . . . POW!"

Jennifer, leaped back and laughed. "But what if he misses?"

"Then they're spooked for the day."

"Would that be so terrible?"

He eyed her seriously. "Why, it would be a disaster."

She walked around the craft studying it. "What would you do next?"

"Well." He squinted and pointed across the lake. "See that meadow?"

Jennifer followed the direction of his finger and nodded. "Yes."

"If you look closely, you'll see a little gully that runs toward the water. I'd get down in it and crawl slowly on my stomach toward the flock, being very careful that the sentry goose doesn't spot me."

She shot a look at him. "What would he do?"

"He'd honk out a loud warning and all the birds would take off in flight. I'd be fouled again."

Jennifer shook her head in amusement. "You men, what you won't do for a goose."

A grin twitched the corners of his mouth and he lifted his brows. "Careful, that could be taken two ways."

She blushed, making him feel bad that he'd made that statement, so he quickly changed the conversation to another direction.

"If I get lucky and bag a goose, would you cook it for me?"

"I've never cooked a goose in my life." Jennifer quickly caught herself and groaned. "Oh my, I'm having a terrible time with words today. Yes, I'll certainly give it a try. Now, let's get off this goose subject." She took a quick breath. "The reason I stopped by is Amelia and I are going into town for the 'Fall Festival'. Any supplies you'd like me to pick up while I'm there?"

"No, but thanks for asking."

"Okay, see ya later." She waved and headed toward the road where she'd parked.

Hawkman stared after her car until she drove out of sight around the bend, then dropped down on his haunches beside the skull boat. "A cooked goose," he mumbled. "Will that be my fate?" He reached up and patted the hard metal in his underarm holster. "Not if I can help it."

⟨┬⟩»⟨┬⟩»⟨┬⟩»⟨┬⟩»⟨┬⟩»⟨┬⟩

After a busy day at the festival, Jennifer could hardly wait to get inside the house and examine her purchases. She first unwrapped a large oil painting of Canadian Geese and held it up against the dining room wall. While inspecting the workmanship, she grinned, thinking about her morning conversation with Hawkman. She now realized that he seemed to occupy a lot of her thoughts lately. No man had interested her since Eric's death two years ago. But this lone, tall, handsome secretive man, had knocked at her heart's door and aroused a feeling she thought she'd tucked away.

Her deliberations were interrupted when she noticed the blinking answering machine out of the corner of her eye. She carefully leaned the painting against the wall and hoped this wasn't another crank call. They were beginning to unnerve her. Clenching her fists, she hesitated a moment before hitting the button.

There were three clicks before a hoarse voice bellowed, "Hanging around the wrong company could be dangerous to your health."

Jolted, she stepped back, almost tripping over the painting. "This has gone far enough," she blared. "Why would anyone leave such a message?"

Punching the rewind button several times, she listened intently, hoping to detect some familiarity in the voice that would help her identify the caller. But he'd muffled his voice beyond recognition. Then a chilling notion struck her. Did these calls have something to do with Hawkman? She glanced at the falcon, who gave her a serious blink. "I'm calling him right now."

She tapped her fingers impatiently on the counter as the phone rang ten times before she hung up. Moving across to the sliding glass door, she looked out over the lake toward his place. Could she be over-reacting? Maybe it's just some kids or some nosy old fogy getting his kicks. She shook her head. No. She didn't think so. Too many things had happened for this just to be a crank call. Her mood subdued, she quickly hung the picture, put away the rest of her purchases and went to bed.

The next morning, she arose early and showered. What a night, she thought, letting the warm water soothe away the horrible nightmares she'd had about phone calls, men with guns and Tom Casey disappearing.

She dressed, then called Hawkman, but still no answer. Glancing up at the clock, she wondered where he'd be at this early hour. A picture of his bloodied head and thigh flashed across her mind. She shivered.

Suddenly, the blast from a shot gun echoed across the lake. She hurried out on the deck and peered toward his place, fearing the shot had come from someone other than a hunter. Perhaps another gunman?

Anxiety clotted her throat. She hurried back in the house and called him again. Still no response. She had to find him. Just as she picked up her purse and headed for the front door, the sound of gravel crunching on her driveway made her dash to the kitchen window. A sigh of relief escaped her lips when she recognized Hawkman's truck.

He tooted the horn and waved for her to come out. She dropped her purse on the counter, stepped outside and stopped short at his appearance. "Good Lord, you're a mess. Mud from the top of your head clear down to your toes."

Holding up a big Canadian goose, Hawkman grinned from ear to ear. "I did it. I got one."

Jennifer's hands were still shaking, so she tucked them into her jeans pockets. "It's clear you didn't use the scull boat."

He glanced down at his mud coated clothes and laughed. "Well, I started with it, but I don't think it fooled them. The whole dang flock spooked. I waited until they returned, then using my sharply-honed hunter's skills, crawled down that gully I pointed out to you, staying well clear of the big sentry goose." He held his prize high. "That's when I got this beauty."

"How'd you do all that crawling with your leg injury?"

His green eye sparkled. "What injury?"

She threw up her hands in despair. "Men! Now what are you going to do?"

"I'll dress this goose out and bring him back for you to cook."

Jennifer looked at him in disbelief. "Tonight? Uh, how about freezing him? Then we'll cook it for Thanksgiving. It's just a few weeks away." Giving him a nervous smile, she noticed the pleading tone of her own voice. She wondered where it came from, along with the sense of relief flooding her chest.

"Yeah, that's a great idea. I never thought of that." He eyed the big bird with a smile. "You sure you have room in your freezer?"

"Yes."

"Okay. I'll be back in about an hour and a half with a clean goose and a clean man." He tossed the carcass into the bed of his truck and climbed into the cab.

Jennifer watched him back out of the driveway, when suddenly, she remembered the phone message. She lifted her arm to halt him, then dropped it to her side. That can wait, she thought. Why put a damper on his jubilation at this moment.

Two hours later, Hawkman returned carrying the cleaned goose in a large plastic bag. "Turned out to be a bigger bird that I thought, close to seven pounds. Took me a little longer to clean him."

She didn't respond and he studied her somber face. "What's wrong? You look troubled."

"Probably nothing," she said, with a half-hearted shrug. "But I want you to listen to something."

Hawkman plopped the goose down on the counter and followed

her around to the phone. She hit the replay and watched all the carefree emotion in his face disappear in a flash.

"Who the hell?" he swore. He flipped the tape out of the machine and jammed it into his pocket.

She looked bewildered. "I'm sure it's no more than a prank call."

"Yeah, and I still believe in the tooth fairy." He slammed his fist down hard on the counter top. "Damn, I knew something like this would happen. I should have the Agency put you into protective custody."

Jennifer gnawed her lip as he paced back and forth. At first, she hadn't believed the danger, but now he frightened her. She'd never seen a man look so cold and forbidding. Trying to hide her own building fear, she grabbed the freezer paper, wrapped the goose and fled out the front door to the garage.

Tears welled, blurring her vision as she plunked the bird into the freezer. Her body shook so hard that she leaned against the cooler door for a few moments. Stuff like this didn't really happen, only to people in books or in the movies. Her life suddenly in danger? What had she done to warrant this? She wiped the tears from her cheeks, shoved her hair behind her ears and walked slowly back into the house.

Hawkman sat at the kitchen bar, drumming his fingers and chewing a toothpick. He glanced at her tear streaked cheeks and softened his voice. "Have you had other calls like this one?"

She sniffed and looked away, nodding her head.

"Tell me about them."

"No messages on any of the previous calls, just heavy breathing. I figured it must be kids, getting their kicks out of scaring someone."

Hawkman frowned. "Give me the names of people who might call you."

Jennifer thought for a moment, then counted them off on her fingers. "Well, there's my editor, Amelia, Mrs. Jordan, the church and I've gotten two calls from John Alexander Jr, this month."

Hawkman shot her a surprised look. "You know him?"

"Yes. This was his parent's house. I bought it from the estate shortly after the death of his father."

He ran a hand over his chin. "I don't believe this."

"He said he knew you."

He jumped up. "What do you mean?"

Puzzled, Jennifer clenched her hands together, not knowing what she'd said wrong.

"What did you tell him about me?"

Her heart thumped. "You're making me very nervous."

He walked around the bar to her side and took hold of her shoulders. "I'm sorry, Jennifer, but I need to know."

She pulled away from his grasp and paced in front of him, relating the story. "About a month ago, I told him about the Ossy incident and how I'd taken the bird to you. He asked some questions, but never mentioned knowing you until this last call.

Hawkman's expression turned grim.

The tension she sensed frightened her. "You two don't like each other, do you?"

"Why do you say that?"

"He told me to stay away from you. You're nothing but trouble."

Hawkman stiffened and turned from her gaze.

She moved in front of him and touched his arm. "He said you worked for his father. I just assumed he knew you lived here and didn't think a thing about it. Was I wrong?"

He exhaled loudly and patted her shoulder. "It's no big deal, don't worry about it." Then he abruptly changed the subject. "Do you have anything planned this afternoon?"

"Why?"

"We need a break. How about dinner in Medford, then we'll take in a movie."

"I do have an appointment with a priest at four. But it shouldn't take over an hour. That should work out perfectly. I'll get ready now."

Jennifer excused herself and went to her bedroom where she changed into a blue silk suit and leather shoes to match. When she walked back into the kitchen, Hawkman glanced up from reading a hunting magazine and whistled. "Wow, you look great. Must be some appointment."

She blushed. "It is."

On their way to town, she told him about her desire to adopt

Sam, a ten year old boy, who lived with the Jordans. "I'm worried though; I'm not sure the adoption agency will even consider a single woman. That's what my appointment with the priest is about."

Her thoughts drifted. But now there's another worry. Would she be putting Sam in harm's way by bringing him into her home? She refused to even consider that thought. Shaking her head, she brought her focus back on Hawkman's comments.

"Well, you won't know unless you ask. But I'm confused. I thought that boy was the Jordan's grandson."

"No. They're his foster parents and would love to adopt him, but they're too old. Now they fear he'll be taken away from the area and placed with a younger family."

"How'd you get to know the boy?"

"We were both at the mailbox at the same time one day. A big package had been crammed into the Jordan's box and he couldn't get it out. Between the two of us and lots of giggles, we finally managed to free it. And we've been friends every since. He and his dog Herman drop by the house almost every day for a treat." She smiled. "I think he and I would do real well together since we're both alone. That's why I don't want to leave right now."

"So that's the reason you won't go? Why didn't you tell me about this earlier?"

"I didn't think you'd be interested."

He turned and gazed at her for a moment. "You've made a very important decision in wanting to raise a child."

Jennifer nodded. "Yes, very. I've wanted a baby for years, but by the time Eric finally agreed, we discovered I couldn't have children. Now he's gone. Who knows if I'll marry again. But, I'm financially stable and can support a child, so I want to do it."

Hawkman turned and stared at the road ahead. "You're some woman."

They drove the rest of the way, conversing mostly in small talk until Hawkman pulled into the parking lot of St. Mary's Church and watched Jennifer touch up her face and smooth down her long brown hair.

She glanced at him and smiled nervously. "Do I look all right?"

"Beautiful," he croaked, jumping out of the truck to run around and open her door. He gave her the thumbs up sign. "I'll be back in an hour. I've got some errands."

Jennifer watched him drive out of the parking lot before she headed toward the entry, praying silently.

An hour later, just as the church door closed behind her, Hawkman drove up. Feeling light hearted and hopeful, she climbed into the 4X4. They drove to the restaurant in silence and it wasn't until after they'd ordered that Hawkman asked. "Well, what'd he say?"

"Father O'Brien seemed receptive to the idea of my adopting Sam. He's going to look into the the state agency rules and advise me. Of course, the ideal situation is adoption by a couple, which I understand. But older children are harder to place. So I might have a chance."

"It sounds like there's some hope. Then the waiting game begins as the sheaves of paperwork are filled out." He shifted in his seat. "By the way, how long does the process usually take before he actually moves in with you?"

"I'm not sure. Maybe a month or two." She searched his face. "Why do you ask?"

He took a sip of his wine and glanced about the room, his expression solemn. "No particular reason. Just interested."

After dinner, they drove to the theater and found the parking lot jammed. Hawkman finally found a spot a fair distance from the entrance. As they hurried inside, neither one paid any particular attention to the man who stepped out from the shadows and leaned against an illegally parked car.

CHAPTER FOUR

Hawkman slowed the 4X4 as it bumped off the pavement onto the gravel road toward the lake. He rounded one of the sharp curves and the headlight's twin beams encircled a frightened deer, frozen to the middle of the road. Knowing better than to brake hard on gravel, he tapped the pedal lightly only to feel it collapse all the way to the floor.

"What the hell?" He pumped furiously, but the truck didn't slow. He turned slightly to the right, avoiding the deer, but the vehicle's rear end began sliding toward the opposite side of the road. "Hold on, Jennifer!"

His knuckles turned white fighting for control on the loose gravel, but all his strength couldn't hold the truck from skidding over the embankment. They bounced to rest against a large oak tree only a few feet from the water's edge. Hawkman took a deep breath and released his death grip on the steering wheel, then glanced at Jennifer whose face had turned ashen. "You okay?"

She rubbed her arm. "I think so. It happened so fast."

He unhooked his seat belt and opened the door. "Something's screwy here. I had this truck serviced last week."

He went around to help her out of her tangled seat belt and heard the approach of a slow moving vehicle, unusual for this road which had little traffic late at night. Quickly, he helped her out of the truck and pushed her toward a stand of pines. "Hide within those trees."

Once she'd disappeared into the shadows, he drew his revolver and crouched behind the truck, his stare focused on the bouncing light beams making their way around the bend. Only when the vehicle passed without slowing did he relax and holster his gun.

He cupped his hands around his mouth and called to Jennifer. "Everything's okay. You can come out."

She stepped up beside him within a few seconds. "Shall we start walking?"

"Not yet. I want to see if I can't get the truck back onto the road."

"But there are no brakes. You could end up in the lake."

"I'll try using the emergency." He climbed into the cab, handed her a flashlight and pointed toward the rear of the truck. "Keep the beam on that steep area so I can judge how far I can go back."

Jennifer guided the light over the embankment and gasped. "Hawkman, be careful."

The truck roared to life and Hawkman engaged the four wheel drive. She held her breath as he maneuvered back and forth within inches of the edge. Then, with one final lunge, he had the vehicle back on the road. "Okay, get in. We'll make it home, the hand brake works fine."

After dropping Jennifer off, Hawkman changed into work clothes and examined the truck. The flashlight flickered and he had to hit it against his hand several times to get a steady beam. The outside body of the truck had a few scratches and one small dent on the fender where it banged against the tree trunk. But the brakes giving out is what really bothered him.

Even though the night had turned pitch black, he secured the truck's wheels with blocks of wood, jacked it up and scooted underneath. Shining the fluttering light along the under body, he noticed the hydraulic tyube glistened with moisture. He ran his finger along the wetness and frowned at the smell of brake fluid. Further investigation uncovered a small nick in the line. His jaw tightened when he realized that some one had deliberately cut it just enough so the fluid would drip out slowly.

Swearing under his breath, he pushed himself out from under the truck, yanked a rag from behind the seat and wiped his hands. He kicked at a stone, sending it through the air to the opposite side of the road. This incident pretty well sealed his suspicions that the strange phone calls to Jennifer were from someone who meant business. They're too close, he thought.

He locked the truck and headed toward the house. The brake repair could wait until morning. When he stepped inside, the absence of the falcon's loud greetings made him lonely. He checked his answering machine and found no messages. Why should he expect any, he'd turned down everyone that had called. One of these days, he had to get serious about this private investigators business.

Yawning, he tugged off his shirt on the way to the bedroom and tossed it over the chair. He used his boot pullers to yank off his boots, then kicked off his Levis, leaving them in a pile on the floor. His shoulder holster and eye patch went on the bedside table and he fell back on the pillow. But sleep wouldn't come. Instead, he found himself staring at the ceiling concerned about Jennifer's safety.

Suddenly, he snapped his fingers and leaped out of bed. He flipped on the light and fumbled through the top drawer of his dresser until he felt the small box far back in the corner. Sitting on the edge of the mattress, he opened the lid and tenderly lifted out a small pearl handled pistol. He turned it over and over in his hand, admiring the beautiful workmanship on the gun. He'd given it to Sylvia a long time ago, but she'd refused to touch it. Not that it would have done any good against a bomb.

The horrifying scene of his wife's exploding car flashed from his memory. He stared into the dark corner of the room, reliving the shock and anger of that day. Tears blurred his vision as he glanced down at the tiny pistol he clutched in his hand. He shook his head to blot out the images. Perhaps if he taught Jennifer how to use this gun, it might save her life. He gently slipped it back into the box and turned off the light.

The next morning, Hawkman awakened to a loud knock on his door. He rolled over and opened his eyes. "Who the hell's that at this hour?" he grumbled, pulling the cover over his head. The knocking persisted, so he dressed quickly, picked up his gun and held it behind his back as he padded bare-foot to the entry.

Wary of intruders, he opened the door only a few inches and glanced down at a pair of blue eyes the size of wash tubs peering out from under a shock of blond hair. A boy about ten years old stood before him, holding a small trapping cage.

Hawkman shoved the revolver into his waistband near the small of his back and covered it with his baggy tee shirt.

The boy hadn't so much as blinked. "Are you Hawkman?"

"Sure am. Who are you?" Hawkman glanced toward the road where Mr. Jordan's familiar pickup waited, the engine idling. His eyebrows rose when it dawned on him that this must be the boy Jennifer wanted to adopt.

"I'm Sam. You fix birds don't ya?"

"Sure do."

Sam held up the cage, apparently not aware of Hawkman's early morning gruffness. "Mr. Jordan and I found this owl on the ground under a big tree behind our house. He's alive, but he won't eat."

Hawkman smiled and motioned for him to come inside. "Bring him in and let's take a look."

He took the box from Sam and placed it on the table. The boy stood at his elbow, watching with an awed expression as Hawkman slipped on leather gloves and opened the trap door. A small pitiful squeak sounded from the young horned owl.

Hawkman gently lifted the listless bird out of the cage and placed him on the table. He sat down on the kitchen chair, stabilized his arms and carefully forced open the owl's beak. Not being able to see down into the small narrow throat cavity, Hawkman pointed toward the counter. "Sam, get that flashlight."

The boy jumped at his request.

"Can you hold that beam so I can see down the bird's throat?"

"Sure."

Hawkman studied the bird's throat for a moment then exclaimed. "Ah!"

Sam's eyes grew wide as he tried to look past Hawkman's hand. "What is it?"

"See that piece of fishing line shining under the light?"

Sam looked again. "Yeah, yeah. I see it."

"Bet there's a hook on the other end."

Sam stepped back, his eyes shadowed. "Really? Won't that kill him?"

"Depends on how far down it got." He peered deeper into the bird's throat. "I think we're in luck."

Sam strained for another look, almost falling onto the bird, but Hawkman caught him just in time. "Will he be okay?" he asked, frowning.

Hawkman smiled. "I think I can get it out. Then he'll be able to eat and drink again, but his throat will be sore. You better leave him here with me for a couple of days so I can doctor him. Then when he's well, we'll take him back to the tree where you found him."

Sam's eyes lit up with a big grin. "Gee, thanks, Hawkman. I'd like to stay and watch, but Mr. Jordan's waiting for me." And out the door he ran.

Chuckling, Hawkman set to work extracting the hook with a pair of forceps. Afterward, he used a large straw like instrument to force-feed the owl some raw hamburger meat, then placed him back into the cage. "You're gonna be just fine, little guy," he said, patting the metal frame.

⟨⊹⟩⊶⟨⊹⟩⊶⟨⊹⟩⊶⟨⊹⟩⊶⟨⊹⟩

Since early morning, Jennifer had been working feverishly in her office, which at one time had been a formal dining room. It shocked her to glance at the kitchen clock and see the time. It's already after twelve and the mail should be here, she thought, pushing away from her desk. She felt good, having made a lot of headway on several wildlife articles that were due within the next two weeks. The locale of Copco Lake had given her quite an advantage to photograph the deer, raccoon, porcupines and birds of all kinds. She'd even caught a glimpse of a mountain lion when she drove up toward Topsy Grade one evening.

Rolling her shoulders, she stood and stretched. She'd been working several hours and needed a break. So she took her time strolling lazily down the road toward the mailboxes. The aroma of baked apple pie from a neighbor's house filled the air, reminding her of the holidays ahead.

She stood for a moment fingering through the mail when the sound of someone approaching made her turn. Hawkman's warnings had made her edgy. A sigh of relief escaped her lips when she saw Sam pedaling his bike so fast that the wheel spokes blurred. He and his black dog, Herman were racing toward the line of mailboxes.

Not sure whether to stand still or jump out of the way, she took her chances and remained frozen to the spot. When he jammed on the brakes, the back wheel skidded around, making dust fly. "Hi, Jennifer," he shouted. Herman bounced and jumped, barking for joy.

She laughed and fanned her hand in front of her face, then gave the dog a dusty pat. "My goodness, what's your hurry, Sam?

"Mr. Jordan's expecting something really important in the mail. So I gotta hurry." He grabbed the envelopes from the box without getting off his bike, then rode off, disappearing behind another dust cloud.

Her gaze lingered after him, praying that she'd convinced Father O'Brien how badly she wanted to give that boy a permanent home. She remembered her own unhappy childhood as a ward of the state. After her parents were killed, she'd been shifted from one foster family after another, never being able to establish roots or form any sort of loving relationships. It just wasn't healthy.

The mail clutched to her chest, she was slowly ambling up the driveway when the crunch of gravel behind her interrupted her train of thought. Hawkman jumped out of his truck and they walked inside. She dumped the mail on the kitchen bar and noticed him silently pacing around the counter drumming his fingers along the top. "What's bothering you?"

Frowning, Hawkman spoke in a dark voice. "Someone cut the brake line on the truck. Whoever did this, gambled that by the time we reached the gravel we'd have no brakes. This was no accident."

She felt the goose bumps raise on her arms, "We could've been killed."

"Exactly."

When he sat down at the bar, she noticed the small box in his hand. He motioned for her to sit opposite him.

She slid onto the stool and he pushed the box forward. "What's this?"

"It's for you."

Removing the cover, she peered inside and gasped. Slamming the lid back on, she shoved the box toward him and jumped up. "I won't have a gun in my house."

His mouth tightening, he lifted the small gun from the box. "It's a 32 caliber semi-automatic. It's made for a woman's hand."

Jennifer shook her head violently. "No!"

He held his hand out with the gun lying across the palm. "I'll teach you how to use it, then you won't feel so spooked."

Shaking her head, she backed away and pointed at him. "They're after you, not me."

"You're missing the point. They'll go through you to get me. Since your not leaving the area, you've got to learn to defend yourself. I want you to keep it near you at all times."

Her face distraught, she turned away. "My parents were killed during a robbery with a gun like that one." Her eyes brimmed with tears. "Take it away." She stormed into the living room and stared out the window, her hands clenched into fists at her side.

Hawkman placed the gun back into the box, then went to her, placing a hand on her shoulder. "I'm sorry, Jennifer. I didn't know about your parents." When she didn't respond, he dropped his hand and changed the subject. "Guess what I have at my house?"

She didn't move. "I haven't the foggiest idea."

"A young horned owl."

Her eyes still glistening with moisture, she turned and looked at him. "Where did it come from?

"Sam brought it over early this morning."

"That's odd. I saw him at the mailbox and he didn't mention a word about it." She waved it off. "Kid's minds run a mile a minute. But I assume the owl was injured if he brought it to you."

"Yeah, the little hooter got a fish hook caught in his throat. A small one." He held up his thumb and forefinger, showing the size. "The hook came right out with no problem and he'll be fine. I told Sam we'd take it back to the tree where he found him in a couple of days."

Her mind churned with an idea for a wildlife article. "Can I get some pictures first?"

"Sure. Come over tomorrow. Then when the bird has recovered, you can go with us when we release him."

"That'll be great."

Hawkman hooked his thumbs in his back jeans pockets. "Well, I better get home and check that little guy. Make sure he's doing okay."

After he left, Jennifer walked into the kitchen feeling their relationship had become quite strained. It seemed they argued a lot and she didn't like that. Then she noticed the gun box still setting on the counter. "Oh no," she said aloud and raced to the kitchen window, craning her neck to see if he'd left already.

She sighed and came down off her toes. Glancing at the box, she thought about how her dad had been an avid hunter, but never allowed a handgun in the house. He'd always kept his hunting guns and ammunition locked up. Ironic that this looked like the type of gun that had killed him and mother.

Shivering, she pushed the box to the wall and began sorting through her mail, throwing the junk into the waste basket, stacking the catalogs in a pile for later reading and the bills in another.

She smiled when she came across the check from her editor and laid it aside. What's this? she wondered, holding up an envelope with her first name scrawled across the front. Strange, it had no stamp or return address. She slit it open and removed a single sheet of stationary. Her heart lurched when she read the message in bold caps: 'STAY AWAY FROM THE HAWK MAN OR ELSE.'

She grabbed the envelope and looked on both sides, it had no visible postmark. A chill crept up her spine. Someone besides the mailman had put this in her box, which meant they were terribly close to her house. She'd never feared being alone until now. The strange phone calls, Hawkman's concerns and now this. She went to the dining room window and searched for any strange cars parked on the road. I'm getting paranoid, she thought, clasping herself around the waist to stop the tremors. Maybe I should learn something about self-defense and I doubt I could find any better teacher than Hawkman.

She wiped her damp palms down the sides of her jeans and moved toward the small box on the counter. Slowly lifting the lid, she gnawed at her lower lip and stared at the gun for several moments. Then, sucking in a deep breath, she made a decision.

"Hawkman," she whispered. "If they come after me, they're going to find a big surprise." She picked up the gun and stroked the pearl handle. Then carefully laying it back into the box, she didn't replace the lid and left it setting close at hand.

CHAPTER FIVE

Hawkman sat on his back porch steps enjoying a cup of coffee while watching Ossy circle and whistle against the morning sky. Hearing a car stop in front, he gulped down the last drop and set the mug on the railing. His hands shoved deep into his pockets, he started around the side of the house only to be surprised by Jennifer, dressed in jeans and a baggy sweatshirt, meeting him halfway. "What are you doing out so early in the morning?" he asked.

Her hazel eyes sparkling in the sunlight, she thrust the familiar small box under his nose. "I've made a decision. I want you to teach me how to use this."

Taking it from her hand, he looked at her sharply. "Are you serious? What changed your mind?"

"Well, you scared me half to death, and then I got those threatening phone calls." She pulled a white envelope from her purse and handed it at him. "And now this came in my mail yesterday."

Hawkman shoved the box under his arm and opened the letter. His jaw became taut and the muscles in his neck rippled. "You found this with your mail?"

"Yes." She pointed. "No address, no postmark, only my first name scribbled on the front. You can tell the mailman didn't put it there."

He slid the note back into the envelope. "Can I hang onto this for awhile?"

She nodded. "Whoever put this in my mailbox was only a half block from my house. That's scary Hawkman. Do you have any idea who's doing this?"

"No, but it sure looks like he's starting to lay a number on you. Now will you take my advice and leave the area."

She put her hands on her hips and glared at him. "I've already told you my answer."

He took a deep breath and headed rapidly toward the front door. "Stubborn woman," he mumbled, gritting his teeth. "Well, at least you've changed your mind about learning to use the gun. When do you want to start?"

Jennifer, side-stepping along beside him, cocked her head up so she could see his face. "Today. The sooner the better."

He stopped and rubbed the back of his neck thoughtfully. "Well, I wanted to release that owl back to the wilds. Let me call Bob Jordan and see if he's home. There's a good target practice area near his place and we could drop the bird off on the way."

"Sounds good," she said, following him into the house.

Just as they got inside, his phone rang.

He paused before answering, wishing Jennifer wasn't standing right there at the moment. Turning his back to her, he picked it up. "Tom Casey, Private Investigator." Then after a few moments, he continued. "I'm booked up right now, but let me have your name and number. I'll get back to you when I have an opening." He wrote the information on a pad of paper, thankful that the advertisement he placed in the Medford paper would expire this week. Sensing Jennifer's stare, he dialed the Jordans.

After hanging up and before she had a chance to make a comment, he picked up his hunting jacket and rifle, then handed her a blazing orange vest. "Bob said it would be fine."

She held up the brightly colored garment. "What's this?"

He slapped on an orange ball cap. "It's deer season and it might prevent you from getting shot."

"Oh," she said, in an almost apologetic tone, folding it over her arm.

He picked up the cage with the owl in it and bustled toward the door, hoping to avoid any questions concerning the call. But she moved in front of him, blocking his way.

"Why did you turn down that job?"

Looking over her head, he gazed outside, rubbing the bridge of his nose with a finger. "It's too dangerous to involve other people in my life right now. Once I get this bastard taken care of, I'll contact the people." He gently pushed past her out the door and headed up the walkway toward the truck.

She trailed close behind, almost running to keep up with his long strides.

"But what if they hire someone else before you can take care of the problem?"

"That's the breaks." He unlocked the cab, set the cage on the seat, threw his jacket in and placed his rifle on the gun rack across the back window. "We'll take my truck. The roads are too rough for your car." Before climbing in, he backed away and scratched his head. "We should take the falcon so he can hunt."

"That's a good idea. Then, I'll just take my car home and get my camera." She placed the gun and orange vest inside his truck cab before jumping into her car.

While waiting in her driveway, Hawkman rummaged behind the seat and found an old towel which he placed over the owlet's cage. He grinned when Jennifer bounded out of the house with the falcon riding on her arm and a camera slung over her shoulder. No wonder that bird feels heavy to her, he's almost as big as she is.

Jennifer climbed into the truck, cooing to the hawk until she placed him on the portable perch. "Okay, I think we're ready to go."

When they approached the Jordans' ranch, Jennifer spotted Sam in the nearby field bordering the road. He ran eagerly to the large gate and swung it open. Hawkman bounced over the cattle guard and parked at the back of the house under the shade of a big tree. Sam danced around outside the truck until Hawkman handed him the cage.

Wrinkling his nose, Sam lifted the corner of the towel and peeked inside. "How come you got him covered?"

Hawkman thumbed toward the falcon. "How would you like that glaring down at you with breakfast on his mind? Wouldn't that make you a bit nervous?"

The boy laughed. "Oh yeah."

Bob Jordan came out the back door and joined them, following

Sam to the nearby oak tree. Hawkman strolled around the trunk, then bent down and studied a small pile of sticks and feathers. "Hey, Sam, come here."

Dashing over to where Hawkman squatted, he stared down at the ground, frowning. "Yeah?"

"See this?"

"Yeah."

"They're the remains of an owl's nest. When the young owls finally venture out on the limbs by themselves, the parents destroy the nest. Is this where you found him?"

"Yeah," Sam said, nodding briskly.

"Then, let's put him in this tree."

"Okay." Sam set the cage down on the ground.

Hawkman handed the boy a pair of leather gloves.

Sam stared at him awe-struck while slipping the over-sized gloves onto his small hands. Hawkman showed him how to pick up the owl without getting clawed by the sharp talons. Directing the boy to a low hanging branch, he instructed him how to place the bird's feet on the rough bark.

"Now, when you let go of the little guy, step back and let's see what he does," Hawkman said.

Sam squealed with delight when the owl twisted his head around, looked straight at Sam, shook his feathers and flapped his wings several times before taking off in flight.

Jennifer put an arm around Sam's shoulder. "You did a good thing by recognizing that little guy needed help. He'll probably be back here to raise his family one of these days, knowing you're his friend."

After watching the bird fly out of sight, Hawkman and Jennifer climbed back into the truck and waved goodbye. The falcon got Jennifer's attention when he shifted on his perch, cocked his head and glared at each of them.

Jennifer scooted back against the seat. "Whoa, what's the matter with him? He looks like he wants us for breakfast."

Hawkman snickered. "He wants to hunt and doesn't understand why I didn't release him."

She shifted into a more comfortable position, farther away from the falcon, fearing he might just take a chunk out of her. The box holding the gun bumped against her hip, so she slid it, along with the orange vest, under the seat out of the way. "Where are we going?"

He pointed toward the tree covered hills. "We'll head up there, away from the houses."

After a few more minutes on the main road, he turned off onto what looked like a deer or cattle path. Jennifer hung on to the door handle as they bumped along. "Good grief, Hawkman, this isn't a road, it's a trail."

A sly grin tugged at the corners of his mouth. "Oh, this is smooth, wait until you see what's up ahead." He threw the truck into four-wheel drive and started up the sheer side of a steep hill.

She let out a moan, closed her eyes and covered her face with her hands. "Oh no, we're going to flip over backwards."

Pretty Boy slipped on his perch, squawked and flapped his large wings for balance, swatting Jennifer's head.

When Hawkman leveled off on solid ground, Jennifer sighed with relief and sat back against the seat, throwing a dirty look in his direction. "I just finished my final prayers."

He grinned. "Shoot, that little incline didn't amount to anything."

Jennifer rolled her eyes and straightened her jacket. When he finally came to a stop, she breathed an audible sigh of relief. "I'm certainly glad that ride is over. I'll try not to think about the return trip."

Hawkman slipped on the long leather glove and extended his arm in front of the falcon. Pretty Boy stepped onto his gloved hand, giving the leather a hard nip, then cocked his head and gave Hawkman a very dubious look.

Jennifer laughed. "Boy, he's not too happy with you."

He waved it off and stepped out of the truck, launching the bird upward. "He'll soon forget all about it." Hawkman watched for a moment as the falcon soared skyward. "Have a good hunt, fellow," he called, tossing the glove back on the seat.

He slipped on his camouflage hunting vest and patted the pockets, making sure the ammunition hadn't fallen out during the rough ride. He reached into a box behind the seat, slipping several empty cans into the game pouch of his vest, then reached for the rifle on the rack. "Put on that vest and grab your gun."

"Which way are we going?"

"We'll head over there." He pointed toward a small canyon. "It's well sheltered for target practice."

By the time Jennifer struggled into the orange vest and fished the box out from under the seat, Hawkman had moved several yards away. She ran to catch up and they continued for a good half mile before reaching the small gorge. Hawkman stopped at a big boulder, stepped off about a hundred yards and set a couple of beer cans upright on another large rock. Jennifer watched with interest. Then he walked up beside her, didn't say a word, hoisted the rifle to his shoulder and fired.

She jumped back and grabbed her ears. "Wow! that's loud."

He grimaced and looked through the scope again. "Damn, the sight's off."

When Hawkman had a gun in his hand, he entered another world. The gun had saved his life many times and must be in perfect working order. To him it was a friend. Then he noticed Jennifer standing wide eyed with her hands clutching her ears. He plopped down on a large rock. "Sorry, should've warned you about the noise." He reached into his pocket and handed her a pair of ear plugs. "Here, put these in your ears." Then his attention immediately went back on the rifle.

"What are you doing?"

"The scope must have bumped against something during the rough ride."

She edged toward him, then stared at the gun and stopped short.

Hawkman glanced at her and let out a disgusted breath. "Get over here, you can't see anything that far away."

She inched around to his side, avoiding the barrel. He shook his head. "You wouldn't be so edgy if you understood how a gun worked. Take this one, for instance. It's a 30-06 Remington rifle. It's used for deer hunting." He held the gun out in front of him and opened the shell chamber, showing her it was empty. He explained how it discharged shells and also pointed out the safety lock. "Here, hold it so you know the feel."

At first she hesitated, then gulping in a deep breath, took the rifle. She made a face and looked at him. "It's heavy."

Ignoring her comment, he stood behind her, placed her left hand under the forearm of the gun and the forefinger of her right hand on the trigger. He moved her head so she could see through the scope and explained how to find the target. Jennifer sucked in her breath when he linked his arms around her, then when he stepped away, she almost dropped the gun.

"It's heavy and awkward," she said. "I can't imagine hitting anything with a gun this big."

"Takes time, but once you've learned how to use a rifle, it's pretty easy."

She handed it back. "I'm not interested in learning how to shoot this thing. I want to learn about the gun you gave me."

"Okay. But first let me check to make sure I corrected the sight."

Jennifer quickly inserted the ear plugs as he put the rifle to his shoulder and fired. One of the cans flew straight up. "Bullseye!" He then put on the safety and leaned the rifle against a rock. "I'll move the cans closer for your gun.

⊷⊶⊷⊶⊷⊶⊷⊶⊷

He set up the target, then showed her how to load the small pistol. "There are three different positions you can use while shooting: standing, with one foot slightly in front of the other for balance: kneeling, one knee on the ground the other up: prone, where you lay on the ground on your stomach, using your elbows to stabilize the gun. Prone's probably the easiest, kneeling is next, but since the ground's so rocky, we'll stand," he said.

Jennifer eyed him. "So what you're telling me, is that I'm going to learn the hard way?"

"Yep." Again, he got behind her and placed his arms around each side of her body. He swallowed hard when a wisp of her hair blew across his face and brought back that sensation he'd experienced earlier when she'd touched him. Only this time it surged through him much stronger. Trying to push the feeling away, he concentrated on showing her how to clasp the gun with both hands. "When you pull the trigger, you'll feel a slight kick, but that's normal." He stepped back, stared at her, and took a deep breath. "Are you ready to give it a try?"

Biting her lower lip, she nodded, squinted and pulled the trigger.

He threw his hands up in the air. "No. You can't close your eyes. If you can't see the target, how do you think you'll hit it? Now keep your eyes open. Okay? Try again."

She lowered the gun and cast her eyes downward. "I'm not sure I can do this."

He folded his arms across his chest. "Yes you can. Now get that gun up and aim."

She stared at the shiny cans sitting on the rock then glanced down at the gun she held in her hand. Maybe if mother had learned how to shoot and had carried a weapon in her purse they wouldn't have died. A strange sensation flooded her. Perspiration popped out on her forehead and trickled down her face, stinging the corners of her eyes. She gritted her teeth and brought the gun up into firing position.

"Are you ready?" Hawkman asked.

She planted her feet solidly and shut out the dark memories. "Yes." Focusing on the target, she pulled the trigger. This time, one of the cans sailed through the air.

Hawkman clapped. "All right. Do it again."

Jennifer squared her shoulders and after several more rounds her confidence grew. Surprisingly, she found herself enjoying this new challenge as she grew more comfortable with the gun.

"You're doing real well. Those last six shots were right on."

Hawkman had her stand back while he practiced with his handgun and fired a few more shots with the rifle. "I think that's enough for today. I'd say you've had a successful first practice."

"It's not as hard as I thought." She unloaded the gun and placed it back into the box, closing the lid with a proud pat. Tucking it under her arm, she turned to follow him, but a movement in the nearby brush caught her eye. She backed up. "Oh no, Hawkman, there's a skunk over here."

He turned around and proceeded walking backwards. "Don't worry, he'll go away if you don't bother him."

She wasn't about to take her eyes off that varmint. The skunk finally meandered around a big rock and she dashed to catch up with Hawkman.

Just as she reached him, he stopped dead in his tracks. His head moved like an animal focusing in on its prey. Suddenly, he grabbed her arm and pulled her into the cover of some trees.

Startled by his behavior, she glanced around frantically. "What is it?"

He pushed her behind him, snatched off his orange hat and stuffed it under his shirt. "Helicopter."

Quickly loading his rifle, he held it against his side so the sun's rays wouldn't reflect off the barrel. Jennifer felt the cold steel touch her leg.

When the chopper came into view, he pressed her hard against the tree, making it difficult for her to breath. His body tensed as the aircraft approached.

"Don't move," he warned over his shoulder in a hushed whisper.

CHAPTER SIX

Jennifer felt Hawkman's body move in the direction of the passing helicopter. When the sound of the popping blades finally died in the distance, he stepped away and yanked the orange cap from beneath his shirt, slapping it against his thigh. "It's gone." He plopped the hat onto his head and walked briskly toward the truck as if nothing had happened.

What the hell is going on? she wondered, running after him. She grabbed his arm. "Wait! Why did you shove me against that tree?"

He kept walking. "Caution. I don't know who's looking for me, but he could have access to a helicopter."

She dropped her hand and stared at his back in shocked silence. This whole thing sounded big-time: helicopters and men with guns who didn't care who got hurt. Fear ballooned inside her.

When they reached the truck, he put the guns away then leaned against the fender and looked skyward. "Now, where's that falcon?"

How can he turn everything off and think about that blasted bird? It amazed her. But she guessed he wouldn't make a good spy if he didn't know how to survive physically and mentally. She shrugged, shaded her eyes and looked skyward. "Don't see him."

The corners of Hawkman's mouth turned down and his eyes clouded. "Like you said, he didn't seem to happy with us earlier. Maybe he won't return." He stuck a toothpick into his mouth and started to get into the cab when a loud squawk sounded. A big grin lit up his features. "Whoa, I almost got into deep trouble."

He quickly grabbed the glove off the seat and barely got his flesh covered before the falcon landed on his strong arm. The bird fluffed his feathers and cocked his head back and forth.

"See, I told you he'd forget about everything." Hawkman placed him on the portable perch. "Man, you're one spoiled bird. So much so, that I doubt you'd make it winging alone in the wild."

Jennifer climbed in on the passenger side. "Yeah, let's see what he thinks after the ride home. We may both leave and try our wings."

They drove back on the same rough trail. Jennifer didn't release her grip on the door handle until the smooth main road came into view. When they were in sight of her house, she slipped the camera strap over her shoulder and placed the extra box of ammunition in her jeans pocket. Then she pulled on the leather glove. "Thanks for the lesson, Hawkman. It's been quite an experience."

"You're mighty welcome. Makes me feel a bit more comfortable knowing you're familiar with a gun."

With the falcon clinging to her arm, she climbed out of the cab and grabbed the gun box. "I'll talk to you tomorrow."

His expression turned serious and he poked his head out the truck window. "Remember what I told you. Be careful."

Jennifer glanced over her shoulder. "I know. I'll be on the alert." Her gaze moved to the falcon. "I've just learned how to shoot a gun, but it's your master who's getting shot at and worried about strange helicopters. And yet, he tells me to be careful. Shish." She grinned and rolled her eyes as she unlocked her front door.

⊹⋇⊹⋇⊹⋇⊹⋇⊹

Hawkman drove home, feeling satisfied with Jennifer's progress. It also pleased him that she'd taken on the challenge without his having to force the issue. He hated to think about it, but it just might save her life. He parked in front of the cabin, removed the rifle from the rack and climbed out of the truck. Suddenly he stopped in his tracks. His well-honed instincts kicked in.

Something wasn't right. He studied the grounds. Then he

spotted it. The scull boat lay upside down in the middle of the yard, not where he'd left it. His chest tightened and his fingers felt for bullets in his hunting vest. He loaded the rifle before walking slowly toward the boat. His keen eyesight searched the area as he reached down and flipped the boat over. Large gaping holes riddled the entire hull. He dropped it to the ground and cursed.

Then he noted the open door of his cabin and crept up the steps, hoping the son-of-a-bitch didn't realize he'd returned. He leaned against the wall, positioned the rifle in front of him and kicked the door open, spinning into the room.

The sight staggered him. The kitchen had been torn apart. All the cabinet doors stood open and his food stuffs had been dumped onto the floor. He searched every room, only to discover the whole damn house had been ransacked and the intruder had vanished. His anger mounted and he felt violated. Kicking a can of beans, he sent it spiraling across the kitchen floor.

He went outside and stomped down the stairs to the storage room underneath the porch. At least the freezer and walk-in cooler were still intact and untouched. He inspected the dock, his fishing boat and searched through the rest of the property. All were undamaged. Satisfied the intruder had left, he went back inside the house and leaned the rifle in the corner behind the door. He stood with fists on his hips and grimaced at the disarray. "Now, where the hell do I start to clean up this mess?"

This couldn't be reported to the local authorities, since it had nothing to do with them. Even if he'd wanted to, the phone lay smashed on the floor with the rest of the clutter. He ran a hand through his hair. "Damn, wait until I get my hands on who did this."

He kicked a path through the loose mattress stuffing that had been strewn across the bedroom floor to the closet where he pulled his sleeping bag from the top shelf. Making room on the floor for a make-shift bed, he thought about what if the birds had still been here tethered to their perches. A shutter ran through him. The maniac wouldn't have thought twice about killing the falcon. Thank God, Jennifer had him and they'd returned the hawk and owl to the wild.

He sat down on the floor, shucked off his boots and removed his gun from the holster. Spotting an unharmed pillow crammed under the bed, he pulled it toward him and shoved the gun under it before crawling into the sleeping bag.

It took him a long time to settle into a restless sleep.

(·⁂·)(·⁂·)(·⁂·)(·⁂·)(·⁂·)

Jennifer ate a light dinner, then left the dirty dishes stacked in the sink for later. She wanted to get to the computer and write about her adventure before any of the details slipped away. After she'd worked for some time, she was shocked when she glanced up at the clock and discovered it was almost midnight. She stretched her arms above her head and yawned, Time to hit the sack.

She snuggled down into the covers and had just drifted into sleep when the falcon squawked. Her eyes flew open. She bolted straight up, holding the covers to her chest. He'd never made a noise at night. Why now? Maybe someone was trying to break in.

She reached for the gun resting on the night table and slipped out of bed. Her heart pounding, she edged around the bedroom door and slipped into the living room. She stood quietly and heard the faint footsteps on the wooden deck. Her heart skipped a beat and she flattened her back against the wall. Staring toward the lacy drapes on the window, she didn't see anything. Then her gaze drifted toward the sliding glass door. Her heart almost stopped. She could make out the silhouette of a man on the other side of the semi-transparent curtains. The clicking sound of the slider lock ricocheted in her ears. The poles she'd inserted in the door runner had so far prevented him from getting the door open, but what if he decided to break the glass? Her legs trembled and her stomach jerked in spasms.

An idea struck her and she slowly inched her way along the wall, her mind working wildly. She stayed within the dancing shadows caused by the moon lit night and crept around the fireplace, never once taking her eyes off the shadow behind the curtained door. When she got to the big picture window that overlooked the lake, she dropped to the floor and crawled beneath the sill. Her gown clung to her sweat-drenched body and her hands grew clammy. She wiped them on the rug so the gun wouldn't slip in her palm.

When she reached the edge of the sliding door, she could

see the intruder still working on the door mechanisms only a few feet away. Suddenly, the slider hit the pole. She almost screamed in terror, but covered her mouth to stifle the frantic sobs. The curtains fluttered as a cool breeze floated through the small slit in the door. Then to her horror, his gloved hand came through the opening, as he groped for the handle. He tried to lift the door out, but she'd planned for that too, by pushing a small round rod into the top runner.

She'd all but stopped breathing, her fear greater than anything she'd ever experienced. Her whole body trembled in spasms. She inched her shaking hand up the wall while her heart pounded loudly in her ears. It seemed like an eternity before her fingers finally found the outdoor light switches. She flipped them all at once. Lights flooded the back yard and part of the lake with enough illumination to make it look like daylight.

The figure jerked around and looked from side to side. He stood for only a second before he dashed across the deck and down the steps. Jennifer darted across the room to the dining room window and peeked out the corner of the drapes. She watched him race across the open lot toward a dark colored car parked on the side of the road. Gravel spewed from beneath his tires as he skidded the car in a circle and sped across the bridge.

Once he'd disappeared from sight, Jennifer's knees dissolved into jelly. She stumbled across the room and grabbed the kitchen bar for support. "Get hold of yourself. You're okay. He's gone," she said aloud.

She dropped the gun on the counter and picked up the phone. Her hands shook so hard that she found it difficult to punch in the numbers. Then she heard that annoying busy signal. "Oh no, Hawkman, of all nights for you to be on the phone."

A few seconds later, she pushed radial, only to hear the same signal. He must have knocked the phone off the hook. Should she call 911? No, she'd talk to Hawkman first. Sleep was out of the question, so she made a pot of coffee, then went from room to room, turning on all the inside lights. Periodically, she tried the phone, only to hear the constant busy signal. She prayed he was all right. But, at this point, her fright wouldn't allow her to leave the house to go look for him.

Hawkman rose early from his make-shift bed and left the cabin. He needed some answers. Passing Jennifer's place, he drove straight to the store. When he entered, Amelia, the proprietor, looked up from reading the paper.

"Well, hello Hawkman, its been a long time since you've graced these doors."

"Good to see you, Amelia. You don't look too busy."

"Pretty slow this time of year."

"Not many tourists?"

"A few stragglers now and then."

"Any strangers lately?'

She folded the paper and placed it on the counter. Pushing wispy gray hair back into the neat bun at the back of her head, she stood, yawning. "Had one come in yesterday I'd never seen before."

Her words piqued his attention, but he didn't want to appear too interested, so he leaned against the counter and chewed on a toothpick. "Oh yeah. Tell me about him."

She looked at Hawkman with twinkling eyes. "Seedy looking fellow. Bought a six pack of beer and junk food."

Taking a handful of peanuts from the bowl on the counter, Hawkman cracked them open and threw the meat into his mouth. "What do you mean by seedy?"

"Grubby, unshaven. Had long black hair hanging to his shoulders in greasy clumps. Doubt it'd seen a comb in a long time. Also, bad acne scars pitted his face." She shuddered. "And he looked like an ape."

Hawkman raised his eyebrows. "How so?"

Amelia put an arm out even with her shoulder. "Oh, he came to about here on me. But his arms were so long that his hands almost touched his knees."

"Sounds like a real woman killer." Hawkman's shoulders jerked with a snicker.

Amelia grinned and shook her head. "Not quite. He looked more like a member of the Mafia with that long jagged scar running down one side of his face." She drew her finger down her own cheek. "He gave me the willies."

Hawkman crunched several more peanuts, making a stack of shells on the counter before he responded. "Has he been back?"

"No. Thank goodness." She wiped the shells from the counter into the wastebasket.

❧•❧•❧•❧•❧•❧•❧

Jennifer poured another cup of coffee and stared bleary eyed out the kitchen window. When she saw Hawkman drive by, she dropped the mug on the counter and ran out the front door.

But by the time she reached the end of her driveway, he'd already disappeared inside the store. She dashed down the road, stopped at the door and took a deep breath, then entered. When she passed Amelia and Hawkman, on her way to the refrigerated area, she overheard Amelia talking about an ape-looking creature giving her the willies. She lifted a half-gallon of milk from the cooler and headed back to the front of the store where Hawkman waited by the door. "Hi Amelia. Put this on my bill, please."

Amelia rang up the purchase and attached the receipt to her book. "You're all set."

"Thanks." She walked outside with Hawkman. "What were you and Amelia talking about?"

"Some seedy looking character that recently wandered into the store. Probably the same slum who broke into my place."

Jennifer twisted her head around and stared at him. "When?"

"Yesterday, while we were out shooting. My cabin's a total wreck. I didn't tell Amelia about it though. Didn't want to frighten her."

Jennifer stared at the ground.

He motioned toward his truck. "Come on, I'll take you home."

She climbed into the cab. "Did you know your phone's out of order?"

"Yeah, it's smashed." Then he gave her a quick side-ways glance. "How'd you know?"

"I tried to to call you several times last night but all I got was that damn busy signal."

He raised an eyebrow. "Why'd you call?"

Jennifer took a deep ragged breath, "Someone tried to break into my house last night."

Hawkman slammed on the brakes in the middle of the road. "What!" He turned and looked at her seriously. "You okay?"

She nodded. "Yes. I would have come looking for you last night, but I was too scared to leave the house."

He took his foot off the brake and coasted into her driveway. When they were inside, she noticed Hawkman glance at the gun on the counter where she'd left it.

"I see you were frightened enough to get the gun?"

She slid the milk into the refrigerator. "After you hear what happened, you'll understand why."

"Start at the beginning."

Jennifer related the events of the previous night, then walked over to the dining room window and pointed out toward the road. "He took off across the open lot and jumped into a car parked over there."

Hawkman's brow furrowed. "Did you get a good look at him?"

She shook her head. "No. He wore a ski mask, dark colored clothes and gloves. About all I can tell you is that he was tall." She folded her arms around her waist. "That doesn't help much does it?"

He stood thoughtfully for a moment, frowning. "You said tall? That sure doesn't sound like the fellow Amelia described."

Jennifer followed him out on the deck and pointed out the scarred marks around the lock. Then she led him down the steps and pointed out the path where the intruder had fled across the open lot. They searched the area thoroughly but found no clues.

When they came back inside the house, the phone was ringing. Hawkman stretched his arm in front of Jennifer to stop her from answering it. "Let's see if they'll leave a message."

A distorted voice came over the machine, "Say, Jennifer, in your pretty little see-through gown. Did I wake you up last night?" A sickening laugh emitted over the line.

Jennifer stepped back, her hand at her throat, horror written across her face.

The message continued. "You've blown your chance and ignored my warnings. That's really too bad, since you're such a pretty little thing. Has Hawk Man told you about Sylvia? Ask him what happened when she got in my way." Another cynical laugh, then the line went dead.

She stared at Hawkman. His mouth had curled into a snarl and his nostrils flared, resembling an angry bull. His clenched fist came down hard on the counter. "Damn him!"

Trembling, she walked into the living room, a chill racing up and down her spine. She closed her eyes and put her fingers to her temples.

"He's using a voice changer."

Not knowing what to say, Jennifer just listened without commenting as he kept replaying the tape until she wanted to scream. "Hawkman, please don't play it again."

He yanked the tape from the machine. "I'm sending this to Bill. This bastard is too close. He knows your name, what you look like and even what you're wearing. I don't like it."

He'd no more popped in a replacement tape, than the phone rang again. When a muffled voice came over the line, she covered her face with her hands and moaned.

"Jennifer, where the hell are you? I hope you're not with Hawkman. For your own good, stay away from him."

Hawkman glared at the machine. "Who the hell is that? That's not the same voice."

Jennifer turned pale. She gripped the back of one of the dining room chairs until her knuckles turned white. Her voice quivered. "Are you sure?"

"Yes. I can tell the difference. The other guy used a voice changer, but this one's covered the receiver with a cloth or something. This voice has different inflections."

She couldn't believe this was happening.

"Have you had any problems at work?"

"None." Her voice hardly audible. "I'm seldom at the office. I do most of my writing at home and either mail it in or drop it off when I'm in town."

Hawkman paced the floor.

Jennifer grabbed his arm and looked up at him with pleading eyes. "Please don't leave me, I'm so scared."

He patted her hand on his arm. "Don't think for one minute that I'd leave you alone. Just consider me your personal bodyguard until I find this guy."

She let out a sigh of relief and collapsed on the couch.

Hawkman leaned over the back and asked. "Didn't John tell you to stay away from me?"

She glanced up at him. "Yes."

"He's probably one of the callers."

"But why would he disguise his voice? It doesn't make sense."

CHAPTER SEVEN

Hawkman moved into Jennifer's guest room with the idea he'd get this problem settled soon. The voices on the phone had promised she'd suffer from associating with him. He shuddered when he thought of what might have happened if the intruder had made it inside her house and thanked God she'd kept her cool and scared the guy off. But for the past few days nothing had happened and he had no new clues to move on. He spent nights staring at the ceiling.

On the fourth morning, Hawkman rose before Jennifer and made coffee. With a cup of brew in hand, he ambled out on the deck and enjoyed the tranquil view. Not a ripple disturbed the lake's reflection. The serenity enveloped him for several minutes, until he glanced at his watch. Time to get on with business.

He returned to the kitchen, sat down at the bar by the phone and keyed in the number, drumming his fingers on the leather-like formica. When Bill's familiar voice finally echoed over the line, he stiffened.

"Did you receive the tapes?"

"Yeah, and you're right. There are two different voice patterns, but I don't have all the results yet."

"Anything on the note?"

"Still analyzing it. Anything new happening there?"

"Things are heating up." Hawkman related the intruder incident.

"I'm worried, Bill. I have no idea how many I'm dealing with. Rush any information ASAP."

Bill paused for a moment, then cleared his throat. "Casey, the Agency wants you to back off. Let us handle this."

Hawkman sensed disapproval in Bill's edgy voice. "You know I can't do that."

"Then at least let us put the Morgan woman under protective custody."

"I've already approached her. She won't go for it."

Bill's voice rose. "Why the hell not? It could save her life."

"I know. But she's in the process of adopting a boy and feels if she leaves it'll screw up her chances."

Bill let out an impatient breath. "Damn. She can't adopt anyone if she's dead. I'll send someone to stay with her."

"No need. I'm here."

"Why the hell didn't you tell me that earlier?"

"You didn't ask."

"Well, that gives me some relief. Give me her phone number."

Hawkman had just hung up when Jennifer came from her bedroom, looking fresh and rested, dressed for the day in her jeans and sweatshirt. Her hair hung straight, still damp and glistening from the shower. She headed straight for the coffee pot.

"Good morning. Who was that?"

"Bill. I checked to see if they had any results on the tape and note, but they're still testing. He'll let me know when they've finished."

Jennifer ran her finger around the rim of her cup, then stared out the window, blowing across the steaming vapors.

Hawkman knew something was bothering that pretty head. "Why so quiet?"

She continued to gaze out the window. "I keep having nightmares about that hooded man and what he might have done to me."

Hawkman immediately crossed the room and put his hands on her shoulders. He gently turned her to face him and looked deeply into her eyes. The stirring he felt within, jolted him so that he fumbled for words. "Don't worry about it anymore. Thanks to your cool head and fast thinking, he didn't get in. I promise nothing's going to happen to you."

Fearful she might sense his alarm, he turned her back toward the window and pointed at the hills. "Let's forget about all this stuff for a while and take a hike to the top of the mesa. We'll take the falcon so he can hunt. And with any luck, we might see a herd of wild horses."

"Really?" She looked up at him, her eyes sparking with curiosity. "I've heard about them. Have you ever seen any?"

"Only once. They're a magnificent sight. A big beautiful black stallion led the herd I saw. But I can't guarantee anything. They wander all over the area." He smiled at her. "It's a long walk. Think you're up to it?"

Raising a fist, she grinned. "Say no more. I'm game." She rushed to the refrigerator and took out lunch meats and condiments. "I'll make some sandwiches to take along."

It pleased him that the idea had lifted her spirits. "I'll go check out the truck while you're doing that." After the brake episode, he didn't trust anything to stay the way he'd left it.

After finding all the mechanics in order on the vehicle, he rummaged through the storage box and found a couple of canteens they could attach to their belts. Jennifer packed the sandwiches into a knapsack and filled the water jugs, then pulled her hair up into a pony tail. Hawkman carried the falcon out and placed him on the portable perch.

They drove as far as possible before Hawkman parked the 4X4 on the shoulder of the narrow road. He released the falcon and watched him disappear toward the north. Then he slung the knapsack over his shoulder and they started the hike up the steep grade toward the mesa.

Midway up, Jennifer stopped and let out a puff of air. "Whew, am I going to be sore tomorrow."

Hawkman laughed. "Yeah, I can feel my legs straining against the slope."

When they finally reached the top, Hawkman dropped the backpack to the ground and flopped down on a large boulder. "That's some hike," he said, wiping the sweat from his forehead with his sleeve.

Jennifer eyed him with an impish grin. Raising her arms high in the air, she took a deep breath. "My, what a nice invigorating climb. Looks like I'm in much better shape than my hiking partner."

He jerked up his head up. "Oh yeah!"

She laughed and started running across the flat ground.

Chasing her down, he caught her by the arm, but immediately put his finger to his lips. "Shhhh, Look." He pointed toward a shallow canyon and gently tugged her toward the ground behind a scraggy bush.

Directly in front of them, not more than a couple hundred yards away, a black stallion pawed the earth. His harem of mares grazed on the lush green foliage while the young stallions bucked playfully, chasing and nipping each other's hind quarters, establishing their rank in the herd.

Jennifer and Hawkman lay on their bellies, whispering. "I count twenty horses altogether," she said.

He nodded. "Looks like the herd has almost doubled and they look healthy. Those shiny coats indicate they're eating well."

They watched the high spirited stallion prance and preen until suddenly, with no warning, the black steed bucked high, pawed the air with his hooves and neighed loudly. When his front feet hit the ground, he ducked his head low and ran full speed out of the gulch. The herd followed close behind.

Jennifer sat up cross-legged with a disappointed look. "Do you think we scared him?"

Hawkman stood and brushed the dust from his clothes. "Maybe he caught our scent."

Just as Jennifer got to her feet, he pushed her back down, throwing his body over hers. "Stay down!"

She forced her head up under his arm and spotted a black helicopter hovering above the area where they'd parked the truck. Hawkman crawled over her, then tugged on her jacket. "Follow me." He led her behind a large boulder where they stayed until the chopper swung up and disappeared in the opposite direction.

Hawkman climbed out from behind the rock and stood, staring toward the air space the copter had occupied. "That's what frightened the horses. They heard it before we did." He scratched the back of his head. "Why the interest in my truck?"

Jennifer walked up beside him, brushing off her clothes. "You're getting paranoid. Pacific Power choppers check the high lines up here all the time."

"That helicopter didn't have any markings on it."

She stood with her hands on her hips and searched the sky. "Well, he's gone now. Shall we eat our sandwiches?"

"Sure." His gaze still scanning the horizon, he stumbled toward a big rock and sat down.

Jennifer fished out the food and sat down beside him. "I can't get the sight of those beautiful horses out of my mind."

Hawkman's thoughts drifted elsewhere and her voice sounded far way. He chowed down his sandwich with a gulp of water and hurried her along. He didn't feel safe on top of this unprotected mesa. They soon returned to the truck and Jennifer pointed skyward. "There's Pretty Boy."

⊰•⊱•⊰•⊱•⊰•⊱

The next morning, Hawkman came out of his bedroom, sniffing the aroma of sausage. After eating, he carried his plate to the sink and rinsed it off. "Thanks for the great breakfast, Jennifer." He rubbed the back of his neck. "As bad as I hate to house clean, I think it's about time I finish cleaning up my place. It's still a big mess."

She glanced up at him. "Want me to help?"

"No, thanks. You should be fine here for a little while. I'll just leave my truck out front and take your boat across the lake." He glanced at her. "That is, if you don't mind."

"Sure, no problem."

"Enjoy your space. It shouldn't take me too long." He stepped out on the deck then turned back. "I almost forgot. Do you have an extra phone? Mine's smashed, but I don't think the the phone jack's hurt."

"I'll get the one from my bedroom. Just be sure and bring it back when you're through." She hurried to her room, returning with the phone and the keys to the boat.

"Thanks. I'll call as soon as I get over there. However, if you don't hear from me, don't worry. There may be more damage than meets the eye."

He glided the Mysterious Lady across the lake and secured her to his dock. Walking slowly up the path toward his cabin, he inspected the hidden traps that he'd set, making sure none were disturbed. When he reached the front door, he squatted and checked the almost invisible thread pulled taut across the bottom, making sure it still held tight. Before entering the house, he flung open the door and stood back, taking no chances that a bomb might go off.

When the cabin appeared clear of booby traps, he went inside and hooked up the phone. The dial tone came on loud and clear, so he first touched base with Jennifer, then called Pacific Power. They assured him all their helicopters were on duty up north, fighting a forest fire. They hadn't flown over the Copco Lake area for two weeks.

He dropped the receiver onto the cradle and stared into space. They'd confirmed his fears. Now, he really wanted a cigarette. Even though he'd quit ten years ago, he never got over the desire. He yanked off his sweat shirt, stuck a toothpick in his mouth and grabbed the broom. His frustration level went down as the house took shape.

Sometime later, while sitting at the kitchen table sorting through stacks of paper, he slowly lifted his head. That inner sense kicked in. Paying attention to that instinct had saved his life more than once. He removed his gun from the holster, crossed to the window and peered out the corner of the curtain. Nothing seemed amiss, but that didn't satisfy him.

He eased out the door and crept to the back of the house where he'd stacked the firewood. Seeing nothing suspicious, he started around the other side then stopped abruptly, ducking under the high deck. A movement in the shadows of the nearby trees caught his eye. He watched the silhouette of a man darting in and out of the shadows making his way to the front corner of the cabin.

The man flattened his back against the siding and inched his way along the wall until he was underneath the kitchen window. He grasped the sill and pulled himself up to peer inside the house. The evening sun glistened off the long blade of a knife he held in his hand.

Hawkman waited for the right moment, then with lightning speed he abandoned his cover and grabbed the man around the neck in a death grip. Gasping for breath, the man cried out in pain as Hawkman yanked his arm backwards into a hammer lock, forcing the knife to drop to the ground.

"What the hell are you doing?" Hawkman demanded, poking his gun into the man's ribs.

"L-lookin' for someone," the man stammered. "I ain't doin' nothing wrong."

Hawkman kicked the knife out of reach. "It looks mighty suspicious when you're waving a knife and peeking in windows on private property." He released his hold on the man's arm, but jabbed him in the back with his gun. "Keep your hands in the air and walk straight ahead."

"Where are you taking me?"

"Inside."

Once they entered the cabin, Hawkman closed the door, snatched a pair of handcuffs from his desk drawer and snapped them around the man's wrists, then shoved him down into a chair. Holstering his gun, he grabbed a rope hanging from a nail on the wall and tied him up. Hawkman's nose twitched and his stomach lurched as the man's dirty body odor invaded his nostrils. "Damn, you stink. Should dump you into the lake for a bath, but I'm afraid you'd pollute it."

Hawkman dragged a second chair around and straddled it. Now facing the greasy character, he twirled his Buck knife in front of him and stared into the small black beady eyes. "Who are you? And what do you want?"

The unexpressive eyes moved away, refusing to meet Hawkman's glare.

Hawkman touched the sharp corner of the knife to the man's chest. "You said you were looking for someone. Who?"

"A man."

"What's his name?"

"Hawk Man."

"Okay, that's me. So, what'd you want?"

His small eyes around the room as he pursed his lips, but he didn't respond.

Moving the knife dangerously close to the man's nose, Hawkman brought his face closer. "I asked you a question."

The man turned his cheek and stared at the wall.

Hawkman got up and circled the chair. What a filthy bastard, he noted. His shirt wore the signs of many days wear: food stains splattered the front and sweat stains ringed the arm pits. His hair fit Amelia's description and the long angular scar running down his cheek did indeed remind one of the Mafia.

He raked the knife point across his back, making him squirm. Then Hawkman noticed the bulging hip pocket of the man's filthy pants. He reached down and yanked out a worn, frayed wallet. The man twisted hard against the rope.

"Hey, you ain't got no right to take that."

"Shut-up." Hawkman flipped open the wallet. Scum, he thought. No professional carries identification on the job. He memorized the pictured driver's license, 'Arthur Velum'.

He crossed the room and dumped the contents onto the table. Shuffling through the stuff, he found a dirty piece of paper with an address, date and time scrawled on it. Could prove to be a valuable piece of information, he thought, stuffing it into his pocket.

Velum's continual struggle against the rope caused Hawkman to cast a side-ways glance. He grimaced at the dirty drops of sweat dripping from the stubble on the man's chin. Shaking his head in disgust, Hawkman turned his attention back to the wallet and ran his finger inside one of the inner pockets. A picture fluttered to the floor and landed face down. Expecting to see a photo of a woman or child, Hawkman reached down and picked it up. The picture caught him by surprise and his jaw tensed. He was staring at a photo of himself, up in the hills releasing the falcon for a hunt. Now, how the hell did someone get so close without me knowing it? he wondered. The adrenalin pumped through his veins, making his neck burn. He must be getting careless.

Turning the picture over, he read the message written in pencil: "Get rid of the Hawk Man or no pay". He narrowed his glare at the man tied to the chair, then stuffed the picture into his pocket.

He made a big issue of shaking the wallet over the table. "Looks like you're broke Velum. But, since you've failed your mission, you won't need any money. All you'll need is a pine box." Hawkman snickered. "You realize, of course, you're in one hell of a mess."

The man's head shot up. He glared, wide eyed.

Hawkman met his gaze. "I'd advise you to tell me who hired you. It's your only ticket to life as I doubt your boss will tolerate failure."

"None of your damn business," he spat.

Hawkman kicked the extra chair out of the way and leaned forward, touching the knife point to Velum's throat. Almost nose to nose, he poked the knife deep enough for a drop of blood to appear on the blade. "You son-of-a-bitch. I'm making it my business."

Never taking his eyes off Hawkman's face, Velum strained against the chair, his Adam's apple working his throat. "I..I.. get my or..orders by phone," he stammered.

Hawkman stepped back, withdrawing the knife. "You stupid idiot. You expect me to believe that you don't know who hired you? Just a voice on the phone."

Velum nodded vigorously.

Grabbing the front of his shirt, Hawkman yanked him forward, forcing the rope taut. "I'm going to ask you one more time. Who gives you orders?"

The small black eyes filled with terror, his voice quivering. "I don't know. I'm telling you the goddamn truth."

"Hawkman slammed him back into the chair, and strolled to the phone, twirling the knife.

Velum watched his every move, eyes bulging with fear.

Hawkman sat down, hiked his booted feet upon the table, letting them fall with a thud and punched in a number.

"Who ya callin?" Velum asked nervously.

He ignored his question. "This is Hawkman out at Copco Lake. I've got a little gift all wrapped up for you." After hanging up, he sat silently, chewing on a toothpick, staring at the scroungy creature in front of him.

Detective Williams was one of few who knew Hawkman's background and had been sworn to secrecy by the Agency. He'd put it together mighty fast without exposing anyone. They'd lock Velum up for a day or so and scare the hell out of him before releasing the scum to the streets.

Close to an hour passed before Hawkman heard a car drive up. He dropped his feet to the floor with such a sudden crash that Velum jumped. His eyes followed Hawkman to the door. Sheriff Donnelly and his partner, Officer Snyder, stepped inside and Hawkman pointed to the captive tied to the chair.

Snyder stood back and eyed the man. "My God, where did you drag that from?"

"The depths of the quagmire. Detective Williams will know what to do with him."

Donnelly untied the rope, grabbed the front of the man's shirt and yanked him to a standing position. "Better remove your cuffs so I can put mine on."

The man's voice trembled. "Where you taking me?"

Hawkman unlocked the cuffs and Donnelly replaced them with his. Then he handed the wallet to the officer and cocked his head toward the door. "Get that piece of garbage out of here before he makes me sick."

Donnelly pinched his wrinkled nose with his fingers. "No wonder."

Following them outside, Hawkman suddenly held up a hand. "Wait. I almost forgot." He glanced at the two officers. "One of you got an evidence bag?"

Snyder pulled one from his pocket. "Yeah."

Hawkman picked up Velum's knife from the ground, holding it by the tip of the blade and dropped it inside the bag. "Here's evidence he didn't come on a social call."

The two officers dragged the resisting Velum to the patrol car and shoved him into the back seat.

Hawkman watched them drive off in the unmarked car, hoping Williams could get something out of that piece of scum. Then he went back inside, sat down at the kitchen table and spread the confiscated picture and pieces of paper in front of him.

CHAPTER EIGHT

A chill snaked down Jennifer's spine as she listened to Hawkman's report of catching the scroungy looking man snooping around his cabin.

"I'm sure he's the one who ransacked my place. And, he actually did resemble a gorilla, just like Amelia described. His finger tips touched his knees." Hawkman shook his head. "He stunk like an animal too."

She'd always thought of the Copco Lake community as being safe and loathed the idea of coming home from town and finding her place torn up. She shuddered. "What do you think he wanted? "

He raised his brows and pointed his thumb at his chest. "Me. And when he didn't find me, he got mad and took it out on my house." He chuckled. "He thought that would put the fear of God into me. Scum like that don't have any brains. They take a job for the money and don't ask questions. They have no idea who they're going after."

Jennifer rubbed her eyes. "Well, I'm glad you didn't get hurt. Now you've got one of the villains out of your hair."

"That's true, but there'll be others."

She frowned. "Why do you say that?"

A look of surprise covered his face, as if she should know the answer. "Because he didn't kill me. The bastard will just keep sending more in. There's no telling how many I'll end up dealing with before it's all over."

Jennifer ran her hands up and down her arms, trying to wipe away the fear that engulfed her. The hit men would soon learn that Hawkman now lived in her guest room. But if he left, she'd be vulnerable. She abruptly stood and pressed her fingers to her temples. "I can't think about this anymore. I'm going to bed and read."

He picked up the paper and moved to the couch. "Talk to you in the morning."

She tried to concentrate on her book but couldn't. Thoughts of men breaking into her house kept running through her mind. She finally gave up and turned off the light. After what seemed like hours of tossing and turning, sleep finally won out.

⟨⫶⟩⟨⫶⟩⟨⫶⟩⟨⫶⟩

The next morning, Hawkman sat at the kitchen bar drinking coffee and watching Jennifer fix breakfast. He couldn't help but notice her unusual quietness and taut lips. Scratching his chin, he tried to think of something that might help ease her tension. Then a thought occurred. "Say, how'd you like to go to the old dump site after breakfast and do some target practicing? Practice makes perfect, you know."

Her grim expression didn't change as she slipped an egg off the spatula onto his plate. "Where's the dump site? I hope it's not on top of some mountain."

He noticed a glint in her eyes and realized she still had her sense of humor. "No, I promise it's not on the top of a mountain." He grinned, hoping she noticed. "It's just up the road a ways."

Jennifer piled the dirty dishes into the sink. "I'll do them later. I want to get out of this house." She marched back to her bedroom and retrieved her gun. "Okay, I'm ready. Let's go."

It took only a few minutes up the road and Hawkman parked on the small shoulder. He pointed toward an open field where the shell of an abandoned car rested. "Many years ago, people used this area for a dump. It's a safe spot for target practice because its tucked in between these hills."

After they'd spent a couple of hours shooting, Hawkman handed her his Colt revolver. "Here, try mine."

Jennifer blinked in surprise. "Really? I always had the impression a gun is very personal."

"It is, but I don't mind. Go ahead and try it. See how it feels."

She took a few pot shots, then handed it back. "It's a lot heavier than mine and has a bigger kick. More for a man than a woman."

He smiled, recalling his words when he first tried to convince her to take Sylvia's gun. "I think you're ready for a permit. We'll drive into town when we're through."

After they returned, a phone message awaited from Bill. He'd sent the report on the tapes by over-night delivery. Hawkman's expression turned solemn. "They must have found something for him to go to that much trouble."

The next morning, he waited outside for the Airborne Express. When it finally pulled into Jennifer's driveway, he took the envelope and ripped it open. He studied the paper for a few moments before going into the house. "Jennifer, Bill's report is here."

She came from the bedroom, looping her hair into a knot on top of her head and securing it with a large hair clip. Hawkman handed her the paper and rested a foot on the hearth as she settled on the couch. Stroking his beard, he studied her expression.

Within a few minutes, she glanced up at him with a shadowed face. "This is hard to believe."

"Those tests don't lie, Jennifer. They show that the voice lines matched those of John Alexander, Sr., but we know he's dead. The next in line is usually a relative, more than likely a child. Of course, it could be a rare coincidence, but I doubt it."

"I just can't picture John as that type of man. When I found his father's journal along with personal jewelry hidden on this property, I turned them over to him instead of the authorities. His gratitude overwhelmed me. I'll never forget that big trailer truck pulling into my driveway carrying the Boston Whaler. I told him I couldn't accept it, but he insisted. Told me to classify it as a housewarming gift. He'd already dubbed the boat 'The Mysterious Lady' in honor of his mother."

Hawkman raised his brows. "That's a mighty expensive gift for the return of personal items." He watched her pace, the report dangling from her hand. She finally stopped in front of him, a hand on her hip. "I gathered from the way you talked about John's dad, that you regarded him highly. Doesn't John have some of the same characteristics?"

He shook his head. "No. His dad dedicated his life to the Agency. John may work hard at what he does, but he hates the Agency."

Jennifer wrinkled her forehead. "Why?"

"It's a long story."

"But I'm not involved with the Agency, so why torment me?"

"It's because of me and my dedication. He must like you as he doesn't want you associating with a dangerous element. Since he couldn't convince you, he decided to scare you into staying away from me."

Jennifer stared at the report in her hand. "It's still unbelievable."

"I understand how you feel, but remember, I also know this man and he's no angel."

"Maybe if I invited him up for a weekend of fishing, we could talk this out."

Hawkman shook his head. "No, that's not a good idea. But a visit from me might work. Do you by chance have his home address?"

"Well, yes. But. . ." She stepped away, her back to him.

"Why the hesitation?"

She faced him, her brows knitted in a frown. "With your obvious dislike for one another and his hate for the Agency, do you think he'll listen?"

Hawkman shrugged. "Depends on how guilty he feels. But it's worth a try."

Jennifer laid the report on the coffee table then sat down on the ottoman, clenching her hands together. "Do you think it's safe?"

Hawkman waved a hand in the air. "Oh, he's not dangerous. Maybe a bit eccentric and weird, but not harmful."

"How can you be so sure? How long has it been since you've been around him? And how do you know whether he had something to do with the hired gunman? Or the vandalism to your place?"

He hooked his thumbs in his jeans pockets and looked puzzled. "You've got a lot of pointed question about a man you don't think would scare you, but yet you're afraid he might do something worse."

She threw her hands up in the air. "I'm confused and frustrated. I need to know your honest opinion."

"Well, that type of modus operandi is not his style. He's got a wife and children that he wouldn't put in jeopardy."

She glanced at the report again. "Bill says they haven't connected the other tape with anyone, that the voice lines are completely different."

Hawkman nodded. "That pretty well clarifies that we're dealing with two different men and two separate situations."

She dropped the paper on the table and folded her arms. "If you decide to make the trip and confront him in person, do you think he'll admit making the calls?"

"As much as he hates the Agency, he does have respect for their procedures. He knows they seldom make an error. I'll take Bill's letter in case I need to show him proof."

"So, you've decided to go? When do you plan on leaving?"

"As soon as you can get ready?"

Her eyes widened and her mouth dropped open. "Me? I'm going?"

"Well, I'm certainly not leaving you here alone."

She put a finger to her chin. "Oh dear, Hillsborough's seven hours away. What if he's not home? Shouldn't you call him first?"

"No, I want to surprise him. Throw in an extra set of clothes in case we have to spend the night." Hawkman glanced at his watch. "Can you be ready in thirty minutes? That would get us on the road by eleven."

"I'll try."

He started for the front door. "I'll be back in a few minutes. I need to get some fresh clothes from my place."

When the door slammed, she waved her hands in despair and ranted on the way to the bedroom. "I'm never going to get any writing done or make my deadlines."

She grabbed a small duffel bag from her closet shelf and tossed it on the bed. Throwing in a few clothes and cosmetics, she zipped it shut and stood for a moment in the middle of the room, worrying about those phone calls. If John really made them, he might be more dangerous than Hawkman suspected.

Her gaze turned to the small gun on her bedside table. Should she take it? Running her finger down the short shiny barrel, she stood for a minute contemplating. The thought of using it on another human being sent a shudder down her spine, but she picked it up anyway and dropped it into her purse.

She heard the familiar rumble of Hawkman's truck returning and grabbed the leather duffel bag from the bed. He walked in the door just as she entered the living room area. "Good, you're ready. Let's hit the road."

She paused before locking the door. "I'm a little apprehensive about this trip."

He waved for her to come on. "So am I. But for the sake of John's father, let's hope we can resolve this without getting the Agency involved."

⊹⊱⊰⊹⊱⊰⊹⊱⊰⊹

Shortly after seven o'clock, they located the address in Hillsborough. Hawkman parked across the street from John's house and started to get out when a black Mercedes pulled into John's garage.

Jennifer grabbed his arm. "That's him."

Hawkman slid back into the cab and closed the door. "We'll give him time to get inside." He studied the large man huffing and puffing as he got out of the car. "Good Lord, he's gained a lot of weight since I last saw him."

The garage door slid shut and they waited a few more minutes before approaching the front entry. Jennifer shifted from one foot to another until a lovely young girl of about sixteen answered the door chimes.

"Yes, can I help you?"

"We're looking for John Alexander," Hawkman said.

"May I ask who's calling?"

"Jim Anderson and Jennifer Morgan."

Jennifer jerked her head around and stared wide eyed at Hawkman.

"Just a moment, please." She shut the door and called in a loud voice. "Dad, it's for you. Jim Anderson and Jennifer Morgan."

Before Jennifer could speak, the large wooden door abruptly

opened. John stared at them for a moment. "Uh, h—hello, Jim, Jennifer. Come in. This is quite a surprise." He stepped back so they could enter.

They followed John into a magnificent study, where he closed the doors and gestured with a shaky hand for them to be seated on supple leather chairs. Jennifer's gaze scanned the walls lined with beveled glass fronted oak bookcases filled with pharmaceutical books of every kind.

After John made his way around a large oak desk and sat down, looking concerned, his eyes bounced off her and then Hawkman. "What do I owe the honor of this visit?"

Hawkman scooted to the edge of his chair, his elbows resting on his thighs, his hands clenched. "I'll get right to the issue, John. I'm sure you've figured out we're not here on a social call. Jennifer has received some threatening phone messages and I had the tapes analyzed by the Agency. The finger points to you and we want to know why you're making these calls?"

John's face turned ashen. "I don't know what you're talking about."

Hawkman shook his head. "Come on, John. You know the Agency's tests don't lie. You made the calls. Why?"

He waved a hand toward Jennifer. "I..I have no reason to threaten her."

Hawkman stood and put his hand out toward Jennifer. "I didn't want to turn this over to the Agency, but it looks like you leave me no choice. Let's go Jennifer."

John quickly raised his hand. "No, no wait, Jim, sit down." He heaved his bulky weight out of the chair and moved to the front of the desk. "Okay, so I did a stupid thing. I made some anonymous calls to her but meant no harm. Just wanted to warn her about you and that damned Agency."

He walked across the floor, gazing into space. "I've received nothing but heartache from that place. They killed my mother and ruined any relationship I might have had with my dad." He wrung his hands, beads of sweat glistened on his cheeks and forehead. "I hate it! Did you hear me, Jim? I hate the whole organization."

Hawkman sat back down and responded in a calm voice. "Yes, I hear you. But I've retired now, so why does it matter to you whether Jennifer associates with me or not?"

Jennifer's eyes followed John back to his desk.

"It doesn't matter, Jim. The Agency will never get out of your blood. Even after my dear mother died such a horrible death, dad still lived and breathed that goddamn place." He slammed his fist on the desk.

Jennifer jumped, her eyes wide.

Hawkman leaned forward. "John, your mother died from a terrible accident. It devastated your father. Don't blame him." He continued in a low soothing tone. "All his life he tried to shield his family from every aspect of the Agency, but certain precautions had to be taken and they restricted your movements. It's not surprising that you built up a resentment."

John whirled around and pointed a stubby finger. "If he hadn't been working on that chemical warfare, mother would never have picked up that lethal canister that caused her death. And Sylvia would still be alive today too, if you hadn't gotten so deeply involved."

Hawkman stiffened at the mention of Sylvia. "Okay, John, I think you've made your point. Now, let's talk about why I'm here. I want to know who else knows that I'm Jim Anderson and living at Copco Lake?"

Averting his eyes, John shrugged. "I haven't told anyone."

"But, someone else does know. And I want to know who."

John shifted his gaze to the ceiling and mopped his neck with his handkerchief. "Maybe I mentioned it when I finished up some business left by my dad."

"That's a lie," Hawkman said, his eye narrowing. "Your folk's lawyer took care of their business. And why would you talk to anyone at the Agency? What are you hiding? Level with me."

John dabbed at the sweat on his brow, then suddenly blurted. "I'm being blackmailed, dammit."

Hawkman shot a surprised look at him and then at Jennifer. "Blackmailed! What the hell for?"

John kept mopping his face. "Some time ago, a strange man called claiming he was from the Agency and wanted my dad's formula. He wouldn't give me his name and when I refused to even discuss it with him, he threatened to expose me for having secret papers in my possession. I hung up on him the first time, but he kept calling back."

"He never even gave you a code name or something to identify him?"

John shook his head. "No, nothing. And he always used a voice changer."

Hawkman raised his brows and thought back to the other threatening phone calls made to Jennifer where a voice changer had been used. Also about Velum, who told him his orders always came by phone. Could it be possible this is one and the same man? He leaned forward. "So you think he's from the Agency?"

He nodded. "Yeah, he knows too much about my dad, his formulae and other technical data a layman wouldn't know." John seemed almost on the brink of tears. "He's causing me all kinds of pain and trouble."

"Why didn't you report it? You know the Agency would have looked into the situation."

John jerked his head up. "And give them a reason to come after me. Hell no!"

Hawkman stared at him. "So how much does this guy want?"

John averted his gaze and looked out the window. "He hasn't asked for money yet."

"Then what else does he want other than the formulae?"

"Information. And if I don't comply, he'll kidnap my wife or one of my children."

Hawkman's nostrils flared. "Only information? Or has he also got you hiring killers and slitting brake lines?"

John yanked his head around and gasped. "You know I'd never get involved in that type of stuff! And let's get this straight. He had nothing to do with my phone calls to Jennifer. Those were my own doings."

Hawkman raised his hands in surrender. "Okay, I believe you. But did you tell this guy about Jim Anderson at Copco Lake?"

John's gaze dropped to the floor. "Yes. He ordered me to report anything about you as soon as I found out. Or else." His shoulders drooped. "I didn't ask why."

"My God!" Hawkman jumped out of his seat and thundered. "Do you know what you've done?"

John stepped back, fear in his eyes. "What difference does it make if you're not with the Agency anymore?"

"Because I have a new identity, you idiot. You've unmasked me with your spouting off. Now, not only is my life in danger, but Jennifer's also." Hawkman shook his fist in his face. "Damn you!"

John slumped down in his chair and dropped his head into his hands. "I'm sorry, Jim. When he threatened my family, I got scared and just did what he said."

"So you have no clue who this man is?"

John raised his head. "I swear to God, I have no idea."

"How do you contact him?

"A phone number."

Hawkman slammed his fist on the desk. "Then give me the damn number and I'll find the son-of-a-bitch."

John cringed as he took a small black book from his desk drawer and flipped it open. He wrote down a number and handed it to Hawkman.

After he stuck the paper into his pocket, he pointed a finger at John. "No more calls to Jennifer. Don't give out any more information on either of us again. If you do, you'll deal with me."

John raised both his hands in defense. "I promise. I won't tell them any more."

Hawkman leaned on John's desk and looked him in the eyes. "I'd suggest you and your family go into hiding. Someplace out of the area and stay away from relatives who can be traced. I'll let you know when it's safe to return. Call me at Jennifer's in a week and let me know your status."

"What if they have her phone tapped?"

"We'll just have to take that chance."

John nodded and stood, then stepped in front of them to open the study doors. Jennifer followed Hawkman out the front entry and into the cool refreshing evening air. The door closed behind them.

⊹⊱⊹⊱⊹⊱⊹⊱⊹

John Alexander leaned against the wall wiping his brow. When he started to return to his study, his wife Elaine stood in the living room staring at him with eyes filled with fear. He gently enfolded her into his arms, holding her for several moments, before leading her up the stairs.

Hawkman and Jennifer rode in silence for several miles before she spoke. "Why didn't you tell me your real name?"

"What purpose would a new identity serve if everyone knew my real name? Jim Anderson supposedly died."

"I understand that, but you could have prepared me for the shock. I only know you as Hawkman or Tom Casey."

"Yeah, you're right, I should have warned you. I apologize."

"How do you think John figured it out? I must have said something that set him off?"

"John and I met a long time ago in college and he knew of my interest in ornithology. When I worked with his dad, I saw him often. He knows how the Agency operates, so it wouldn't have taken him long to put it together. And he more than likely learned of my eye injury somewhere along the line."

She sighed. "And I talked about the hawks, so that gave him a good clue."

"Don't blame yourself. You knew nothing about my relationship with John's family. Plus, if I'd known his parents had owned your house, I probably wouldn't have moved to Copco Lake." He shrugged. "It's just sort of crazy the way things worked out."

"You think he'll stop making those calls now?"

"There's no reason for him to continue. However, he's in a mess of trouble. I'd like to help him, but I don't know how I can keep the Agency out of it." He took a deep breath. "I have this strange feeling that the same guy giving John fits, is the one terrorizing you. The M.O. is just too similar.

Jennifer yawned. "This whole mess is mind-boggling. Not only am I scared, but I'm exhausted."

He glanced at her. "You want me to stop and get a motel?"

"No, I'd like to go on home, unless you're too tired to drive."

"I'm fine. Why don't you lie back and rest."

While she slept, his mind worked over the visit with John and the things he said. The more he pieced together, the more concerned he became. He didn't like the way things were developing.

The late hour and minimum traffic had him in Jennifer's driveway in record time. He nudged her with his elbow. "We're home."

She sat up rubbing her eyes. "What time is it?"

"Almost four in the morning."

"Did you go over the speed limit?"

"Not me," he said, mischievously. He picked up her purse and handed it to her. "My word, that thing's heavy. What in the heck do you have in it?"

She turned her eyes down sheepishly. "My gun."

His face lit up. "Hey, you went prepared like an agent. That's great."

"Well, I didn't know what to expect."

"You did the right thing." He patted his holster. "Now you understand why I'm always armed."

Hawkman ambled around to the passenger side and had just opened the door for Jennifer, when he suddenly whirled around and pulled his gun. "Get down," he ordered harshly.

✦✦✦✦✦✦✦

Startled and fully awake, Jennifer dropped behind the dashboard. After a few seconds, she raised up and peeked through the windshield. Hawkman had disappeared into the darkness. Her heart thumped against her ribs. She pulled her gun from her purse, pushed in the clip and slid out the partially opened door. When her feet hit the ground she went into a crouch and listened intently for any sound. She heard nothing and started inching her way toward the front of the truck, keeping her head below the top of the fender.

Suddenly, gun shots exploded from the dock area. Her heart leaped into her throat as she dashed from the truck to the corner of the house. Hugging the side of the building, she stayed within the shadows, making her way to the back. Trembling, she dropped to her knees and crawled underneath the high back porch and crept silently forward. She almost screamed in terror when she came nose to nose with a warm body. Realizing a deer had decided to bed down under the porch, she took a ragged breath and leaned heavily against one of the supporters of the wooden frame. The alarmed animal fled quietly out the other end.

Her heart still loudly pounding in her ears, she groped her way toward the wooden lattice that decorated the front of the porch. She peered between the crisscross pattern in search of Hawkman. But all she saw was the wake of a boat racing away from the dock.

CHAPTER NINE

When Hawkman reached the back corner of the house, he spotted a small boat floating next to the Mysterious Lady. Using the blackberry bushes as cover, he crept closer to the water's edge and could make out the silhouettes of two men, whose muffled voices drifted across the water. They were hunched over in their boat, examining something under the narrow beam of a flashlight.

He inched forward, hoping he could decipher their conversation, but a covey of roosting quail erupted from the bush next to him, loudly clicking their warning signals as they flew in all directions. Both men jerked up their heads, one aiming the flashlight toward the shore, catching Hawkman in its beam.

He stood and aimed his gun at their heads. "Police! Hands up or I'll shoot."

Immediately the flashlight went out. "Let's get the hell outta here!" one of them yelled. The boat's engine roared to life and they navigated sharply into the channel, leaving a spray of water in its wake.

Hawkman fired a couple of warning shots over their heads, but they quickly disappeared into the darkness. He shoved his gun back into the holster and headed back toward the front of the house. Just as he reached the corner, Jennifer emerged from underneath the porch, holding her gun in her hand.

"What the hell are you doing under there?"

"I thought you might need some help."

He took her arm and led her toward the front. "They're gone."

"What were they doing?"

"Messing with your boat. And I need to check it out. Do you have a lantern or a big flashlight?"

"Well, yes. But, what were they trying to do, steal it?"

"No, I think they planted a bomb."

Jennifer froze in her tracks.

He turned and looked at her. "I want to make sure they didn't succeed."

She hurried past him, retrieved her purse from the truck and started to go inside, but Hawkman seized her hand.

"Wait." He pointed toward a tree near the house. "Go stand behind that."

She backed away, staring at him. He waited until she'd reached the sheltered area, then using his own key, in one swift movement, he unlocked the door, flung it open and jumped back.

Jennifer started to come forward, but Hawkman raised his hand. "No. Stay there until I tell you it's safe." Then, he disappeared inside. Within a few minutes, he poked his head out the door and waved her in. "It's okay, you can come inside."

The falcon rustled his feathers at the sight of her and cocked his head. She frowned. "I'm so tired of being cautious."

"Had to make sure they hadn't been in the house. Now, if you'll find me that flashlight, I'll go check the boat."

"Do you know anything about bombs?" she asked, reaching into the utility closet and handing him a lantern, along with a large flashlight.

"Yes, I know enough to be careful. But I don't want you down there until I'm sure it's safe."

⋅⫟⋅⟩⋅⫟⋅⟩⋅⫟⋅⟩⋅⫟⋅⟩⋅⫟⋅

Jennifer switched on the the outside lights and stood on the deck. She leaned on the railing, her eyes watching every movement of the lantern, expecting any moment to see her boat, dock and Hawkman go up in a big fire ball. Finally, he waved for her to join him.

She hurried down the gangplank, trusting his wisdom. When she arrived at his side, he pointed the flashlight beam on wires dangling over the side of the Mysterious Lady, flipping precariously in the breeze. "Looks like I interrupted their mission in the nick of time." Then he moved the light to the ignition area, where a small pack of plastic explosives lay next to the steering wheel. "They never got it connected."

Her hand went to her throat. "One of us could've been badly maimed."

Hawkman gave her a black look. "Or killed."

Thinking of Sylvia's brutal death, her voice shook. "What if one of these days they succeed?"

"We won't let them. We're going to take extreme caution. Before you take your boat or car out, I want to check it thoroughly."

Jennifer clenched her trembling hands together and took several deep breaths, trying to suppress the fear growing inside her. Her stomach felt like a huge knot and her insides shook so hard that she couldn't speak.

Hawkman climbed into the boat. "I think I'd better remove these plastic explosives."

She glanced out across the dark body of water. "You think they'll come back?" Her voice quivered.

"I doubt it, but I'm not taking any chances. It'll soon be daylight, but we'll leave on the outside lights anyway. I'll nap on the couch in the living room and keep watch."

⊹⊱◈⊰⊹⊱◈⊰⊹⊱◈⊰⊹

A couple of days later, Jennifer awoke to the loud honking of Canadian geese flying over the house. She groaned, rolled onto her stomach and pulled the cover over her head. But her eyes flew open when a dog barked. "That came from the living room. What the heck's a dog doing in my house?" She jumped up and threw on her robe.

Poking her head out the bedroom door, she saw Hawkman sitting on the living room floor with Herman in his lap and Sam leaning over his shoulder. She combed her fingers through her hair and headed toward the threesome. "What's happened?"

Hawkman held up a porcupine quill. "Herman tangled with a varmint last night and got the raw end of the deal."

"Oh, Herman, you poor thing." She knelt beside the dog and patted his head. He let out a low mournful whine.

"There," Hawkman said, giving Herman a healthy pat on his rear, "that's the last one. Now you're all fixed."

The dog's tail thumped loudly and before Hawkman could stand up, he received a big slobbery dog kiss. Jennifer and Sam laughed at Hawkman's grimace as he wiped his cheek with the back of his sleeve.

He put a hand on Sam's shoulder. "Be gentle with Herman for a few days. Try not to run him too much. That quill buried in his front paw went pretty deep, so he'll probably limp a little. I've already medicated it, but if it gets puffy or looks infected, bring him back so I can doctor it again."

Sam gave Herman a big hug and Jennifer handed him a biscuit for the dog. "Don't worry, I'll watch it. Thanks for fixing him up."

While Herman munched his treat, Sam turned inquiring blue eyes toward Hawkman. Putting both hands on his hips, he tilted his chin upwards. "Is Hawkman your real name?"

Glancing at the flaxen headed boy, Hawkman grinned. "No."

"Then how come people call you that?"

Winking at Jennifer, he pointed toward the perch. "You see that bird?"

Sam turned his head toward the falcon. "Yeah."

"He's a member of the hawk family. I found him injured up in the hills. He'd have died if I hadn't brought him home and nursed him back to health. When the people living here first saw me with him on my arm, they started calling me the 'Hawk Man'. . . and it stuck."

The boy's eyes grew wide with wonder. He glanced from Hawkman to the falcon and back. "Why didn't he fly away?"

Hawkman shrugged. "I don't know, Sam. I've given him plenty of opportunities to go back to the wild, but he always returns.

After a few thoughtful moments, Sam reached down and grabbed Herman's collar. "I better get him home. Thanks again."

Hawkman and Jennifer watched Sam walk slowly down the driveway with his dog. They heard Sam tell the animal, "Wow,

Herman, wait until I tell Mr. Jordan about that falcon. But we can't run now. We'll just take our time and tell him when we get there."

Chuckling, Jennifer went into the kitchen and poured herself a cup of coffee. "What a wonderful way to start your day, helping a little guy and his dog in distress."

He nodded. "He's a neat kid. I like him. I can understand why you want to adopt him."

⊷⊶⊷⊶⊷⊶⊷⊶⊷

That afternoon, Hawkman received a call from Jake. He punched on the speaker phone so Jennifer could hear.

"I'm worried about Herb and Elsie Zanker," Jake said. "They're an older couple that live up past Topsy Grade. I've tried calling them several times and so has Amelia, but we keep getting a busy signal. I'm afraid either their phone lines are down or something's wrong. The roads are deeply rutted up that way due to the heavy rainfall and the graders won't go up that far until spring. And I know Herb won't take that new truck of his out of the garage as long as the roads are bad."

"I'm going to be up in that area tomorrow. Want me to check on them?" Hawkman asked.

Jake's voice sounded relieved. "That would be great. I can't get away before next week. Let me give you the directions to their place."

After writing down the instructions, Hawkman turned to Jennifer. "Looks like we have a goodwill trip tomorrow."

She smiled. "It'll be a nice outing."

The next morning, they climbed into the 4X4 and after thirty minutes of a rough and bumpy ride, they finally reached the long winding driveway that led to the Zankers' ranch. When they approached the dwelling, a couple of large dogs charged from behind the barn and barked menacingly until a man stepped out the front door and called them off.

Hawkman climbed out of the truck. "You Herb Zanker?"

The man strolled toward him and extended his hand. "Sure am. And from what I know about you, I'd say you're the Hawk Man."

He grinned. "You got that right." He gestured toward Jennifer as she came around the front of the truck. "This is Jennifer Morgan."

She shook Herb's hand. "Jake and Amelia are worried about you folks. They've been trying to call you all week and couldn't get through. We told them we'd check on you since we'd be in the area."

Herb cocked his head. "That's mighty nice of you." Then he turned toward the house. "Come on up and meet my Elsie."

An older woman with a shawl draped over her frail shoulders and a face wreathed in smiles hurried down the porch steps.

Herb put his arm around her and introduced Elsie to Jennifer and Hawkman.

"It's so nice to have company." She motioned toward the house. "Won't you come in for a spell?"

She put a small arthritic hand on Jennifer's arm. "I heard you say that Amelia had tried to call. Our phone has been out of order for some time, but it's supposed to get fixed today."

Jennifer patted her hand. "You be sure and call her the minute you can. She's worried about you."

"I'll do that this afternoon."

Once inside, Elsie poured coffee for everyone. Then they congregated in the living room, sitting around the cozy fireplace. Herb eyed Jennifer above his spectacles. "So you're the young widow who moved into the Oxnard's house?"

But before she could answer, he turned suspicious eyes on Hawkman and pointed the stem of his pipe. "And someone tried to kill you not too long ago. Why was that? You got enemies?"

Taken back by the man's boldness, Hawkman cleared his throat. "Mr. Zanker, I wish I knew the answer, but I don't."

"Call me Herb. Copco Lake's become a haven for mysterious characters these past few years. Lots of strange happenings." He turned back to Jennifer. "Now, take that house you live in." His eyes twinkled. "A strange couple lived there. They visited only in the summer. Never during the cold months, mind you."

Elsie straightened in her chair and nodded. "My Herb's right. They were a peculiar couple. Why, Mrs. Oxnard never left that house. There were a few people who lived across the lake said they saw her sitting on the dock a few times. But even with their binoculars they couldn't make out her face because she always wore wide brimmed floppy hats and sat under a big droopy umbrella,"

Herb packed his pipe with fresh tobacco. "Then, the big black helicopter came."

All eyes turned toward Herb.

"I saw it land on the meadow."

Jennifer shot a look at Hawkman while Herb sucked on his pipe.

"On my way home from town one day I saw that chopper hovering, so I pulled to the side of the road and watched it set down behind the trees. It pulled back up into the air within minutes and disappeared over the hills." He snapped his fingers and his bright blue eyes danced. "Then in a little while here comes Mr. Oxnard in his truck, heading back toward the Lake." Herb leaned back in his chair and took a long drag on his pipe while he watched their faces. "No one ever saw Mrs. Oxnard again."

"Do you think that helicopter took her somewhere?" Jennifer asked.

Elsie scooted forward on her chair and wagged her finger. "We think she might have been terrible ill, or something wrong with her, as Mrs. Oxnard never befriended any one. No one ever saw her up close. Amelia told me she never visited the store, only Mr. Oxnard. She said, he always wore sunglasses and a hat pulled low over his eyes. He'd buy something, put cash on the counter and walk out. Never said a word or waited for his change. They just weren't friendly people."

Herb turned his attention toward Jennifer. "Tell me young lady, did you know about all this mystery before you bought that house?"

Jennifer coughed and her gaze leaped from Herb to Hawkman. "Huh, a little. The realtor showed me newspaper clippings and told me about Mr. Oxnard dying in a plane crash. I just assumed she'd died several years before as they spoke of Mr. Oxnard as a widower."

Herb put his elbows on his knees and pointed his pipe stem in the air. "You know, after Mr. Oxnard's death, men in uniforms blocked anyone from going near that house. But I noticed a few unmarked trucks inside the fence. I wondered if they were carpet layers, painters or some sort of repairmen. But I never saw any work going on."

Jennifer spoke up. "I know there were several house repairs done before I moved in, but I find it strange that there were uniformed guards around the house, unless Mr. Oxnard was a government official and had secret documents inside."

Herb puffed on his pipe before answering. "Hard to say. But I went into the store one day and this tall red-headed man stood chattin' with a short stocky fellow as they drank a soda. They seemed to know each other real good."

Hawkman immediately slid forward in his chair and rested his elbows on his knees. He held his cup with both hands and gave his full attention to Herb.

"The two men spoke in low tones, but I heard the tall one say that he couldn't find a thing. Now, that don't sound like no carpet layers or painters." Herb leaned back in his chair with a satisfied grunt.

"That could fit in with what Jennifer suggested. The man could have been an agent or some top level government official," Hawkman said, in a noncommittal tone.

Herb bent forward again, his pipe waving in the air and continued as if he hadn't heard Hawkman's comment. "Being I'm not shy, I walked right over to this tall guy and asked him what the hell's going on at that house."

Hawkman eyed the older man. "What did he say?"

"Well." Herb's gaze locked with Hawkman's. "He stared at me with the coldest blue eyes I've ever seen, drilled right through me. He pointed a finger at my nose and said, 'Old man, don't concern yourself with something that's none of your business.' Then, he and his friend walked out of the store." Herb knocked the ashes from his pipe into the fireplace before glancing back at Hawkman. He lowered his voice. "If you ask me, that red-headed one looked like a mean S.O.B."

The women then cut into the conversation, changing the topic, but Hawkman's thoughts remained on what Herb had just related. Several things swirled into his mind. The Agency was definitely involved with the operation Herb described. They were making sure that Mr. Alexander, alias Mr. Oxnard hadn't left any high security papers behind. They obviously didn't find them, as Jennifer discovered the secret formulae documents later in a remote hiding place and turned them over to John. When they whisked John's mother away in the helicopter, she'd become to ill to stay at the summer house and eventually passed away in the hospital. But the part that bothered Hawkman the most was the description of the tall red-headed man in charge.

Jennifer's hand on his shoulder interrupted his deliberation. "It's getting late, and it sounds like rain outside. Maybe we should think about leaving."

Hawkman nodded and stood. "We better hit the road before it gets bad out there. That howling wind sounds like another storm's brewing."

Herb walked over and extended his hand. "Hawkman, thanks for checking in on us. Appreciate it and it's been a pleasure talking to you. You tell Jake and Amelia we'll call them real soon."

Hawkman took his hand. "Will do." He then turned toward Elsie. "Thanks for your hospitality, Mrs. Zanker."

She nodded and smiled. "You tell Amelia I'll get in touch as soon as my phone's fixed.

"We'll let them know all is well here," Hawkman said, as they stepped out onto the porch.

A blowing, rainy wind met him and Jennifer as they scurried to the truck.

The storm developed into a downpour by the time they reached home. Jennifer jumped out of the truck and almost lost her balance when a gust of wind whipped around the corner of the garage.

"This is some storm," she yelled above the roar.

They hurried inside and Hawkman quickly stoked the fire. The falcon let out a small squawk, welcoming them home.

"That bird certainly likes this place," he said. "I've never seen him so content and I must admit he's acquired quite a personality."

Jennifer smiled. "He probably thinks he's human. I talk to him all the time."

Once the fire kicked in, the heat soared through the room. Jennifer shrugged off her coat and busied herself making hot cocoa. When they were both settled on the hearth, their backs to the fire and sipping warm chocolate, she glanced at Hawkman. "Why were you so interested in the story Mr. Zanker told about that tall red-headed man with the piercing blue eyes? Did you know the man he described?"

Hawkman straightened his back and let out a long breath. "Sounded like someone I knew a long time ago."

Suddenly, the lights flickered and went out.

"Uh, oh," Jennifer said, "better build a bigger fire. With this storm, the electricity won't be back on for quite awhile."

Jennifer got out of the way while Hawkman placed another log on the pile. She moved over to the couch and snuggled down, pulling a coverlet up over her shoulders. It didn't take long before the hypnotic dancing flames lulled her to sleep.

When Hawkman noticed, he placed another small lap blanket over her. He stood for a moment gazing down at the small body, then reached down to brush a few strands of hair from her face. When his fingers touched the velvet skin of her cheek, his heart surged. At that moment, he realized he wanted to be more than a body guard to this woman.

CHAPTER TEN

Jennifer awakened to the inviting aroma of freshly brewed coffee. She rubbed her eyes and pushed off the coverlets. Thank goodness the power had come back on. She got off the couch and meandered into the kitchen, glancing out the window as she poured a mug of coffee. Hawkman was busy cleaning up the front yard of the storm debris and raking it into a big pile.

She took her cup and ambled back to the bathroom where she indulged in a warm shower. The water pulsed against her back and she thought of how nice to have a man around who's helpful, rugged and handsome. She instantly felt shamed for having such thoughts. Don't forget he's in your house for one reason, to protect you. She quickly dried, dressed and left the bathroom.

When she entered the kitchen, Hawkman had just dropped the phone into the cradle. "Good morning. Who have you been talking to so early?"

He glanced up. "Bill."

She felt tension creeping into her chest as she poured another cup of coffee. "Did he have anything new to report?

"No, but he is concerned about all that's happening."

"What did he say about the guy trying to break into my house?"

"He thinks it's all connected and has his whole crew working over time."

Her expression serious, she looked at him from the opposite side of the kitchen bar. "While you were with the Agency, did things like this happen often?"

A slight grin curled the corners of his mouth. "Let's just say, never a day went by without some sort of action."

Jennifer went to her computer after breakfast. "Hawkman, if I don't get some writing done, I'm not going to get paid."

"I know it's rough with me in your face." He drummed his fingers on the counter, then glanced at her with a smile. "Tell you what. I'll change the oil in your car and tune it up. That will get me out of the house awhile so you can work without interruption. What do you think?"

She smiled gratefully. "That's a splendid idea."

"Good, give me your keys and I'll get started."

Just as she dug them out of her purse, the phone rang. Without thinking she lifted the receiver to her ear before Hawkman could stop her. The color drained from her face.

Hawkman quickly leaned over the bar and pushed the speaker button, but it was too late. Her jaw taut, she slammed down the phone.

He laid his hand over hers. "Who was it?"

"I don't know." Her voice broke. "But why don't they leave me alone."

"What did he say?"

She wrenched her hand away and turned her back to him. "Hawkman will die," she whispered.

"Did it sound like John?"

She rubbed her temples with the tips of her fingers. "No. It sounded more like the other muffled voice, but I'm not positive."

"Don't answer the phone any more. Let the machine pick it up. That way we'll have a recording of his voice."

"I know, I shouldn't have answered it." She dropped her hands to her side. "I just didn't think."

He patted her on the shoulder, then headed for the outside, keys jingling in his hand. "We'll get some answers soon," he called over his shoulder. The door slammed behind him.

⊹⊱•⊰⊹⊱•⊰⊹⊱•⊰⊹

The next day, Hawkman sensed it was time for another break and suggested they take the falcon hunting. Jennifer seized on the moment, shut down the computer and grabbed her jacket.

"Sounds good to me."

When they reached an open, flat area, Hawkman released Pretty Boy. Then they strolled around enjoying the warm sunshine of the crisp fall day. Suddenly, Hawkman shaded his eyes and gazed toward the air-cutting sound of chopper blades.

Jennifer pointed to the aircraft that had just turned toward them. "There it is."

He grabbed her hand and practically drug her toward a cluster of pine trees. "Hurry, we've got to get away from the truck and under cover. He jerked his revolver from his holster and yelled over the noise of the chopper bearing down on them, "When we get into the trees, find some thick bushes and hide under them."

The helicopter advanced rapidly, flying over the truck. The blast of rapid gunfire and the sound of shattering glass ripped through the air.

Ducking under the protective boughs of the trees, Hawkman shoved Jennifer under some dense shrubs and fell on top of her, pointing his gun skyward. A sporadic round of bullets hit the ground nearby making the dust fly. He could see the rotors through the breaks in the branches and felt the downdraft of the chopper passing over them.

Jennifer covered her head with her hands and screamed. "God, they're going to kill us."

He jumped up and grabbed her arm. "Not if I can help it." He knew the chopper would circle, so he ran deeper into the trees, dragging her behind him.

"Where are we going?" she cried, ducking the tree limbs as they ran.

"I don't know," he shouted, "but he's coming back."

Hearing more shots, he shoved her under another bush and again shielded her body. As they lay, panting heavily, he heard the bullets hit the ground. But this time, much farther away. Finally, after what seemed like an eternity, the popping sound of the rotor blades faded into the distance.

Hawkman kept her pinned underneath him, listening intently

until he was satisfied the helicopter had left. He helped her to her feet and brushed off her jacket. "You okay?"

"I'm still alive, I think," she said, still breathless from the experience.

Looking at her with concern, he gently pushed her chin to one side and took a handkerchief from his pocket. "Looks like I got a bit rough shoving you into those bushes." He placed the soft cloth on her neck. "You're bleeding a little."

Her eyes were still wide with fright and her voice trembled. "It's better than getting hit with a bullet."

He handed her the blood spotted hanky and directed her hand toward the worst scrape on her neck. "Hold this on that cut until the bleeding stops. I'll clean it when we get back to the house."

They weaved through the trees until they reached the perimeter of the forest. Hawkman held up his hand. "Let me check and make sure the coast is clear."

"He flew so low." Jennifer said, stopping in the shadows. "Could you see anyone inside?"

"No." Hawkman then cautiously stepped out into the open and searched the sky. After a few moments, he holstered his gun and motioned for her. "Looks like he's gone."

She grabbed his hand and they headed for the truck. He stared at the shattered windshield. "Damn, that sure took care of that. Let's pray that's the only damage." Taking off his hat, he wiped his forehead with the back of his arm, then plopped it back on his head. He surveyed the hood and gave a sigh of relief that there were no bullet holes.

When he opened the truck door, pieces of glass rained down onto his boots. He brushed off the seat, jumped into the cab and shoved the key into the ignition. When the engine roared to life, he broke into a big smile. "Hallelujah! Let's get the hell out of here."

She jumped inside and they sped back to the house where Hawkman phoned Bill, leaving a message for him to call back as soon as possible.

Glancing at Jennifer, he noticed the dried blood on her neck. "I almost forgot, sit over here on this bar stool and I'll clean those scrapes while we're waiting for his return call."

She fidgeted and kept glancing at her watch as he tried to wipe her neck with a gauze pad soaked in hydrogen peroxide. "What the hell's the matter with you? Can't you sit still for a a moment?"

Impatiently, she pushed his hand away and jumped off the stool. "Why hasn't Bill called?"

He shook his head and threw the pad into the trash. "Be patient. He'll call as soon as he gets my message."

When the phone rang, she stood over it waiting for the recorder to click on. The minute Bill's voice came over the line, Hawkman reached over and punched on the speaker phone.

Jennifer listened intently as Hawkman related their close call.

"Did either of you get hit?"

"No. Jennifer's a little shaken and scratched up from the bushes we hid under. Otherwise, we're both fine."

"Recognize any markings on the chopper?"

"No."

"How many inside?"

"Could only see the silhouette of one man, but there could have been two. We were so busy scurrying for cover that I didn't have a chance to check real close."

"Okay, let me see what I can come up with, then I'll get back to you."

"Also, another call came in this morning. This one threatened my life."

"Did you get it on tape?"

"Unfortunately, we didn't. But we will if he calls again."

"Keep a record, regardless. I'll get on this helicopter thing right away."

"Thanks, Bill."

After the conversation, Jennifer crossed over to the living room window, her arms wrapped tightly around her waist. She stood staring out over the lake.

Hawkman was beginning to get concerned about her erratic behavior. "You all right?"

"Not really. My insides are shaking something awful."

He went to her, brought her close to him and held her tightly. She put her arms around him and laid her head on his chest.

He rested his chin lightly on the top of her head and closed his eyes. "Everything's going to be all right. I'd die before I let anything happen to you."

Jennifer wondered if he really meant what he said, or was he just being a sympathetic agent protecting an innocent party. She slowly pulled away and her gaze fell on the empty perch. "Oh my gosh. We left Pretty Boy out there."

Hawkman hit the heel of his hand to his forehead. "Damn, I forgot all about that hawk. We better go find him."

They dashed outside and both stopped abruptly, bursting into laughter. There on the white fence sat an indignant falcon with ruffled feathers. He cocked his head and gave them a scolding squawk.

Retrieving the leather glove from the seat of the truck, Hawkman shook it free of glass, then slipped it onto his hand. "I see you know your way home." He grinned when the falcon stepped on his arm. "Good to have you back, fella."

Jennifer suddenly broke into a run toward the house. "The phone's ringing."

Hawkman raised his free hand. "Let the machine pick up." He hurried in behind her and put the bird on his perch. Bill's voice broke the silence.

Hawkman picked up the receiver. Several minutes later, he hung up and glanced at Jennifer who'd been staring at him intently. "They found the chopper abandoned in a field. They're dusting for prints. Let's hope it's not another dead end."

CHAPTER ELEVEN

Wanting to get out of Jennifer's hair so she could finish her overdue articles, Hawkman wandered outside to the garage. There he lounged against the side of the building watching the workman replace the riddled windshield of the truck. She seemed especially uptight since the helicopter incident. And he wanted the 4X4 back to it's normal appearance as soon as possible, so it wouldn't keep reminding her of their horrible experience. In fact, he'd paid extra for the man to come out to the house.

Two hours later, he ambled inside for something to drink, found the computer idle and Jennifer no where in sight. His chest tightened until he spotted her out the living room window, sitting on the dock, doing what she loved best, casting her line out over tranquil water. He stood for a moment appreciating her beauty before making his way back to the kitchen.

He snatched a beer from the refrigerator and decided he'd join her since the workman had finished and left. But, just as he stepped out the sliding glass door, shots rang out. Bullets ricocheted off the dock and splashed into the surrounding water. Jennifer screamed, dropped her fishing pole and in her attempt to dash for the house, stumbled over one of the wooden chairs. Hawkman's beer fell from his hand as he vaulted over the railing and raced toward her. By this time, she'd regained her balance and managed to get halfway up the ramp. Hawkman positioned himself between her and the sniper's bullets as they ran toward the sliding doors. Once inside, he guided her deeper into the interior, away from the large windows. "Are you hit?"

Her eyes wide with fear, she frantically ran her hands over her body. "No, I don't think so." She clutched his arm. "Why is someone trying to kill me?"

Hawkman took her into his arms and held her trembling body. "They're playing games," he said in a controlled voice.

"How can you say that? Those bullets were splashing all around me."

He stared toward the dock. "If they're serious, they don't miss."

Abruptly, he pushed her away, grabbed the binoculars from the hutch and dashed back out on the deck. Scanning the bank directly across the water, he saw nothing suspicious. He bolted down to the dock and did a quick examination of the bullet punctures. Racing back up to the house, he grabbed a clip for his gun from his bedroom and headed toward the front door. "I'm going to find the sniper."

"No!" Jennifer cried, jumping up from the couch. "Don't leave me. He might come back."

"The shots came from across the lake, he'd have to pass me to get here. Get your gun and keep it beside you until I return." He charged out the door, almost running into Amelia.

"What the hell's going on?" she asked, grabbing his arm. "I heard shots and Jennifer's screams."

"Stay here. I'll be right back." Hawkman darted past her and jumped into his truck. He hit the accelerator, squealed out of the driveway and sped across the bridge.

From the angle of the bullet marks on the dock, he figured the shots came from the top of the hill across the lake. If the sniper knew the area, he wouldn't go up the front incline: an unstable area with frequent rock slides and sloughing soil. So, Hawkman threw the truck into four-wheel drive and climbed to the back side of the decaying volcanic mountain.

When he turned off his ignition, he heard the revving of a another engine. Grabbing the binoculars from the seat, he scrambled up the slope just in time to see a motorcycle climbing up a deer trail on the neighboring hill. Hawkman focused on the helmeted rider with a rifle strapped to his back, before he skidded over the top and disappeared.

"Damn, just missed him," he swore, kicking at the ground. Then he caught the glint of several empty shell casings scattered over the dusty surface. He glanced toward Jennifer's dock and took a bearing, figuring the sniper must have stood in this exact spot. Searching through his pockets he found an old business envelope and used his ball point pen to lift the casings and drop them inside. While down on his haunches, he discovered footprints made from biker boots leading down the hill. He followed them until they stopped under a tree-sheltered area where drops of oil, scorched grass and the impressions of knobby tires indicated the sniper had parked the bike while tending to his wicked mission.

Hawkman searched the area and and had almost given up on finding any more clues when he pushed back a clump of tall dead grass. Tucked near the roots lay a black pager. Sparked by the find, he hooked the belt clip on the back of the small box with his pen and carefully lifted it above the grass and dropped it into the envelope. He folded the flap and tucked the package into the pocket of his jeans jacket, giving it a final pat.

He probed around a few more minutes, but found nothing more, so he returned to the house. When he entered the door, Amelia whipped her head around and Jennifer hurried toward him. "Did you find him?"

"No. But I spotted him charging up a deer path on a motorcycle."

Amelia put her hands on her hips. "Why didn't you chase him?"

"The 4X4 couldn't have made it up that narrow trail."

Amelia let out an impatient breath and raised her hands. "Why didn't you flatten one of his tires?"

Hawkman shot her an annoying look. "I didn't have a rifle, only my pistol."

She dropped her arms in disgust. "Oh great. Now he's free to pull this stunt again."

He opened the refrigerator, pulled out a beer and popped the tab. "I doubt he'll return."

Amelia brushed back some loose wisps of hair that had drifted over her eyes. "Well, since you're here, I'd better get back to the store."

Hawkman saw her to the entry. "Thanks for staying." But before closing the door, he caught the drift of her ranting as she made her way down the driveway. "Good Lord alivin', what's this lake coming to?"

He suppressed a smile and shook his head, then ambled into the living room where Jennifer sat on the couch, her fists clenched in her lap. "Are you settled down now?"

She glared up at him. "No. I'm scared to death. When is this all going to end?"

He sat down beside her and pulled the envelope from his pocket. "Soon. Real soon." Pushing on the ends of the envelope so she could see inside, he pointed with his pen. "I found these shell casings which will tell us what kind of a gun he used. But best of all, this."

She studied the black box without touching it. "That looks like a pager."

"It is. And, hopefully there's a record of ownership. If you're up to it, we could go into Medford today before the stores close so I can check it out. We'll just plan on having dinner in town."

She nodded. "Okay, but let's take my car. I'm in no mood to ride in that rough truck tonight."

They arrived at the MobileComm office in Medford and went inside. Hawkman spoke to the manager, explaining he'd found the pager out in the country and would like to return it to the owner.

"There's usually a serial number." The man pointed at a small area on the pager. "But looks like its been scraped off on this one. Which means it has either been reprogrammed by a different company or it's stolen. Without that number, there's no way we can trace it."

When they returned to the car, Hawkman, disgusted, flopped down in the seat and chewed on a toothpick.

Before Jennifer turned on the ignition, she glanced at the envelope in his hand. "Any numbers showing on the display?"

He jerked his head around, as if startled she was there, and glanced down at the envelope. "Great idea." Throwing caution to the wind about smudging fingerprints, he yanked it out and pushed the button. "Yeah, there is."

"Better write it down before the batteries go."

"Got a pen?"

She pulled a small pad from her purse. "Give me the number."

❖❖❖❖❖❖

They found a restaurant and while waiting for their order, Jennifer leaned back in her chair and studied Hawkman from across the table. She marveled at his calm demeanor. Her insides hadn't stopped quivering since this mornings horrifying experience of almost being killed. When their meal arrived, she glanced at the food and wondered why she'd even considered eating. She wasn't even hungry. "Hawkman, how do you do it?"

He glanced at her, one brow raised. "How do I do what?"

"How can you be so detached from what's going on?"

"A trained agent learns that emotions can get you killed."

"Well, I'm not an agent and someone tried to kill me this morning. My stomach's so twisted in knots I'm not sure I can eat."

He brushed his napkin across his mouth and leaned back. "Just because I don't mention it, doesn't mean I'm not worried."

Jennifer dropped her gaze and fingered the napkin on her lap. "Well, I wish you would discuss it. Maybe it would help me."

Hawkman cut his steak and examined the bite on his fork. "Well, so far there's really nothing to talk about." He slid the piece into his mouth. After a few moments, he glanced at her. "Hey, don't worry. I'm not going to let anything happen to you."

She pushed her plate away and glimpsed at the other patrons. Certainly easy for him to say, she thought. So, he's trained. Big deal. How does he think for one moment that I can push being shot at out of my mind?"

On the way home, they rode in silence. Hawkman must have sensed that she was irked with him, as he'd tilted his seat back, letting his cowboy hat ride over his eyes. His heavy breathing indicated he'd drifted off.

She glanced into the rear view mirror making sure they weren't being followed. Then it dawned on her that in the short time she'd known him, he'd taught her through his actions to be cautious. She smiled to herself. A man trained to speak few words. Maybe her edgy nerves made her read more into his silence than she should.

She tried to relax and enjoy the solitude, but when she crossed the bridge nearing the house, her headlight beams bounced off a dark car parked at the side of the road. She stiffened and grabbed Hawkman's arm.

He sat straight up, his hat tumbling to the floor board. Snatching it, he plopped it back on his head. "Yeah, what is it?"

Her voice trembling, she pointed out the window. "That car."

Squinting, his gaze followed the direction of her finger. "What about it?"

"That looks like the car the intruder drove."

He motioned for her to slow down. "I need to get a closer look."

She eased off the accelerator while he scribbled down the license plate number on the back of an envelope.

"Get as close as you can." He strained his neck to see inside the car. "Looks empty."

Just as she braked to pull into her driveway, he grabbed the wheel. "Go on down the road and turn around in front of the Perluck's place."

Not understanding why, she nervously obeyed his order. When she made the u-turn, her bright headlights lit up the area where she'd seen the parked car."

Her eyes searched the roadside. "Hawkman, that car's gone."

He pointed across the lake. "There he goes. Head lights just went on."

Jennifer's stomach knotted. "Could it have been the same guy who tried to get into my house?"

"Hard to say."

She noticed he seemed to be in deep thought, so she continued up the road slowly and again started to turn into the driveway. But he raised his hand. "Stop right here."

Her nerves raw, she hit the brakes harder than necessary, throwing him tight against his seat belt. "Why in the middle of the street?"

"A hunch." He took the flashlight from the glove compartment and removed the garage door opener from the cubby above their heads. "Don't pull in. I'll be right back."

Not knowing what to expect, she sat tensely, gripping the

steering wheel with both hands, as she watched him move toward the house.

⟨⊹⟩×⟨⊹⟩×⟨⊹⟩×⟨⊹⟩×⟨⊹⟩

Hawkman guided the beam around the facing of the front door, examining the small pins he'd placed over the hinges to alert him if anyone had tried to jimmy open the door. Nothing seemed disturbed. He walked around the house and checked each window and sliding glass door. After finding nothing amiss, he went back to the front yard and eyed the garage door for several seconds before stepping back a few yards. He pointed the opener at the big door and pushed the button. It slid silently open. He paused a moment, staring at the interior of the garage, then hit the button again. An explosion ripped through the air, knocking him off his feet. Long fingers of flame burst forth from the garage and licked at the sides of the house.

Jennifer leaped from the car and screamed. "Hawkman, are you all right?"

On his feet and running for the water hose, he yelled. "Set the alarm off at the fire station."

She whirled around, dashed across the street and shoved open the emergency door which set off the alarm. The siren wound up, and its wail echoed across the lake and throughout the hills.

By the time the volunteer firemen arrived, flames lit up the sky and were endangering the rest of the house. But the tile roof, the watering done by Hawkman and the quick action of the fire fighters saved it. They were soon rolling up the hoses and dispersing.

Fire Chief Ruskin rubbed the stubble on his chin. "From the looks of things, an explosion caused this fire. Either oily rags near the water heater or a faulty gas can. People should be more careful."

Hawkman didn't deny the fire chief's conclusion. "Thanks, Ruskin. I'll certainly give Ms. Morgan your warning."

He waited until the chief had left before removing a long screwdriver from his truck's tool chest. Using the flashlight and the wrench, he crouched down in the middle of the wet, black muck and began prying through the debris. He flipped up pieces of charred material at random, turned them over in his hands then tossed the black chunks back into the pile.

Jennifer sat on the stoop, elbows on her knees and chin resting in her hands. "Hawkman, what are you doing?"

"Trying to find the source of the fire. Oily rags or a leaky gas can didn't cause this. That, I definitely know."

She stepped cautiously through the black ash until she stood beside him. "What did?"

Without looking up, he flipped over another burned piece. "A bomb."

Stepping back into a soft pile of charcoal, she put a hand to her mouth. "Oh God, Hawkman. It's not safe to stay on this lake any longer. We're going to end up getting killed."

He stood, tapping the flashlight against his thigh, his face set with stern lines. "This proves what I've said all along. It's dangerous for you to be around me." He stared at her. "I want you out of here tonight. Pick some place to go and I'll take you to the airport. Either that or I'll have Bill arrange a secure place for you to stay."

"And what about you?"

"I've told you before, I'm not leaving here until I find the bastard who's responsible for this."

Her eyes narrowed. She put her hands on her hips and threw back her shoulders. "Well, then I'm not leaving either."

Hawkman shot a sideways look at her and turned off the flashlight. "Look, I'm staying because I want this ended, but I want you safe.

Jennifer tilted her chin stubbornly. "Then I guess we'll see this through together."

He immediately knelt back down and started digging through the debris, swearing under his breath. "Damn stubborn woman."

She bent over, resting her hands on her thighs. "At least let me help you find whatever you're digging for."

Annoyed, he continued raking through the burned pieces without glancing up. "You wouldn't recognize a piece of bomb if you saw it."

Jennifer threw up her hands and turned toward the entry. But before she got inside, she threw a glance over her shoulder when she heard him speak.

"Ah, here's a piece." He lifted a blackened object into the air, then placed it on the ground beside him.

She shook her head and closed the door.

After digging for over an hour, he figured he had all the pieces that were large enough to spot. He balanced them in his hands and carried the charred material into the house.

Jennifer quickly placed a piece of newspaper on the counter where he dumped the unrecognizable blackened chunks. "That's it?"

He dusted off his hands. "All parts of a triggering device that set off the explosion."

She touched one of the burned fragments and looked at him questionably. "What good are they now?"

"Hopefully, it'll tell us where it came from and something about the person who set it up."

She put a finger to her lips. "You mean they can find out all that information from these burned pieces?"

Hawkman arranged the black stuff in a pattern and nodded. "Yep. They can find out a lot."

Jennifer grew quiet and stood staring at the twisted objects.

He knew when she got silent there were questions going through her mind. "So what else is bothering you?"

She took a deep breath. "I can't figure out why that guy hung around. He'd already planted the bomb. So what was he waiting for?"

"To make sure the trigger device worked."

Her concerned gaze shifted to his face. "And if it hadn't?"

"He'd have set if off with a remote control."

"So you're saying he hid nearby."

"Probably in that shadowed area behind where he had the car parked."

She frowned. "But he left before the explosion."

"Yeah, but he never got out of the remote's range. More than likely he parked on the road across the lake until he heard or saw the blast."

Jennifer visibly shuddered. "Thank God you had a hunch and we didn't pull into the garage."

He eyed her a few seconds. "We'll catch him. I promise."

"I hope so," she whispered.

Hawkman continued to rearrange the blackened pieces on the

paper. "Do you by any chance have a box big enough to hold this stuff, plus the casings, pager and plastic explosive? I certainly can't send it through the mail. Bill's going to have to send the helicopter."

She headed for the linen closet. "I'll see what I have."

Later that night in the guest room, Hawkman sat on the edge of the bed and mulled over the number on the pager that Jennifer had written down. It looked familiar. He took the paper that he'd taken from Velum's wallet off the top of the dresser. His eyebrows shot up and he grabbed a note pad. Bill would be interested in this. He included it in the box with the other items.

The next morning, he informed Bill about the bombing. "Here's the license plate number of the car we spotted. Run a check and see if it's significant. I can't send this stuff through the mail, so you're going to have to send in the chopper.

⟨⊹⟩»⟨⊹⟩»⟨⊹⟩»⟨⊹⟩»⟨⊹⟩»⟨⊹⟩»⟨⊹⟩

After the insurance adjuster read Chief Ruskin's fire report, which indicated the probable cause of the fire was due to a faulty gas can found in the debris, he shook his head. "People don't understand the dangers of a leaky gasoline can."

Hawkman didn't argue. After giving Jennifer instructions on sending in the bids, the adjuster left. She got busy right away and found a contractor within a week. Construction on the new garage began.

The noise of the renovation became unbearable and Jennifer found it impossible to concentrate on her writing. She tried running to the computer during the men's lunch hour, but couldn't collect her thoughts fast enough before they were back.

She stared at the blank monitor, then dropped her head onto her arms. Suddenly, above the pounding hammers, she swore a dog barked. Anxiously, she dashed to the front door and smiled when she found Herman sitting on the front stoop wagging his tail. Sam, perched on Mr. Jordan's ATV in the driveway, looked like he'd grown a foot. The sight made her heart swell.

She waved at the boy, trying to catch his eye. When that didn't work, she yelled, hoping her voice carried above the racket. "Hey Sam." Finally getting his attention, she motioned for him to come inside. Closing the door after the two entered, she leaned against it and wiped her forehead with the back of her arm. "There's so much noise out there I can't hear myself think." She clasped her hands in front of her. "It's sure good seeing you two. How about some juice and a cookie. And I think I have a milk bone for Herman."

Sam hopped onto a bar stool. "Sure."

Herman sat on his special rug, cocking his head and pleading with his big remorseful eyes. When Jennifer didn't move fast enough with his treat, he gave her a friendly bark to the tune of a thumping tail.

After inhaling his cookie and slurping down the juice, Sam rested his elbows on the counter, putting his chin in his hands.

She eyed his thoughtful gaze. "What's on your mind?"

He sat up straight with a serious expression. "I just hope you're making that garage big enough."

Jennifer raised a brow. "Oh?"

"Well." He raised upon his elbows. "When I come over here to visit in the rain, I'll need a place to park the ATV."

She turned her head to stifle a laugh. "I see what you mean."

About that time, Hawkman walked in and tousled the boy's hair. "Hey Sam, how's it going?" But before Sam could answer, he continued. "I'm thinking it's time to take that falcon out for a hunt. Want to come?"

Sam's eyes grew big as saucers. "Boy, you bet. But I'll have to check with the Jordans first."

After getting permission, Jennifer and Sam climbed into the cab with the falcon. Hawkman lowered the tailgate allowing Herman to jump into the back. Jennifer worried about having Sam along. Would it make any difference to a sniper if a child accompanied them?

CHAPTER TWELVE

Dirk Henderson sat on a park bench in front of his office building surveying both sides of the street. Finally, he folded the newspaper under his arm and sauntered over to the phone booth. He glanced up and down the sidewalk one more time before he stepped inside and closed the door. Sheltering the phone with his body, he slyly placed a voice changer over the receiver, then keyed in the number.

On the other end the phone rang and rang. No answer. Tapping his foot impatiently, he scowled and pushed down the receiver button with his finger. "I'll take care of him later." He then dialed another number. A deep male voice answered.

"Hello."

"How come I haven't heard from you? And don't give me any of your damned excuses." Dirk listened for a few moments, his eyes narrowing to slits. "So, what you're telling me is that you bungled the goddamn job."

He snatched the voice changer from the receiver and stepped out of the booth, slapping the newspaper against his hand. If the idiot had shot straight and just injured Jennifer like he'd been ordered, Hawkman would have had no choice but to take her into the city to the hospital away from that damned remote Copco Lake. But no, the numskull couldn't even hit the dock.

He hurried toward his office, mumbling, "Can't anyone follow orders? Nobody got any brains anymore?" Sweat ran down his red sideburns and prickling heat gathered at the back of his neck. He hesitated at the door of the building, his blue eyes flashing against his ruddy skin. Suddenly, he whirled around and jogged back down the steps toward the parking lot.

After two hours of driving, he turned his dark green sports car onto the familiar gravel road. He passed Copco Lake and continued up Ager Beswick Road toward Topsy Grade. He'd stop at one of the fishing accesses to plan his strategy.

He noticed a vehicle on the road ahead kicking up the dirt, forming a thick dust cloud. He lifted his foot from the accelerator and dropped back.

When the air cleared, he could see the truck and straightened in his seat. A wicked laugh escaped his lips. "I'll be damned! How lucky can a fellow get?" He slowed and dropped farther back. "Can't let him spot me in his rear view mirrors."

When the 4X4 turned onto a logging road and headed toward the foothills, Dirk pulled to the side of the road and stopped. Yanking his tie down mid-chest, he focused on his enemy dropping the tailgate, letting a big black dog jump out, then stroll around to the passenger side of the truck and brought out a large bird perched on his arm. "You bastard, what the hell are you doing?" he questioned aloud, observing the hawk lift into the sky, circle overhead then fly away. He swiftly brought his attention back to Hawkman and Jennifer as they ambled leisurely toward the hills, the boy and dog racing in circles around them.

Dirk finally lowered the binoculars and patted the rifle which lay on the seat beside him. "This is going to be easier than I expected."

He put the glasses back to his eyes and scanned the area up the road. A tree covered knoll about a half mile ahead caught his eye. He grinned. "Perfect."

He hid the car deep inside the cluster of trees behind the hill, picked up the gun and started up the incline. When he reached the top, he mentally calculated the distance between himself and the group. A smile curled the corners of his mouth. They're well within range. He stepped back into the shaded area, hoisted the rifle to his shoulder and aimed the telescopic sight at Hawkman's heart.

Just as he tightened his trigger finger, a loud screech and the sound of flapping wings distracted him. He jerked around but not before he felt the razor sharp pain across the top of his head. Frantically trying to fend off the angry bird, he accidentally squeezed the trigger. The sound of the shot echoed against the hills. Another screech sounded in his ears and he whirled about to see the large bird's outstretched talons coming straight for him again.

Waving the rifle in front of his face, Dirk scrambled down the hill and jumped into his car. He jabbed the key into the ignition, bore down on the accelerator and hit the road hard.

He touched the painful area of his head and pulled back a blood covered hand. "Damn! How'd he train that dumb hawk to attack?" His knuckles went white around the steering wheel. Then he let out a scream of primal anger. "What's he got? A guardian angel in the form of a falcon? And how come he always got the best assignments and any woman he wanted?"

‹⊹›‹⊹›‹⊹›‹⊹›‹⊹›

Hawkman went for his gun at the sound of the shot. He immediately checked for Sam, who'd stopped playing with his dog and stood frozen like a statue. After a moment, he raced toward Hawkman with Herman at his heels. "Somebody's shooting a gun."

He quickly slipped his weapon back into his holster to avoid frightening Sam. "Yeah, I heard. We should have thought about it being hunting season. None of us are wearing our vests so we might be mistaken for a deer. I think we better get out of here."

Their attention diverted to the sound of squealing tires, the three looked toward the road. A dark colored car emerged from a dust cloud and sped toward the west.

Jennifer stepped up alongside Hawkman and whispered. "Something tells me we weren't mistaken for a deer."

He nodded. "You're absolutely right." Eyeing the hill, he mentally calculated the distance and raised his brows. "I can't figure out why he missed. We're definitely in range."

She put her hands on her hips and faced him. "Well, let's be thankful for small favors."

Hawkman stared toward the road, still puzzled by the shooter's departure. "These guys don't miss, they're pros," he said, more to himself than to Jennifer.

She frowned. "You're always saying that. Maybe these aren't professionals. And who knows, maybe seeing Sam nearby changed his mind."

He shook his head. "Nope, even if they aren't pros, seeing a kid around isn't going to make any difference if they have a job to do. But, something scared him off. And what's strange is, I don't see another soul around."

Jennifer squared her shoulders, "Well, I'm glad he missed, Shows even a pro can goof."

Hawkman grinned at her attempted humor. Nearing the truck, he spotted the falcon fly from the clutch of trees. He motioned for Sam and Herman. "Looks like Pretty Boy's ready to go."

He slipped on the glove and whistled for the hawk. Sam hung his head out the window and watched the falcon land.

With the bird still on his arm, Hawkman dropped the tailgate for Herman. Once he'd secured the dog inside, he started toward the cab, but stopped short because of Pretty Boy's fidgeting and almost falling off his arm.

"What's the problem boy?" Hawkman studied the hawk's attempts to get something off his talon. Finally, he had to help the bird untangle a mess of what looked like human red hair from around his spur. He rolled the strands between his fingers into a small ball and put it into his pocket. A closer observation revealed spots of blood spattered on the falcon's feet and under feathers. Hawkman raised his arm to shoulder level and looked the hawk in the eye. "I think I know what distracted the sniper, Pretty Boy. This makes us even. I saved your life and today, you saved mine."

Dirk slammed the door of his small apartment and went straight to the bathroom mirror. He examined the deep gouges on the top of his head and grimaced. "I should have killed that damn bird." He jerked open the medicine cabinet and took out cotton swabs and hydrogen peroxide. Touching the swabs to the raw wounds, he grit his teeth at the smarting pain.

The more he thought about the incident, the angrier he became. The red blotch forming around his neck spread upward, turning his cheeks a hot crimson. "That goddamned Hawk Man's trained bird turned my perfect shot into a disaster." He swiped his hand across the counter, sending comb, deodorant and peroxide to the floor. Then he kicked the wastebasket with such force, it flew out the bathroom door, sailed across the bedroom and banged against the opposite wall with a loud clamor. He gripped the sides of the sink, taking several deep breaths in an attempt to calm his emotions. But it didn't work, so he paced back and forth, from one end of his apartment to the other.

⟨⊹⟩⟨⊹⟩⟨⊹⟩⟨⊹⟩⟨⊹⟩

The morning after the shooting, Jennifer came out of her bedroom and discovered Hawkman with his thumbs hooked in his jeans back pockets staring out the living room window. He didn't turn when she greeted him. His grim expression worried her. She crossed over and stood behind him. "Why are you trying to fight this man alone? You know he's dangerous."

He took a deep breath and turned around, rubbing the back of his neck. "Yeah, I know."

"He keeps showing up where you don't expect him. It's like he's got spies."

He nodded. "Yeah, we're being watched, no doubt. He's smart, trained and has contacts. He's one dangerous bastard." Turning back to the window, he gripped the back of a chair. "I had a strange dream about a faceless man last night. "But when I woke up early this morning, the face had filled in and flashed through my mind."

At the tone of his voice, Jennifer felt a chill travel down her spine. "Did you recognize him?"

"Yes. A guy I worked with years ago. When I got transferred from Oklahoma to D.C., I lost track of him."

"Did he have red hair like the man Mr. Zanker described?"

"Yes. And blue eyes that pierced your soul."

Her heart pounded when she thought about the story the old man had told. "Do you remember his name?

He nodded. "Dirk Henderson."

Jennifer started to say something, but the phone rang. She clamped her mouth shut and looked at Hawkman.

He motioned for her to go ahead. "But, punch it on the speaker phone and push the record button."

She followed his instructions then answered. "Hello."

"Jennifer, this is John. Jim around?"

She stepped back so Hawkman could move closer to the phone.

"Yes, John."

"I took your suggestion, and my family's out of here."

"Where are you?"

"In another town, under a different name. Not even my wife knows where I am. I'm going to keep moving, don't want to stay in the same spot over a day."

Hawkman shifted from one foot to another, his expression solemn. "Good thinking."

"How long do you think I'll have to continue this charade?"

"Until I tell you it's safe. Hopefully it won't be too long. We're closing in."

John's heavy breathing hissed over the speaker phone. "I keep thinking about this guy wanting my dad's formulae. Dad had vowed never to release another one without an antidote because of mother's death. All the ones listed in his journal had none, so I hid the book. Now I'm thinking maybe I should turn it over to the Agency. But, dammit, Jim. I don't know anyone I can trust but you. And you're not with them any more."

Hawkman stroked his beard. "I have someone in mind that you can trust. I'll contact him when this mess is over."

"That relieves my mind. When shall I call you again?"

"Give me a week." John hung up and Hawkman thoughtfully tapped the phone with his finger, hoping John had hidden his family well. He knew that as soon as the bastard found out that John had disappeared, he'd start looking for John's pretty little daughter.

CHAPTER THIRTEEN

The telephone rang just as Hawkman stepped out the front door to talk to the garage workmen. Jennifer's fingers hung over the keyboard while she waited anxiously for the ringing to stop. Since the last threatening call, Hawkman had replaced the old answering machine with one that logged the date and time of each incoming message. After what seemed like an eternity, the machine finally picked up. "This message is for Jennifer Morgan from Father O'Brien."

She leaped from her chair and grabbed the phone. "Hello, Father, this is Jennifer Morgan."

"Ah yes, Jennifer, nice to hear your voice. How are you my dear?"

"I'm fine, thank you."

"I have some good news and I have some bad news."

She sat down and braced herself, not sure how she'd hold up under much more negative stuff.

"The state is very reluctant to consider adoption by a single woman. However, I told them your story, also Sam's age, and persuaded them to give you time with him so you could prove yourself."

Her heart hammered. "What do you mean?"

"They're going to require that you become his foster parent, so that you're sure adoption is what you really want. They feel the more time you and Sam spend together, the better for both of you. If all works out, then we'll start the gears in motion for adoption. Now, this may take a while. First, you'll need to fill out an application. Then a social worker will interview you, inspect your home and process the license. There'll be a lot of paper work. Probably take a couple of months. But I'm starting on it right now. How does this sound so far?"

Jennifer sighed in relief. She liked the idea. The timing sounded perfect. She didn't want Sam at her house with the killer loose, nor did she want Father O'Brien knowing the dangers that surrounded her life right now.

"It's an excellent idea, Father. At least they didn't turn me down completely. This sounds encouraging."

"Oh my dear lady, it's very promising. I've talked with the Jordans and they'll keep Sam until we get everything in order. Then they'll turn him over to you."

"I'm thrilled, Father. Thank you so very much for all you've done."

"Things run rather slowly here, but hopefully you'll have your first interview in about a month."

"Sounds perfect, Father. Thank you."

"God bless you, my dear. I'll be in touch."

Jennifer hung up, leaned heavily against the wall and hugged herself.

Hawkman walked in the door. "Hey, what got you looking so happy?"

"Father O'Brien."

"Obviously good news."

She related the conversation to him. "I'm so relieved things won't start for a month or so. I couldn't bear putting Sam in any danger."

Hawkman went to the refrigerator, pulled out a soda and held it toward her. "Want one?"

"Yes, thank you."

He joined her in the dining room and sat down at the table. Lifting his can in the air, he solemnly toasted. "Here's to good news."

Jennifer shot him a puzzled look. "You don't sound very enthusiastic."

"Sorry, didn't mean to put a damper on it, but thinking about you raising a boy by yourself bothers me."

She stiffened and stared at him. "I think I can manage."

"A boy needs a man in his life. Someone who can teach him to track game, hunt, fish and handle a boat."

Her eyes narrowed. "I know how to do most of those things and am very capable of teaching him."

"You're missing my point. Camaraderie between a man and a boy is very important. Boys need a role model."

She shifted uncomfortably, knowing he had a good point. "Mr. Jordan is here. And what about you? Won't you be around? You said you thought Sam was a good kid and you liked him."

Hawkman got up and ambled into the kitchen. "Of course. He's a great kid." Fidgeting with his beard, he strolled to the sliding glass door and back to the kitchen again.

Jennifer's gaze followed him. The vulnerability and uncertainty she suddenly saw in him were both puzzling and endearing.

He returned to the table and faced her, his thumbs hooked in his back pockets.

She sensed he felt suddenly uncomfortable. Did he want to say something to her but didn't know how? Then she noticed the twinkle in his eye and looked at him with suspicion. "What's going on in that clever brain of yours?"

A slow smile crept across his mouth, making him look like a sly fox that had trapped his prey. "You'll find out."

She laid a hand on his arm. "Hawkman, don't do this to me. I can't stand guessing."

His expression turned serious and he looked deep into her eyes. "The answer to your question: Yes, I'll be here, if that's what you want. But, I need to know how you feel about this long-haired, bearded, patch-over-the-eye guy that's been living in your house."

Her gaze softened and dropped to the soda in her hand. "Well, I don't know what I'd have done without him."

"I'm not talking about being a body guard."

Her heart started vibrating with an urgent stacco beat. "Oh?" She rose quickly and carried her soda to the kitchen counter. "Then what are you talking about?"

Striding over, he took her by the shoulders and turned her

about to face him. "Well, should I plan to stay here after all this stuff is settled? I need your input." His beseeching expression engulfed her senses.

She swallowed and stared back into his mesmerizing gaze. "If you're speaking job wise, I don't think a private investigator would do too well at Copco Lake, but maybe in Medford. . ."

He released her shoulders, turned his back to her and took a deep breath. "No, I mean, do you think there's any future for me in your life?"

Her heart thumped harder, even though this is what she'd hoped to hear. "You mean, you and me?"

He turned around and looked steadily at her. "Yes, that's what I mean."

She put her hand to her throat and sank back into a chair. "Well, that's a little different. I guess a lot depends on you. Do you think you could actually share a future with a free-lance writer who wants to adopt a boy?"

His face broke into a wide grin. He took her by the hands, gently pulled her up and enclosed her tenderly into his arms. "More than you'll ever know." He smoothed her hair back with both his hands and warmly kissed her.

⋅⊱⋅⊰⋅⊱⋅⊰⋅⊱⋅⊰⋅

After the workman left for the day, Jennifer returned to her computer while Hawkman leaned over the coffee table studying the blue prints of the house. He planned to install an alarm system and needed to familiarize himself with the electrical wiring. He'd started making some sketches on his scratch pad when the phone rang.

Jennifer shot a look at him. He poised his pencil in the air, waiting for the message. A distorted voice boomed over the line. "Hawk Man, if you're home, pick up. I know you're staying with Jennifer. Why don't you answer? Afraid to talk to me?"

Hawkman slowly turned his head and stared at the phone. He threw his pencil down on the table. His jaw set, he moved toward the phone and punched the speaker button. "Who the hell is this?" he spat through clenched teeth.

A loud cynical laugh echoed across the line. Hawkman folded his hands into tight fists.

"You're going to die, Hawk Man, so keep that pretty little woman and that kid out of my way. I'd hate for them to get hurt," the voice sneered. "And keep that damn bird in his cage or next time I'll shoot him out of the sky."

The line went dead. Hawkman's fist came down hard on the speaker button. The muscles in his back twitched. He spun around to face Jennifer, who sat frozen to her seat, her face drawn tight with fear.

He pointed a finger at her. "Go get your gun."

She flinched and half rose from her chair, her eyes wide. "Right now?"

"Yes. That son-of-a-bitch is nuts and could be right here on the lake."

Jennifer stumbled back to her bedroom and returned with the gun.

He took it from her and pushed in the clip. "This guy's gone over the edge. So keep it loaded with the safety on. But carry it with you everywhere. I mean everywhere. Down on the dock, to the mailbox, even to the store. Don't leave this house without it." He held the gun out to her.

Her hand trembled as she took it from him. "This is getting scary."

"And mighty dangerous."

She glanced down at the gun. "How am I going to carry this everywhere without people noticing?"

"Put it in your purse."

"I don't always carry my purse. Especially down on the dock or to the store."

He marched over to the entry, snatched his hat off one of the coat pegs and slapped it on his head. "We'll take care of that problem right now. Let's go."

Flustered, she shut down her computer and grabbed her jacket. "Why do you always have these sudden brainstorms when I've got things to do? Where are we going anyway?"

He had already gone outside and gotten into the truck. When she got to the door and peered out, he hung his head out the window. "This brainstorm is very important. Just make sure you bring your gun."

She slipped it into her pocket and rushed out.

Hoisting herself halfway into the truck, she stopped. "Wait a minute, I forgot my purse."

He'd already started backing up. "You won't need it."

Flopping down in the seat and slamming the door, she sat in silence as they sped toward Yreka. On the outskirts of town, Hawkman made an abrupt turn onto a small, winding road. She frowned and glanced at him. "What's up this way?"

He grinned like a little boy with a secret. "Leon's Leather Works."

"Never heard of it."

"Leon's been in this area for as long as anyone can remember. He's probably as old as these hills. He specializes in making original and out-of-the-ordinary leather goods. I just hope he hasn't closed for the day."

"Maybe we should've called before we left."

Hawkman shook his head. "Leon's got no use for modern conveniences, especially phones. He doesn't like being bothered while he's working."

Jennifer rolled her eyes. "Oh, one of those."

He grinned with the anticipation of seeing Jennifer meet Leon. When the road narrowed to a single lane, he made a sharp turn onto a dirt driveway and came to an abrupt stop. Jennifer stared at the picturesque log building directly in front of them. A single wooden sign hung over the door with 'L.L.W' carved in block letters.

Hawkman jumped out of the truck and rushed around to open her door. "Come on. You'll like him."

After he knocked, they waited a few moments before a thin voice called out. "Come in."

Hawkman opened the door for Jennifer and she stepped into a small room where the distinct smell of leather invaded her nostrils. She blinked against the dimly lit interior. When her eyes adjusted, she scanned the walls. They were covered with leather goods hanging from nails and hooks. Everything from water bags, fringed vests, hats, belts, and holsters. She even spotted a pair of boots in a far corner. Against one wall of this one room warehouse were several saddles displayed on saw horses. Bridles and reins hung from a rope secured across the ceiling.

She gasped. "I've never seen so much leather stuff crammed in such a small space."

The only light in the whole place was a single light bulb in the far back corner of the room. Hawkman guided her toward it. They approached a table heaped with leather scraps. Over the pile, Jennifer could barely make out the figure of an old man hunched over another small table. When he raised his head and glanced at them, she stepped back in awe. The old wizened man with his long white hair and a beard that hung to his waist, looked like an elf in a children's fairy tale. When he smiled, his face transformed into a wreath of wrinkles and his deep set, blue eyes sparkled. She could swear she'd just stepped into a magical, make-believe world.

His eyes twinkled brightly at the sight of Hawkman. "How good to see you."

Jennifer couldn't help smiling as he walked around the table to greet them. When he grasped Hawkman's hand, he looked no taller standing than if he were still sitting on his stool at the table. His smile widened and he pointed a crooked finger at Hawkman's head. "Ah, you're wearing the hat I made." The old man chuckled. "I told you, once you put it on your head, you'd never take it off."

His bright-eyed gaze went from Hawkman to Jennifer. "My, my, now who do we have here? Someone much too pretty to be seen with the likes of you."

Hawkman laughed and drew her forward. "Leon, this is Jennifer Morgan, a good friend of mine."

Leon shuffled toward her and reached out, clasping her hand between his two. She looked down, amazed at how soft the old man's wrinkled and leather stained fingers felt as they wound around her hand. She liked him immediately and smiled into the blue eyes of the withered face.

The old man turned and cleared off a couple of wooden chairs, then motioned for them to sit down. "How can I help you?"

Hawkman explained what he wanted and the old man's eyes grew wide with excitement. He rushed back to his corner and rooted through pieces of leather, throwing remnants every which way.

Hawkman shook his head and grinned.

Suddenly, the old fellow tossed a pelt in front of them. "Feel this."

Hawkman picked up the piece and fingered it, then handed it to Jennifer.

She caressed it against her cheek. "Oh my. How did you get this so soft?"

"An old Indian technique called 'brain-tanning'." His eyes gleamed. "You like it?"

"Yes, it's wonderful."

"Good, then that's what we'll use." He sat back in his chair a moment and closed one eye. And as if talking to himself, he whispered. "Now, what we want to do is hide this holster, but still give the lady quick access."

Leon leaned forward in his chair and winked at Jennifer with an all knowing look. Then out of the blue, he pointed a curved finger at Hawkman. "This man leads an exciting life."

He scooted around the table and motioned for Jennifer to stand up. He took her arm and turned her around, taking an eye's account of her size. "I will make you such a soft holster you'll never know you're wearing it." The old man became serious and turned to Hawkman. "Did you bring the gun so I can get the exact measurements?"

Jennifer pulled it from her pocket. "Yes, here it is."

Leon glanced up at her and nodded in approval. "A 32 cal. semi-automatic. Good choice, young lady." He placed the gun on the table and pointed at Hawkman. "You go for a walk while Jennifer and I do business."

‹⊤›‹⊤›‹⊤›‹⊤›‹⊤›

Hawkman tucked his hands into the pockets of his jeans jacket and tramped up and down in front of the log cabin for what seemed like an eternity. He stopped once and stared at the old fashioned oak front door, wondering how many years Leon had been here. He didn't tell Jennifer how he'd actually learned about Leon. The Agency occasionally hired him to make custom holsters, as well as other specially ordered leather goods with secret pockets and slits.

He turned and started down the road again, kicking a pod, sending it into the ditch, then threw a pebble as far as possible into the adjacent field. A scolding bird flew up. "Whoops, sorry about that fellow, didn't mean to startle you."

After about an hour, the sun sank toward the horizon and he sauntered back toward the shop. Jennifer had just stepped out the door and glanced up the road in the opposite direction.

He ran toward her. "Here I am."

She held out her arms and turned in a circle. "Well, how do you like my holster?"

He scanned her up and down, then looked confused. "Where is it?"

She winked at Leon. "It's on me. Can't you see it?"

The old man chuckled from the doorway.

Hawkman walked around her several times, then stopped and scratched his head. "I don't see it."

Jennifer reached under her blouse and pulled out the small revolver. "You did a good job, Leon. He sure couldn't spot it." She put her hand on her hip. "But, I'm too slow in getting the gun out."

Leon's laugh crackled. "That'll just take some practice."

She glanced at Hawkman. "Leon designed the holster so that I can position the gun right side up, upside down or side ways. Whichever turns out to be the best for me."

He scratched the back of his head, pushing his cowboy hat toward his eyes, almost covering them. "I'd like to see how it's made."

She laughed. "Well, I'm not taking it off out here. If you'll excuse me, I'll be right back." She returned in a few minutes and handed the leather harness to Hawkman.

He examined the workmanship on the bra-like shape. The holster had a hook and loop tape design on the flap, which prevented the gun from falling out. A clip on the holster attached to a soft breast plate that Leon had uniquely designed. The leather harness fit under her bra, the holster part could nestle between her breast or be tucked under one, whichever she felt more comfortable with or found less visible. The holster shifted so the gun could be drawn from any angle.

Hawkman chuckled and handed it back to Jennifer. "Leon, you're a genius."

She rubbed it between her hands. "The leather's so soft I don't even feel it against my skin. The gun makes it feel a bit bulky, but Leon says I'll get use to that."

Hawkman patted the old man affectionately on the shoulder. "Great job."

"Do you use the same 'brain-tanning' technique on all your leather?" Jennifer asked.

Leon shook his head and smiled. "Only for special customers."

Hawkman paid him and they left.

Jennifer found the soft leather incredible and fondled it most of the way home. "What a fascinating old man. He set my imagination on fire. How'd you ever find him away up here?"

"Somebody told me about his work and I drove around in these hills for the best part of a day until I finally stumbled onto his place."

Jennifer glanced up at his head. "Now I understand why you're so fond of that hat."

"Yep, just like he said. I've loved the thing from the very first time I slapped it on." He fingered the soft brim. "Felt like I came into this world with it on my head."

Jennifer stretched across the seat and gave Hawkman a big kiss on the cheek. "Thank's for getting me the holster, I really like it."

He smiled.

Jennifer, fascinated with her new toy, talked about it and fondled it the rest of the way home. But Hawkman's thoughts centered on her adjusting to the holster and learning to draw the gun swiftly. He knew that one of these days soon, she'd have to draw that gun real fast or die. How he wished he'd succeeded in persuading her to leave the area until he caught the bastard. He found her one of the most stubborn ladies he'd ever encountered. Slipping a sideways glance at her, he grinned to himself. Maybe that was one of the traits that attracted him so.

CHAPTER FOURTEEN

Suddenly, Hawkman made a U-turn in the middle of the road,
Jennifer glanced at him with surprise. "Did you forget something?"

He grinned. "No, just decided we might as well run up to Medford for dinner."

"That's a nice idea, but I'm not dressed to go out." She pouted. "Plus, I don't even have a comb or lipstick with me. Remember, you told me to forget my purse, I wouldn't need it?"

He scrutinized her for a moment, then smiled. "You look great."

She pulled down the mirrored visor and grimaced at her reflection. Her hair needed a good brushing and she felt she looked pale without any lipstick. "That sounds just like a man. Exaggeration of the year."

"Women always worry about how they look. I bet if you ask somebody tomorrow what you had on today, they couldn't tell you."

She shoved up the visor. "Hawkman, you're not funny." But she felt a ripple of laughter inside.

When he pulled into the parking lot of the steak house on the outskirts of town, she breathed a sigh of relief. She knew the establishment and they didn't require fancy dress. But they did have excellent food.

Hawkman drove through the packed lot several times before he finally found a parking spot. Once inside, they only had to wait a few minutes before the hostess led them to a booth.

Mid-way through the meal, Jennifer noticed Hawkman seemed preoccupied and had become unusually quiet. He changed his position several times, but when he raised his hand to shield one side of his face, she knew something was wrong. She glanced around the room trying to find the reason for his behavior, but nothing suspicious caught her eye. Finally, she leaned across the table and whispered. "What is it?"

He put a finger to his lips and shook his head.

Her stomach immediately congealed into a knot. She continued to observe and concluded that the two men sitting directly behind him were the reason for his actions.

When the men finished eating and left, Hawkman confirmed her suspicions by immediately getting up, crossing the room and peering out the window. He returned to the table with a grim expression covering his face.

"Who were they?" she asked.

"I'll tell you later."

They finished their meal and hurried toward the truck. Hawkman grabbed her arm a few yards from the vehicle. "Wait here until I tell you it's safe."

She stood back, wondering how many times since she'd met him that he'd told her to 'wait here until its safe'. He raised the hood of the 4X4 and examined the engine compartment. Then he got down on all fours and thoroughly checked the under side of the truck. Once satisfied with the outside, he opened each door, standing behind them for a few seconds to shield his body. Then he climbed inside and searched the interior.

Apprehension filled her as she watched his movements. She knew he suspected some type of explosives. She eyed each person coming and going from the restaurant and anyone loitering in the lot, but she saw no one resembling the two men who had left.

Hawkman finally stepped out of the truck and beckoned her. "You can get in. Everything looks clean."

She always said a little prayer that he hadn't missed something. When they were safely on their way, she turned sideways in the seat so she'd be facing him. "Okay, what was that business at the restaurant all about?"

"Did you get a good look at those two men?"

"Yes. And I also heard tidbits of their foreign conversation.

"That's right, they were Iranian. I know that language well." His jaw tensed. "Those two are paid assassins."

Her eyes opened wide. "You mean they just talked about it right there in public?"

"Oh, yes," he scoffed. "They figure no one understands their language. But when I heard them mention Copco Lake and our names, it really piqued my curiosity."

Her eyes clouded with fear. "Our names? You mean yours and mine?"

"Yes. They have orders to kill us."

Jennifer swallowed hard and fell back against the seat. "Oh my God!" Then she raised back up and stared at Hawkman. "I don't understand. Why in heaven's name would Iranians be after us?"

He shook his head and let out a long breath. "I don't know. But this whole mess is pointing more and more toward someone who's within the Agency." He slapped his hand against the steering wheel. "I'm going to get to the bottom of this yet."

Her heart in her throat, Jennifer turned and kept an eye out the back window, watching for any signs of a tail. When they finally pulled into her driveway, she slumped in relief. No cars had followed them. Before entering the house, Hawkman ran a check on the outside. When they got inside, he locked all the windows and doors, then closed the drapes.

Jennifer watched him take out his gun and lay it on the coffee table. His jaw set, his mouth grim, he glanced at her. "You go on to bed but leave your door open. Be sure your loaded gun is near."

It shocked her that he thought she'd be able to just fall asleep with visions of assassins waiting to kill her racing through her mind. No use arguing with him, so to appease his wishes, she went to the bedroom.

She washed her face with cold water several times and took several deep breaths, hoping to relax her mind and body. Putting her gun on the bedside table, she crawled under the covers, but sleep eluded her. She flipped on the light and tried to read. That didn't work either, so she spent most of the night tossing and turning, staring at the ceiling and listening to the darkness.

Very early the next morning, not being able to stand the bed any longer, she arose, dressed and went into the living room. Hawkman stopped his pacing in front of the large living room window overlooking the lake. He looked tired, with dark circles under his eyes. His thumbs hooked in the back pockets of his jeans, he stared at the floor, his face full of remorse. "I'm sorry you're involved in all of this mess. I'm afraid it's getting pretty sticky."

She pushed back her shoulders. "Don't blame yourself. I asked for it, being such a stubborn woman." Gnawing her lower lip, she continued into the kitchen and poured herself a cup of coffee, then joined him in the living room. She sat on the hearth where the embers of an earlier fire warmed her back and stared at the mug she balanced on her knees "Do you really think those two men will come here?"

Hawkman nodded slowly. "Yes. They have a contract on us."

Jennifer felt her heart compress. "When?"

He didn't meet her gaze. "Soon. But I don't think they'll try anything during daylight hours."

"So we're just going to sit here and wait to be killed?"

"No, you're going with Amelia and Jake to San Francisco. They have a trip planned to visit friends. I'm sure they'd love to have you along."

She stood up with her hands on her hips and faced him adamantly. "And where are you going?"

He pointed to the floor. "I'm staying right here."

"I'm not going with Amelia and leave you here alone to face those two killers. You know I'm very capable with a gun. You've told me that yourself."

He stared long and hard at her. "I can't have you getting in my way. You know nothing about the dangers of this game."

She turned on her heel, her back to him and crossed her arms. "Well, I guess you'll have to give me a quick lesson before nightfall because I'm not leaving my house." She knew he couldn't order her to leave her own home. But it wouldn't prevent him from giving her orders.

Hawkman took a deep breath and went into the kitchen. His jaw taut, he pointed a finger at her. "If you're going to stay here, then listen closely. I talked to Bill this morning. This is to be a clandestine operation, which means these guys don't leave here alive."

She looked at him in horror. "Are you saying we kill them?"

"That's right. Unless you want to die. It's us or them."

She went to the kitchen bar and slumped down on one of stools. "Dear God," she whispered, dropping her head into her hands. After a few minutes, she collected her thoughts and looked up at him. "How do we keep this from the residents on the lake?"

"I've already done some checking. Your closest next door neighbors are gone, we know Amelia's closed for the weekend, and the house across the street to the east is locked up tight. So that leaves us fairly isolated from people who might hear or see something."

Jennifer grimaced. "You don't miss a thing, do you?"

"I can't afford to." He picked up his mug and headed for the coffee pot, but froze when he glanced out the kitchen window, his cup hanging from his fingers.

Jennifer noticed his change in posture and moved to his side. When she looked out the window, a dark gray Ford sedan with two men inside drove slowly by the house. She grabbed his arm. "That's them, the two men who were in the restaurant."

His gaze followed the car down the road. "They're casing the area. They'll be back."

A chill ran down her spine. "Hawkman, I'm scared. Shouldn't we call the police?

"No."

"Can't the Agency help us?"

"Not enough time. We'll have to take care of this ourselves."

"How?"

He patted her hand. "Let's get ready."

Throughout the day, Jennifer followed him and hung on to every word he said, as he prepared her for what might happen. That evening, they arranged pillows under their bed covers, giving the appearance of someone sleeping there.

Hawkman glanced into Jennifer's room as she put the last touches on the fake figure. "Hey, where'd you get that hair?"

"It's an old wig I had stored up in the closet. I figured the hair flowing across the pillow would really make it look more authentic."

"It would fool me. Especially in the dark."

After running through the check list once again, they decided

they'd done all they could. Now, they'd play the waiting game.
Hawkman sat on the couch next to Jennifer and screwed a silencer
onto his gun.

She pointed at it. "I heard those don't really help."

He grinned. "Sounds like you've been doing your homework.
You're right. Compared to your little popcorn popper, mine sounds
like a cannon, but the silencer will help muffle the noise."

Soon, darkness engulfed the house as they sat silently. Jennifer
felt the tightness in her chest as the minutes dragged. Even the soft
ticking of the kitchen clock resonated in her ears like Big Ben. Her
body jerked when a drop of water splashed into the kitchen sink,
sounding like a shot. Her nerves raw, she rolled her shoulder to ease
the tension which felt like millions of needles pricking her flesh.

Suddenly, Hawkman grabbed his gun, dashed to the dining
room window and peered around the edge of the lacy drapes. She
hadn't heard a thing and her heart lurched to her throat, fear gripping
her. Watching Hawkman's every move, she clutched her gun in both
hands. He stood like a statue for several minutes. Her stomach
churned and knotted while waiting for him to say something.

Finally, he came back to the couch. "Only a deer."

Relieved, she slumped back and closed her eyes. When she felt
Hawkman's hand on her shoulder, her eyes flew open and she leaped
up. "What is it?"

"Everything's okay. You dropped off to sleep. They didn't show,
so we'll go through this again tonight. I want you to go get some rest.
Otherwise, you won't make it through another twenty-four hours."

Jennifer ducked her head, ashamed that she'd let him down. She
didn't realize her exhaustion. What if those men had come? Lots of
good she'd have been. She shuddered at the thought. "You're right."

Determined not to let this happen again, she headed for the
bedroom. Before closing the door, she poked her head around the
corner. "I'll take a nap, then you take one, okay?"

He nodded. "Sounds like a good plan."

After she rested, then fixed the dummy back in her bed, she
sent Hawkman to his room. She knew he hadn't slept in two days
and, regardless of his training, humans need sleep to be at their best.
Jennifer kept a close surveillance out the kitchen window and fixed
some light snacks while he rested. They didn't need anything heavy
on their stomachs to cause drowsiness.

She practiced pulling her gun from the holster, but still felt awkward maneuvering the new harness and decided this wasn't the time to experiment. Leaving the gun beside her or in her hand made her feel more secure.

‹-‹-›‹-‹-›‹-‹-›‹-‹-›‹-‹-›

When evening descended upon them, they felt refreshed and more prepared for the vigil. Their eyes adjusted rapidly to the dark house.

Hawkman sat down on the raised hearth, resting his elbows on his knees, his honed senses tuned to the outside. Jennifer served the snacks at midnight then sat on the couch opposite him, waiting in silence. Nearing two in the morning, Hawkman slowly raised his head and focused on the kitchen. He put his finger to his lips, picked up his gun and crept toward the window. Jennifer watched him wide eyed. Again, she hadn't heard a thing; but when he didn't move for several moments, she picked up her gun.

He hurried back and crouched beside her, keeping his voice low. "They're splitting up." He motioned with his gun. "One is coming around the east side, the other around the west. Don't fire unless they break in. Then shoot to kill."

She gripped his shoulder and whispered. "Should I watch from my bedroom?"

He shook his head vehemently "No, we'll stay together."

Silently, he crept to the dining room window. Jennifer saw his head jerk toward the laundry room. Then she heard the sound of someone trying the outside steel door. Hawkman slipped over and stood next to the inner wooden door that separated the laundry room from the kitchen.

Jennifer twisted around on the couch. Using the back rest to steady her gun, she aimed toward the laundry room. But at that moment, she heard light footsteps on the deck stairs on the south side of the house facing the lake.

She turned her head and squinted through the loosely woven drapes covering the picture window and could barely make out the shadow of a man huddled on the steps that led out to the dock. Crawling over to the swivel chair, she moved it inch by inch until the back didn't block her view. Resting her gun on the arm, she aimed at the man on the steps.

She no longer heard the intruder at the steel door and noticed Hawkman had eased back toward the window. He stood there a few moments before slipping across the room and squatting next to her. She pointed at the man on the steps. Then their attention switched to the other one trying to loosen the latch on the sliding glass door. But again the poles did their job and the door didn't budge.

The man left there and slithered past the window toward Jennifer's bedroom where he got the same results. He soon joined his partner on the stairs. They appeared to talk in whispers and gestures for a few seconds before they took off in a run around the west corner of the house out of sight.

Jennifer whipped around and whispered frantically. "I forgot about the slider in that extra room."

Hawkman grabbed her hand and pulled her behind the couch so they'd be facing that area. "That's where they'll get in."

The minute she felt the brush of cool air hit her feet, she knew they were inside and poised her gun. Hawkman followed suit. Two shadowy figures appeared in the small hallway. One turned to his right, quietly opening Jennifer's bedroom door and at the same time the other man turned to his left, opening Hawkman's. Instantaneously, both men raised their assault weapons and fired. The hollow sound of bullets hitting the mattresses made Jennifer shiver.

When the two men examined their victims and discovered they were dummies, they dashed into the living room, waving their guns in front of them. Hawkman and Jennifer opened fire and the two men went down.

Hawkman ran to the fallen bodies and kicked the guns from their hands before checking each man's neck pulse to make sure they were dead. He flipped on the lights and grabbed the phone. "Bill, it's done. We need the helicopter ASAP. Tell them not to waste any time. It's getting light."

⟨⊹⟩ ⟨⊹⟩ ⟨⊹⟩ ⟨⊹⟩

When he spun around, Jennifer stood staring at him with glazed eyes. Dear God, he thought, I've no time for this. He snapped his fingers in front of her face. "Jennifer, come out of it. The chopper will be here within the hour. You've got to help me load these men into the truck." When he saw no reaction, he took the gun from her hand. In her dazed condition, she might turn it on him.

Suddenly, she rushed to the kitchen sink and bent over as vomit spewed from her mouth. He hurried to her and clasped her shoulders until she stopped heaving. Then he tenderly wiped her cheeks and mouth with a dampened cloth.

She gasped and started to cry. "I'm sorry, but I can't believe what I've just done."

He kissed her forehead softly. "I know. I know. But right now we have some work to do, we don't have time for emotions."

She took a ragged breath and patted her face with a towel. "I'm okay."

Hawkman rifled through the Iranian's pockets and found a set of car keys that he tossed to Jennifer. "Hold on to these. Their car must be nearby."

She dropped them into her pocket, then grabbed the feet of one of the bloody victims, helping Hawkman drag him outside. After a few moments of struggling with the two bodies, they finally managed to get them loaded into the pick up bed, then sped off toward the logging road.

Hawkman spotted the helicopter lights in the distance and bore down on the accelerator. They made it to the designated site just as the chopper set down.

Between Hawkman, Jennifer and the pilot, they heaved the bodies inside the aircraft in short order. The helicopter lifted into the air just as the faint rays of sunshine flickered over the tops of the hills.

On the way back to the house, Hawkman searched the shadowed areas for the assassin's car. Pulling over the bridge, he pointed down a short road that led to the water's edge. "There it is. Toss me those keys and I'll put them inside. Bill's men can handle it from here on out."

When he climbed back into the truck, he noticed that Jennifer hadn't taken her eyes off the dark colored sedan. Her face was deathly pale, her chin quivering uncontrollably. He leaned over to embrace and comfort her until she sighed and seemed to regain her composure.

⟨⊹⟩•⟨⊹⟩•⟨⊹⟩•⟨⊹⟩•⟨⊹⟩

Dirk sat in his apartment at the formica table in his kitchen, drumming his fingers loudly against the surface while glaring at the wall clock. Suddenly, he slammed his fist down and shouted. "Why haven't they called? They've had plenty of time."

He spent another hour restlessly pacing from one end of the the small apartment to the other. A gut feeling told him he'd never hear from those two assassins again.

He snatched up his car keys and headed out the door. "Guess it's time I took things into my own hands." He backed out of his driveway, rammed his foot against the accelerator and careened around the corner, leaving black tire marks on the street.

CHAPTER FIFTEEN

Later that night, Jennifer clutched her pillow to her chest. Her mind wouldn't let go of the sight of the two bloody bodies lying on her living room floor. What were their names? Did they have wives and children? What drove these two men to take on such a horrid job? How could anyone kill for a living and be able to look at himself in the mirror?

Tears filled her eyes. She'd always respected other people's lives, but no one had told her what to do if hers got threatened. The fact that she'd actually used her gun to kill another human being gnawed at her heart, even though she knew she didn't have a choice. Hawkman's training had taught him how to control his emotions. Would she ever be able to do that and sort it out on her own?

When she finally drifted off, the same nightmare of running for her life invaded her sleep over and over. Then, in the pitch darkness, the phone jolted her completely awake. She grabbed the receiver.

"Hello."

She could barely hear the muffled voice. "After Hawk Man dies, then I'll have your pretty body." A high-pitched laugh echoed over the line. Slamming down the receiver, she glanced toward her bedroom door. Hawkman stood silently with his hand on the knob.

Sobs wrenched through her and she dropped her head into her hands. He rushed to her side and enfolded her quivering body into his arms.

"Who was it?"

"He threatened to rape me."

Hawkman stiffened, taking her by the shoulders, he looked steadily into her hazel eyes. "Mark my word, he's never going to lay a hand on you."

Once she'd calmed down, he reached over and unplugged the phone. "You don't need this ringing in here."

He left her door ajar. She stared numbly at the ceiling, trying to suppress the fear crawling around the edges of her mind. Finally, the soft light of a new day filtered into the room. She got up and showered, letting the warm water cascade over her for several minutes, soothing the raw nerves.

After drying, she strapped on the leather harness and pushed the pistol into the holster. Hawkman had insisted she continue wearing the gun, keeping it loaded at all times. Remember, he told her, the number one bastard hadn't made his appearance yet.

She tried to force the phone call from her mind by scrutinizing her petite frame in the mirror. Her well endowed bust line did a good job of concealing the gun. She'd chosen to wear the holster under the fold of one breast, which put it an angle that made it easier for her to reach. Turning from side to side, she saw nothing that indicated a concealed weapon.

Placing her hand on the pearl handle of the gun, she wondered why a surge of excitement sweep through her every time she strapped it on? A feeling she found hard to handle. Was it normal? Some day she'd ask Hawkman if he experienced such sensations.

A ragged breath escaped her lips as she relaxed her shoulders. If someone had told her this time last year she'd be wearing a gun, she'd have told him he was crazy. She stared at her reflection and realized her face had changed. It had taken on a different, more mature look. She brushed her hair into a pony tail, then put on a touch of lipstick.

Maybe if she started the day on a lighter note, it would help ease the heaviness she felt in her heart. Tempting Hawkman out of bed with the smell of food always brought a smile from him. While the big iron skillet heated on the stove, she pulled strips of bacon apart, dropping them one by one onto the hot surface. She delayed turning on the stove fan until the tantalizing smell had weaved its way through the house.

Soon, she heard heavy footsteps clumping down the hall. Glancing in that direction, she tried to conceal a grin. Knees locked, arms extended, Hawkman marched into the kitchen like a sleep-walking robot. "I smell food. I smell food," he chanted in a monotone voice.

Not being able to contain herself any longer, she laughed out loud. "Hawkman, food will be your downfall."

He sniffed the air, rubbed his stomach and smacked his lips in jest. "Ah, but what a way to fall!" He clunked down stiffly on the bar stool, keeping his arms straight in front of him. She placed a plate piled with bacon, eggs and toast on his outstretched hands. Smiling, she fixed a plate with more moderate helpings for herself.

But her light mood disappeared after breakfast, her thoughts drifting to the shooting and the midnight phone call. It must have shown in her face, for Hawkman stopped sopping up the last of his egg with a piece of toast. "What's eating you?"

"I have this terrible feeling of guilt." She played with her fork for a second, then dropped it on her plate. "Did you have any qualms or regrets when you killed the first time?"

He laid his toast on the plate and stared toward the window, "My first time was also a case of self defense. I didn't have the luxury of deliberating the rightness or wrongness." He turned his dark, encompassing gaze on her. "You did the right thing. You had no other choice. Time will help erase your feeling of guilt."

She thoughtfully sauntered to the sink and rinsed her plate, then turned toward him, clutching her hands in front of her. "After I saw those men ruthlessly shoot into our beds, I knew we wouldn't have a second chance. But it still doesn't make me feel any better that I helped wipe out two lives."

Hawkman laid his hands on each side of his plate. "They were hired to kill us. Nothing would have stopped them but a bullet. So, don't be so hard on yourself."

She wiped her hands across her face. "I understand. But it's going to take some time for me to get over this." Taking a deep breath, she moved across to the bar and leaned heavily on her hands. "And then came that phone call. Do you know what it means when a woman gets threatened like that? It not only scares her to death, but tears away her dignity."

He abruptly stood. "He won't touch you. I won't let him."

She carried his plate to the sink, then faced him, frowning, a shiver running through her. "What if he kills you first?"

He shot a determined look at her. "That's why you have a gun. You empty it into him. Don't even think about it. Just point and fire until you have no bullets left."

She gripped the material of her sweatshirt so tightly that it appeared like a spider web at her neck when she released it. Not sure she wanted to hear any more, she still had questions about the two dead men that had to be answered. "What will the Agency do with those men's bodies?"

"They'll try to identify them through tests. Then they'll cremate or bury them."

Her eyes widened with horror. "What about their families?"

"They'll notify the next of kin. That is, if there's a record of their names. But, who the hell knows where they've migrated from." Hawkman waved a impatient hand in the air. "Jennifer. I want you to quit worrying about those two murderers. Just be thankful you're alive."

She took a deep breath. "It's not that easy. I feel like a murderer too."

"Jennifer, look at me."

She met his gaze which looked agitated. "Get it through your head that if you hadn't defended yourself, you'd be the dead one. Now, I'm telling you, don't dwell on what happened yesterday." He snapped the pencil he held in two pieces. "Remember, we're not through."

Visibly shaken by his scolding, she turned around and stacked the dishes on the counter. "Yes, I know. The bastard hasn't made his move yet." The thought of that horrible creature still out there made her tremble. How dare him call and say such terrible things.

Hawkman tossed the pencil pieces onto the bar. "You need to get your mind off this stuff. Let's go target practicing. You need more drill on pulling that gun from you new holster."

Jennifer put the dishtowel down on the counter. How he thought that would take her mind off the killings, she wasn't sure. But it was a better idea than being idle in this house. "You're right." She closed the dishwasher. "Let's go."

❦❦❦❦❦❦

They took the falcon and went to the dump site. Hawkman released the bird and leaned against the fender of the truck, observing Jennifer as she practiced. She was good and he knew she possessed a lot of inner strength. It would just take time for her to overcome that sense of guilt. He admired the fact that she had a mind of her own, but would still listen and learn. Nothing must happen to change that.

An idea hit him and he pushed away from the truck. He waited until she'd holstered the gun, then he grabbed her around the neck. "Now, what would you do if you were attacked?"

Startled, she squealed, grasped his arm with her left hand, wrenched the gun out of her holster with her right and poked the barrel into his stomach.

"Very good," he said, roughly pushing her to the ground and putting his foot on her back. The first time she couldn't get away. But after several repetitions of the maneuver, he noticed she fell with an arm underneath her body, sucked in her breath and wrenched the gun out of the holster.

"Good thinking."

They soon tired of the violent activity and rested on a large boulder near the truck. Hawkman patted her shoulder. "You perfected some good moves, now let's hope you can just remember them in case a similar situation arises. We better head back to the house, but we'll do this again. After all, practice makes perfect."

She clicked her heels and saluted. "Yes sir, teacher Hawkman."

Pretty Boy had waited patiently on a tree branch and flew down immediately when Hawkman gave the signal.

❦❦❦❦❦❦

They returned to the house and found the large contractor's truck blocking the driveway, so Hawkman pulled over near the stack of firewood and parked. A workman hailed Jennifer before she entered the house.

"Excuse me, Ms. Morgan." He handed her a long white envelope. "A man stopped by and left you this note. He said he'd drop by another time."

"Thank you."

Hawkman had already taken Pretty Boy inside and waited for Jennifer in the kitchen. "Is there a problem with the construction?"

"No. Someone stopped by and left a message." She pulled a single sheet of paper from the long white envelope. "Terminate with extreme prejudice," she read aloud. Looking puzzled and confused, she handed it to Hawkman. "I don't get it. What does it mean?"

He grabbed the note and dashed out the front door.

Jennifer watched from the kitchen window, wary of his reaction. He went straight to the workman who'd given her the envelope.

After a few moments, he stormed back into the house and tossed the note on the counter. "The bastard's here. Our waiting game is over."

Jennifer felt her knees almost buckle. She didn't know how much more fear she could handle. "How can you be sure?"

"The workman described a very tall guy with brown hair, strange blue eyes and driving a dark green sports car."

"Brown hair?"

"He's either dyed it or wearing a hair piece, but nobody has eyes like his."

"Where'd he go?"

"Hard to say. The workman said he headed toward the back route, so he might have left. But I doubt it. He's probably hiding out somewhere."

She picked up the sheet of paper with trembling fingers. "What do these words mean?"

"It's spy talk."

"That doesn't answer my question."

Hawkman leaned his hip against the counter and stared at the wall. "It means he's going to try to kill me."

Jennifer slammed her hands on the bar top. "We can't just stand around here like sitting ducks. We need help."

He motioned for her to calm down. "I need to think." He paced for a few moments, pinching the bridge of his nose with his fingers. "This is the first time we've actually known he's in the area. Doesn't mean he hasn't been here, we just didn't know it. But, he probably doesn't have a firm plan on what he's going to do next. It might give us some extra time."

"How can you be so sure?"

"I'm not. But it indicates that he's given up on his goons and is going to take the job on himself. His first step was to put the fear of God into you with the phone call and now the note."

Jennifer fidgeted with the envelope. "Well, he's definitely accomplished scaring me to death. I don't know how much more of this I can stand." She put her hands to her cheeks. "Maybe we should both leave the area. That would really foul up his plans."

Hawkman rubbed the back of his neck. "It's still not too late for you to leave."

She pointed a finger and stared at him with narrowed eyes. "Stop. I'm not going anywhere unless you come with me. I couldn't stand the anxiety of being away from you, wondering whether you're alive or dead." Resting her clenched hands on the counter top, she chewed her lower lip. "I just wish it would all end."

Hawkman put his arm around her shoulders. "The waiting game isn't easy, but sometimes safer. I want him to make the first move. He's frustrated and I'm counting on him to make a mistake."

Jennifer lifted her head, her eyes sober. "I hope you're right."

He gave her an affectionate squeeze and picked up the phone. "It's time I installed that alarm system."

⋆⁂⋆⁂⋆⁂⋆⁂⋆

The components for the system arrived and Hawkman went to work. On the second day of solid labor, he strolled into the dining room, wiping his hands on a rag. "Ready to see if this thing works?"

Jennifer glanced up from her computer, her eyes lit up with anticipation. "You're finished?"

"Yep. Follow me."

He led her outside and closed the front door. Pulling a small card from his pocket, he held it up. "This is the activator switch."

She took the card and examined both sides. "It looks like a Visa."

"It's the latest technology. The magnetic strip has a code on it just like a credit card." He pointed to a small narrow groove he'd made in the wall. "When slid into this slot, it senses whether the unit is on or off. Right now it's off." He slid the card in and pulled it out. "Now it's on. Open the door."

Not knowing what to expect, Jennifer squinted her eyes, grasped the knob and shoved it open. The siren blasted through the house and off the roof from the speakers on each side of the chimney, echoing off the surrounding hills.

Jennifer jumped back and clamped her hands over her ears. "Turn it off," she yelled.

A couple of customers at the store plus Amelia ran into the street and peered toward the house. Hawkman waved them off and quickly shoved the card into the slot and silence reigned.

"Thank goodness," she said. "It's way too loud."

He laughed. "Hey, it works. But, you've got a point. It's pretty damned loud. I'll turn it down."

When they went back inside, Hawkman fiddled with the control panel while Jennifer removed a bottle of champagne from the refrigerator.

He looked at her curiously. "What have you got there?"

"I've been chilling this for the past two days. We haven't had much to celebrate lately so I thought now that you've installed the alarm, we'd toast the activation."

She took two frosty crystal glasses from the freezer while he popped the cork. They cheerfully toasted 'The Alarm Project'.

Hawkman downed the last of his champagne, then searched through the many instruction envelopes scattered across the coffee table. "It's here somewhere," he mumbled.

Jennifer picked up several loose ties and wrappings, wadding them into a ball for the trash. "What are you looking for?"

"Here it is." He pulled out another access card. "Keep this with you at all times. Neither of us should leave the house without turning the alarm on."

She slipped it into her jeans back pocket. "What about while we're inside?"

"That's when we'll need it the most, especially at night. And, you know, it wouldn't hurt to tell Amelia, now that she's heard the siren, to call for help immediately, if she hears it go off again."

A wry grin tugged at the corners of Jennifer's mouth. "She's going to wonder why I need an alarm system when I have a body guard."

⊹⊱•⊰⊹•⊱⊰•⊱⊰•⊰⊹

Dirk parked in a clump of trees off Teal Drive. With his long lanky stride, he made his way up the mountain toward the mesa. His camouflage suit blended well with the large boulder he'd been hiding behind for the past two days, spying on Jennifer's house.

There hadn't been much movement around the place except for when Hawkman climbed up on the roof and installed the alarm system horns on each side of the chimney. Too bad he didn't slip and break his ugly neck, Dirk thought.

He had them in view when the siren went off. "My, my," he scoffed, "doing all this for my benefit. It won't work, you son-of-a-bitch. I'll find my way around your stupid alarm."

He dropped the binoculars, letting them hang from his neck. In deep thought, he studied the house for several minutes before he sauntered down the hill and climbed into his car.

CHAPTER SIXTEEN

Baffled by what he'd just read, Bill Broadwell closed the file and leaned back in his chair. How had that rogue agent managed to get away with his corrupt and unprincipled behavior for so long? And now his drive for revenge has put Jim Anderson, alias, Tom Casey, in serious danger.

He whirled his chair around and stared out the large window behind him. His thoughts traveled back to the years when he and Jim had worked together as agents in other countries. Jim's extraordinary foreign language capabilities gave them the edge in any situation. He recalled Jim's words when they were on an assignment in Turkey: 'Keep your mouth shut or we'll end up rotting in jail. Leave the talking to me.' Bill smiled as his hand rasped across the day old stubble on his chin. Jim had been right

He slapped his hands on the arms of his chair and said aloud. "God, I hated to lose him to that eye injury." Then a frown creased his forehead when Sylvia's image floated before him. What a beautiful woman and how Jim had loved her. They'd just begun their life when she died that violent death. Grimacing, Bill remembered how Jim, single-handed, searched out and killed the ones responsible for her death. That is, all but one. The leader.

He turned back around in his chair and brought his fist down hard on the bulky folder. "It took us awhile, Jim, but we'll get the bastard now," he proclaimed to the empty space surrounding him.

Bill heaved his muscular bulk from the chair and paced thoughtfully before he stopped in front of his desk and pushed the intercom. "Steve, you busy? I need to talk."

"Come on down."

Bill buttoned his collar button and pushed his loose tie knot back up where it belonged, then hustled down the hall toward his superior's office. When he entered, Steve Warren motioned toward a chair.

"So, what's on your mind?"

Bill pulled the chair to the front of the desk and sat down. "I need your authorization to go to the west coast and help a former agent who's in trouble."

"What's his name?"

"Used to be Agent Jim Anderson, new identity, Tom Casey." Bill then gave him a quick run down of the situation.

As Bill talked, Steve's bushy gray brows knitted deep into a sour frown until they almost touched at the bridge of his nose by the time Bill finished. Steve leaned forward, resting his clasped hands on top of his desk. "This sounds like a very serious situation and definitely doesn't look good for the Agency. I think you better get out there as fast as you can and take our culprit alive. He has a lot of answering to do. Our ex-Mr. Casey might not be so lenient."

Bill nodded. "My thoughts exactly."

Steve pulled his scheduler toward him. "How does your week look?"

"Nothing pressing."

"Good. Stay as long as needed. I'll handle this end. But, I think you better get on your way tonight."

Bill stood. "I'll notify Casey. All he needs to know right now are the bare facts. If I give him Dirk's name and everything I've discovered, he'll kill the bastard before I get there."

"Good idea. Have you issued any preliminary orders?

"Henderson's under surveillance, but that's it so far."

"You better move quickly. Sounds like he could well start taking things into his own hands since his hired thugs have failed." He closed his scheduler. "Need anything done right now from this end?"

"It wouldn't hurt to alert the Medford and San Francisco offices. Just make sure none of these details leak to Dirk Henderson."

"Done." Steve stood and extended his hand. "Be careful and good luck."

Bill hurried back to his office and made a call.

Jennifer sat silently at the kitchen bar deep in thought, both hands gripping her coffee cup. When the phone rang, she jumped, spilling her coffee across the counter. "Good grief, I'm so skittish."

Hawkman snatched a handful of paper towels and sopped up the mess before it dripped to the floor. When Bill's voice came over the machine, he grabbed the receiver, a pad of paper and a pencil. "Hello, Bill."

Jennifer watched his face turn grim.

"So the leak's in Medford. Who is it?"

She flinched at the cracking noise when he snapped the pencil in two pieces. He hastily scribbled a note with one of the halves and hung up. She watched him rub his hands across his face and readjust his eye patch. When he looked at her, his expression sent a shock wave through her system. She didn't even recognize the cold, forbidding man standing in front of her.

He spoke in a low and menacing voice. "They know the bastard's identity. Bill's flying out."

Her stomach turned a flip-flop, a mix of relief that Bill would soon be there, and anxiety about what might happen before he arrived. She crossed over to the coffee pot and refilled her mug. "So what are you going to do until Bill gets here?"

"I'm going to find the son-of-a-bitch and kill him."

Her hand shook so hard she had to set the mug down on the counter. "Did Bill tell you his name?"

"No. But I know."

She stared at him. "Who?"

The hairs in his beard quivered, his eye narrowed. He yanked the gun from his holster and laid it on the counter. "Dirk Henderson."

Placing a hand to her throat, she stared down at the gun. "You can't just kill him outright." Her voice caught.

His head whipped up. "Why not? He killed Sylvia without a second thought. Sent those creeps out here to do us in. And made a bunch of threatening calls to you. He doesn't give a damn about anyone."

She walked around the bar and put her hand on his arm. "If you stoop to murder, then you're no better than he is. Why don't you let the Agency deal with him?"

He shook off her hand. "Butt out, Jennifer. I've lived with this hell long enough. That bastard doesn't deserve to live. He isn't getting away from me this time." He wiped down his weapon then shoved it back into the holster.

Her hands dropped to her side. "He's a cold blooded killer. What if he gets you first?"

He walked away from her. "He won't have a chance."

She dashed around to his front and put her hands against his chest. "Hawkman, please don't do it."

He grabbed her shoulders in a punishing grip. "Check all the window locks and barricade the doors," he snarled. Then he jerked away and stormed out the front door.

Fighting back the tears, she hurried to the kitchen window and watched through blurry eyes as he ran down the driveway, onto the road and toward the hills. When the garage blocked her view of him, she came down off her toes, tears sliding down her cheeks as she clenched her arms around her waist in fear.

❖➤❖➤❖➤❖➤❖➤❖

Hawkman knew he had to get out of the house before he exploded. Jennifer's pleading had gone straight to his heart and it hurt like hell to know he'd upset her. But he'd felt a surge of adrenalin pump through his body when he'd talked with Bill. He had to let it dissipate.

The more he thought about the scum who'd destroyed his earlier life, the harder he pounded the ground. That son-of-a-bitch would have to die before he could have a life of his own. Jennifer didn't understand the hatred that burned deep inside him. Naturally, she'd felt grief with the loss of her husband, but that was an accident. Sylvia's death was cold-blooded murder. Tears stung his eyes as the wind whipped around his beard and face. He'd never forgive himself if he gave that piece of filth another chance at killing someone he loved.

Not wanting to get out out of sight of the house, he turned and headed back in a dead run. Dirk's ability to stay one step ahead bothered him greatly. Trained by the Agency like himself, the man knew all the tricks. Maybe he couldn't whip him alone. Maybe his best revenge would be to let the Agency have him. At least he'd never get away from them. But, he feared if he ever got his hands on Dirk, he wouldn't be able to resist killing him on the spot.

Hawkman stood in front of the house a few minutes and inhaled deep breaths of clean mountain air. He felt much calmer and slowly jogged up the driveway. After Jennifer unbarricaded the door and he got inside, he noticed her red swollen eyes and pulled her into his arms. "Dammit, you're right. I'm going to let the Agency have him." Then he held her back at arm's length and looked deeply into her eyes. "But I'm warning you right here and now. I won't hesitate to kill him if I have to."

She sniffled and wrapped her arms around his neck. "Neither would I," she whispered.

⊹⟩⋆⟨⊹⟩⋆⟨⊹⟩⋆⟨⊹⟩⋆⟨⊹⟩

Bill dropped the phone on the cradle and hit the desk with his fist. The Agency had lost track of Dirk. "Damn, didn't get things rolling fast enough."

An announcement blared over the intercom that a car for Bill Broadwell awaited at the curb. He grabbed his luggage and the office door slammed behind him.

When he reached Dulles Airport, he hustled out onto the tarmac and boarded the Lear jet. Copco Lake was clear across the country and even though a chopper would be waiting at Medford to airlift him to the lake, it would take hours to get there. Time was of the essence and he feared that Dirk might already be at the lake, setting up his plan of action.

Once in the air, Bill opened his briefcase and reviewed some of the papers from the bulky file. After refreshing his memory, he leaned back in his seat. Better get some rest, he thought. These next few days wouldn't allow much time for sleep. Soon, Bill's chin relaxed on his chest, his mouth fell open and his snores mixed with the drone of the jet.

Down on her knees restocking some lower shelves, Amelia groaned when the phone rang. "Why does that blasted thing always go off when I'm in this position. You'd think they did it on purpose." Using the shelves above her for a hand hold, she hoisted herself up to a standing position and walked stiffly toward the front. "I'm coming, I'm coming." She leaned across the counter and picked up the receiver. "Copco Lake Store."

"Is this where I call to rent a cabin?"

"Yes, it is. How can I help you?"

"I'd like a place on the north side of the Lake."

"Oh dear, I'm not sure anything's available. How many will be sharing the cabin?

"Just one."

"Hold on, let me check my list." Mumbling, she limped stiffly back to her office. "Hmm, just one, that's unusual. Shouldn't be a problem if I have a vacancy." After sifting through the papers on her desk, she picked up the extension. "You're in luck, I have a cabin for one week only, starting tomorrow."

"Perfect."

She reached for a pad of paper and pencil. "What's your name,

"Brad Swenson."

"Come to the store when you get here. I'll have your key and directions.

"What if you're closed when I arrive?"

"No problem. I live in the apartment above the store, just take the stairs on the side. See you when you get here, Mr. Swenson."

Amelia hung up muttering. "A one man hunting trip. I guess I've heard of stranger things." It still puzzled her how business had boomed all of a sudden. Two weeks ago, she couldn't give a cabin away. She shook her head. Maybe hunting season's better than I heard.

She picked up a rag and dusted off a row of canned beans. "Thank goodness all the cabins are clean. I'd hate to think of doing that job tonight on top of everything else." She let out a moan as she got back down on her knees in front of the shelf.

CHAPTER SEVENTEEN

Smirking, Dirk replaced the receiver on the cradle and patted it. "Everything's falling into place like clock work." He peeked out the corner of the drape and eyed the blue Buick parked in front of his motel unit. A nice low profile car, he thought. One that won't attract much attention. He let the curtain fall, sneering, as he rubbed his hands together. "I'm only forty-five minutes from you, Hawk Man and tomorrow night I'll only be a stone's throw away."

His biceps quivered with anticipation as he picked up the briefcase from the floor and placed it on the bed. He flipped it open and stared at the contents for a moment before pulling the Sokolosky .45 from its leather holster. Holding it in front of him, he turned the gun from side to side so the lamp light flickered off the shiny barrel, sending iridescent streaks onto the surrounding wall.

After screwing on the silencer, he held the gun high in the air. "Here's to you Hawk Man. I'll empty this baby into your big ugly heart." With that he dropped to one knee and pointed the gun at the motel door. "Pow! you're dead, Hawk Man."

He fell backwards laughing, the hideous sound bouncing off the walls and filling the room. Rolling over, he wiped his eyes with his sleeve and crawled on his knees back to the attache case on the bed. He removed a patch cloth, took off the silencer and gently buffed the barrel until it glowed. Satisfied with the shine, he placed the gun back into its sheath and slid it into the valise. He then concealed the case under the extra pillow on the bed.

Next, he opened his suitcase and took out a long-sleeved, brown plaid shirt and a pair of army green pants. He shook the wrinkles out as best he could, then hung them in the closet. The camouflaged hat had gotten crushed so he hit it against his thigh a couple of times before tossing it onto the closet shelf.

From one of the zippered compartments, he brought out a matching wig and beard. He plopped the wig on his head, but cringed at the forgotten, yet still tender scratches. Going into the bathroom, he admired himself in the mirror, then placed the false beard against his chin. It drooped down a shade long, making him appear a bit eccentric, but that pleased him. The salt and pepper color also gave him the appearance of being much older. He viewed his new image for several minutes, then pulled off the wig and placed it with the beard alongside a pair of sunglasses on the bedside table.

He went back into the bathroom to fill a glass with ice from the ice bucket and again glanced into the mirror. He rearranged his hair with his fingers, trying to cover the streaked red spots. "Damn bird. Another couple of days and there won't be a Hawk Man, Jennifer or bird."

He went back into the main room and lifted a bottle of Jack Daniels from a brown paper bag sitting on the dresser. The bag slipped to the floor and he kicked it under the bed. He poured a stiff drink, flopped down into the chair, placing the bottle on the floor between his feet, then turned on the television with the remote control. "Might as well relax tonight, Tomorrow the bird shit's gonna fly."

⊹⊱•⊰•⊱•⊰•⊱•⊰⊹

Hawkman sat straight up in bed. It only took him a moment to realize he'd been jerked out of a deep sleep by the siren from the alarm system. He leaped out of bed, grabbed his gun and dashed across the hall to Jennifer's room. He shoved open the door only to find her sitting in the middle of the bed with her gun aimed at him. "Don't shoot! It's me!" he yelled, quickly jumping back around the door jamb.

Her eyes wide, Jennifer joined him in the hallway. "Do you think someone's trying to break in?"

"I'm not sure, but I need to get to the main control and see which side of the house is being disturbed. Stay close and cover me in case they're still inside."

She followed him into the living room, her gaze scanning the windows as they made their way into the kitchen. From what she could see, nothing appeared disturbed.

They finally reached the control box where Hawkman switched off the loud siren, then studied the blinking light. "Looks like someone tampered with one of the living room windows. I'll check it out."

He started across the room just as a flash of light illuminated the kitchen. Ducking back out of the headlight's beam, he stepped toward the entry, his gun poised.

Within seconds, someone pounded on the front door and shouted. "Everyone okay?"

"Who's there?" Hawkman asked.

"Fire Chief Ruskin and Jake Arnold."

He dropped his gun hand to his side and opened the door. "Boy, you guys don't waste any time in getting here."

Jake stepped inside. "Amelia told me you've had some problems and if that alarm went off, to get the police here pronto."

"Appreciate it," Hawkman said.

"Have any idea what set it off?" Ruskin asked.

The indicator shows tampering of one of the living room windows. I haven't checked it out yet."

Ruskin stepped back outside. "While you do that, Jake and I will search the grounds." They drew their guns and started around the corner of the house.

Jennifer flipped on the outside lights.

Hawkman crossed the room to the window that had set off the alarm and removed the pane. He yelled out the window to the two men. "Never mind, I've found the culprit."

Ruskin and Jake scurried up the steps to the deck and watched Hawkman pull a dead bat from between the screen and window. "Looks like this little guy's radar fouled up."

Jennifer put her gun on the counter and joined the men. "That's the second time that's happened. But no alarm system went off the first time."

Hawkman held up the bat between his thumb and forefinger. "Sure sorry to have pulled you guys out of bed for this."

Ruskin holstered his gun. "No problem. I'd rather it be a bat caught in the screen than a burglary in progress." With that, he and Jake strolled back around the house to their car.

Hawkman tossed the dead bat out into the yard. "He'll make a nice meal for a raccoon."

Jennifer put her hand on her chest. "My heart's still pounding."

"I'll check all the screens tomorrow and make sure they're tight so nothing can get inside them. We definitely don't need that kind of scare."

After they locked up, Jennifer picked up her gun from the kitchen counter and headed back toward her bedroom. "At least we know the alarm works. Good night."

⊹⊱•⊰⊹⊱•⊰⊹⊱•⊰⊹⊱•⊰⊹

She climbed into bed, her stomach still in knots from the scare. Feeling utterly exhausted, she wondered if maybe she'd made the wrong decision and should have left for awhile.

The next morning, she found Hawkman leaning against the kitchen counter and staring out the window, a cup of coffee in his hand. "I heard you stirring around an hour ago, but I fell back asleep."

He kept gazing out the window. "Yeah, I've been up awhile."

She moved over behind him and stood on her toes, trying to see over his shoulder. "What's so interesting out there?"

"A lot of strange men coming and going around the store."

Jennifer came down off her toes and shrugged. "Probably hunters."

Hawkman shook his head, "Nope, these aren't the kind of hunters you're used to."

Again, she strained her neck trying to see out. "But I don't see anybody."

He strummed his fingers on the sill of the window. "They've already gone. But I've got a gut feeling things are going down and

Bill has sent in some men." He stepped away and ran a hand over his beard. "Can't figure out why we haven't heard from him. He should have been here by now."

She reached into the cabinet for a cup. "He'll probably call soon."

Abruptly, he grabbed his hat and jacket off the coat rack. "Let's run over to the store. I want to talk to Amelia."

She waved him off. "Why don't you go ahead. I'll be all right." Opening the refrigerator, she shook the almost empty milk carton. "Pick up a carton of milk while you're there, and get a newspaper, please."

"Okay, but don't let anyone in, not even someone you know." He shrugged on his jacket and plopped on his hat. "I'll be back shortly."

"I hear you," she sighed, watching him deactivate the alarm to get out, then activate it again on the outside. She combed her fingers through her hair, thinking how she felt like she lived in a jail. Everything was so closed in and complicated. She couldn't even go to the dock without carrying her gun or fussing with that damned alarm system

⊰•≺⦂≻•≺⦂≻•≺⦂≻•⊱

Hawkman walked down the road with an uneasy feeling. His instincts screamed warnings and he felt as though red flags were waving in his face. A chill slid down his spine, yet he saw nothing out of the ordinary. When he stepped inside the store, Amelia poked her head out of the office area near the back. "Hi, Hawkman, be right with you."

It always amazed him how she knew when someone walked into the store. There were no wires leading back to the office indicating any sort of warning system and no bell hung from the front door. She just had one hell of a sensor system in her body. He smiled to himself. Maybe the Agency should hire her.

He went back to the cooler and took out a half gallon of milk. Amelia came out of the office and joined him, walking toward the register. "How's it going?" he asked, laying a paper beside the milk.

She rang up his order, gave him his change then looked at him with one arched brow. "Is the hunting exceptionally good this year?"

"Why do you ask that?"

"Well." She hesitated a moment and busied herself with straightening the counter. "I've rented every available cabin on this lake in the last two days. Normally, this is the slowest time of the year and I end up closing the store until spring." She threw her arms out in skepticism. "I just don't understand it."

"Hey, don't knock it. Be happy with the clients."

"True, and if it continues, I might not close at all. But it just doesn't add up. Never happened before in all the years I've been running this place."

"Maybe some hunting club got wind of good deer hunting at Copco Lake?"

"Darned if I know. Usually I'll get a call from some official if a club's interested. They like to check on how many cabins I have, then they send a retainer to hold them." She shook her head. "I've gotten no calls from clubs." Then she pointed a finger at Hawkman. "But I'll tell you something. These guys don't look like the run-of-the-mill hunters."

"Oh. Why's that?" he asked, furrowing his brow.

"For one thing, they're not wearing the right clothes." She leaned on the counter toward him. "And the second thing is their gun cases are odd. They definitely don't contain hunting rifles or shotguns."

He shrugged. "Maybe they're trying out some new fangled guns and have them broken down. And as far as I've heard, the deer season's been about average. So, afraid I can't help you explain the boom in your business. But, I'd say enjoy it while it lasts." He left the store, his suspicions confirmed. The Agency had arrived. But where was Bill? Heading back to the house he sensed the uncomfortable feeling that had haunted him earlier, still lurking in the back of his mind. He tuned all his senses up to maximum pitch.

The minute he stepped inside, he called to Jennifer. "Any calls?"

She glanced up from her computer and shook her head.

He immediately went to the phone and dialed Bill, but he could tell by the clicks and pauses that the call had been rerouted.

"Steve Warren here."

"Steve, Tom Casey at Copco Lake. I'm trying to reach Bill."

"He's on his way. Should arrive anytime."

"Did he station men out here?"

"Yes, but I don't know how many."

"That explains a few things. Thanks."

⟨∗⟩⟨∗⟩⟨∗⟩⟨∗⟩

Jennifer stopped working on her article and listened while Hawkman talked. She observed how pensive his mood had become and wondered if he'd learned anything from Amelia. Then out of the corner of her eye she noticed the milk sitting on the counter and got up to put it in the refrigerator. Even though she brushed right by him, he didn't say anything and seemed occupied in deep thought as he headed back toward his bedroom.

After putting the milk away, she followed and stood at his door. He knelt at the closet, pulling out an attache case that he plopped on the bed. His expression grim when he glanced her way.

She watched with interest. "Did you find out anything helpful at the store?"

"Yes. My suspicions were correct. The Agency's men are here. But I'm not sure Henderson's on the lake yet."

Jennifer leaned against the door jamb, nervously running her hands up and down her arms. "What do we do now?"

"We get prepared. Just like before."

Her insides tightened at his comment.

But this time, I'll use a few different tactics" He snapped open the briefcase. "Do you have on your gun?"

"Yes. I've worn it every day since Leon made the holster."

"Good. Don't take it off. Even wear it to bed." He then brought a strange object out of the case, flicked his wrist and it opened up like a flower.

Jennifer gasped and stepped forward. "What's that?"

"A blossom."

She blinked as it opened and closed. "What do you do with it?"

"You throw it at your aggressor. It won't kill him but it will disable him enough for you to escape."

She reached out and touched the sharp corners. "This would definitely leave an ugly wound." Then she peered down into the opened case. "My word, this is full of gadgets. Have you used them all?"

He nodded. "At one time or the other." He picked up what looked like an old fashioned fountain pen and held it out for her to see. But when she reached out to take it, he pulled it back. "Don't touch it. It's full of a special gas and if activated would paralyze you for about four to six hours."

She quickly retracted her hand. "What if it leaked out while you were sleeping?"

"It won't. But I'd advise you not to touch anything in this case. You could activate something if you don't know what you're doing."

She backed away, her eyes wide. "Don't worry, I wouldn't touch anything in there with a ten foot pole."

He showed her the Clipitt knife, a form of the switchblade; an umbrella with a sword in the end that folded up; another fountain pen with a lock pick inside and 'bugs' you hide in a room to transmit voices.

Then he held up a round item. "This is a voice changer. It's the instrument Dirk used when he made those calls to you and John."

By this time, Jennifer had regained some of her confidence and eased closer to the case. Her curiosity forced her to ask one question after another.

After he finished showing her the items inside, Hawkman placed a few selective tools on the bed and closed the briefcase. "Even this," he said, pointing to several different areas on the the case, "can be rigged with everything from poison gas to a hidden camera."

She waved her hand over the items he'd put on the bed. "What are you going to do with these?"

"I'm going to carry them for the next few days."

Standing silently, her hands twitched at her side as she stared at the forbidding objects. "When is this going to end?"

He stepped beside her and put an arm around her shoulders, squeezing her close to him. "Real soon."

CHAPTER EIGHTEEN

Dirk didn't want to arrive at Copco Lake too soon, so he slept until nine o'clock. After dressing in the camouflage hunting outfit, he took the suitcase to the car and stowed it in the trunk alongside the ice chest, tossing the paper sack with the wig and beard onto the passenger seat. He returned to the room, dropped the key on the dresser, scrutinized the area to make sure he'd left no telltale signs of his visit, then grabbed the briefcase holding his gun. He wanted the valise within reach, so he nestled it between his left leg and the car door.

Making a quick stop at the grocery store, he packed the ice chest with bags of ice and food. He couldn't help but snicker. People would think him just another hunter on his way to stalk game.

While having breakfast at the local cafe, he gazed out the window and noticed the museum across the street. He checked his watch and realized he needed to kill more time. A trip through the museum would just about do it. As he left, local residents and visiting hunters gave him casual nods and a wave, wishing him luck. He returned their greetings and grinned. If they only knew what he stalked.

At the museum, he meandered through the aisles of displays, letting his mind wander, paying no attention to the other visitors. When someone touched his arm and asked an innocent question, he jerked away. But then realizing his reaction, quickly pulled himself together, smiled and nodded. This place held too many people in close quarters to be comfortable, so he headed for the car.

When he reached Ager Beswick road, he followed it north to the cut-off to Copco Lake. A surge of exhilaration raced through his body when he thought about having Hawk Man in his gun sight again. This time nothing would interfere.

A few miles from the lake, he found a spot on the road wide enough to park without impeding traffic. He took the wig out of the paper sack, and pulled the snug fitting hair piece over his head, tucking the loose strands of red hair underneath the tight band. Next, he patted the beard into place along his chin line. He tugged on the camouflaged hat, slipped on the sunglasses, then scrutinized his reflection in the mirror. The disguise had completely transformed his appearance. No one would ever recognize Dirk Henderson. He chuckled to himself as he pulled back onto the road.

When he crossed the bridge to the other side of the lake, he saw the construction trucks parked in Jennifer's driveway. He noted with interest that the garage would soon be back to normal. But when his eye caught sight of Hawkman's familiar 4X4, obscenities spewed from his mouth.

He fixed his gaze on the store and pulled into the parking lot. His watch showed five-thirty on the nose. Perfect. He pulled the key from the ignition and locked the car.

A few customers still lingered inside, so he roamed through the aisles studying the shelves. He stopped in front of a poster depicting 'Noah's World of Water' rafters coming down the Klamath River through 'Hell's Corner Run'. Maybe I'll do some white water rafting when I finish with the Hawk Man, he thought, a smile curling his lips as he traced his finger over the colorful scene. After the last customer left, he ambled up to the counter.

Amelia barely looked up from the register. "And what can I do for you?"

"I'm Brad Swenson. I have a cabin reserved."

"Oh yes, Mr. Swenson. I'll get the contract and key for you." Locking the cash drawer, she hustled back to her office, returning within a few seconds with the paper in her hand. She gave him a pen and pointed. "Sign on that line, please."

At that moment, a boy dashed into the store and ran toward the ice cream freezer. "Whew, I thought you'd closed," he said, out of breath.

Amelia took his coins and buffed his head. "Sam, you made it just in time."

He eyed the man standing next to him. "Wow, are you tall!" he exclaimed, and ran out the door.

Dirk scowled, but didn't respond, recognizing him as being the same kid he'd seen with Hawk Man and Jennifer the day the bird had clawed his head.

Meantime, Amelia had walked over to the confection counter to retrieve some candy bars which had fallen to the floor.

Dirk cleared his throat loudly. "Where's the cabin? I'd like to get settled."

She hurried back around the counter. "Forgive me, Mr. Swenson, it's been a busy day." Picking up the contract, she slipped on her glasses and glanced at his signature, then pointed out the window. "See that two story log cabin behind the fire station?"

Dirk's gaze followed the direction of her finger. "Yes."

She handed him the key. "That's yours for the week. Enjoy yourself."

"Thanks." Dirk left and whistled a melody on the way to the car while tossing the key in the air. But before getting inside, he spotted the boy he'd just encountered running up Jennifer's driveway with a big dog at his heels.

He quickly jumped into the car and drove to the rental cabin. Grabbing the binoculars from the seat, he dashed up the front steps and unlocked the door. He bounded up the stairwell that jutted upward right in front of him, taking two steps at a time. It only took him a few seconds to find the room with a perfect view of Jennifer's house. Smirking, he put the glasses to his eyes and watched Hawk Man talking to the boy in the front yard.

Soon, the boy took off down the road and Hawk Man disappeared inside. Dirk lowered the field glasses, but his glare stayed riveted on the house. Several minutes later, he forced himself to move away from the window and go downstairs.

He lugged in the ice chest and suitcase, then locked the door. Tossing the wig, hat and sunglasses onto a chair, he mussed his thick red hair with his fingers. Carefully removing the beard with its sticky tape, not sure if he'd need it again, placed it gently on the table. It would be best to park himself in that upstairs room and use it for his observation point. Dashing up the steps, his blue eyes sparkled with anticipation.

⟨⁘⟩⋇⟨⁘⟩⋇⟨⁘⟩⋇⟨⁘⟩⋇⟨⁘⟩

Jennifer stood at the kitchen sink peeling carrots when she glanced up and spotted Sam and Herman running up the driveway. "Hawkman, Sam and Herman are coming to the door. They shouldn't be here. It's much too dangerous for them."

Hawkman rose from the chair, dropping the newspaper to the floor. "I'll handle it." And sauntered outside to meet the boy. "Hey, Sam, how's it going?"

Sam stood in the big opening where the garage door would be installed. "Great. Hey, looks like it's almost finished."

"Won't be long now." Hawkman scanned the area and strolled over to the other side of Sam so that he stood between the boy and the road. Sam stared at him strangely and grew very quiet. This disturbed Hawkman for a moment, hoping the boy didn't sense his anxiety. "Why so quiet, Sam?"

"Oh, just wondering how tall you are."

Hawkman chuckled in relief. "Six foot two inches. Why?"

"Well, I just saw a guy at the store that I bet's taller."

His interest piqued, Hawkman raised a brow. "Really. Who?"

Sam shook his head. "I don't know. Just some old guy with a long gray beard." Then his attention switched back to the construction.

They examined the new cabinets and hot water heater. Hawkman explained all about the electrical plugs until Sam tired of the technical stuff.

"Guess I better get going, it's about supper time." He whistled for Herman, waved goodbye and ran down the road toward home.

Hawkman watched him go, then walked back inside the house. "He's some kid. I do believe he asks more questions than you do."

Jennifer smiled and tossed an apple to him, "Here. Sweeten up that mouth of yours."

When night fell, Hawkman went through the house and closed the drapes. "No sense in being a clear target."

⸰⟨·⟩⸰⟨·⟩⸰⟨·⟩⸰⟨·⟩⸰

Jennifer couldn't sleep, her senses so keyed to the outside that she heard every sound from the crickets, fish splashing in the lake, to the night owls hooting a long distance away. It made it difficult to concentrate on her reading. But soon sleep overtook her and as she drifted off, she could still hear Hawkman moving about the house.

The next morning, Jennifer found him in front of the living room window, staring out over the lake. She put her hands on her hips. "Did you ever go to bed?"

He shook his head. "No."

"Why? You need sleep to be at your best."

"I know. But there's something's wrong. I feel it."

She ran her hand along the back of the couch. "I'm afraid I agree. I had a very restless night."

"Walk over to the store with me. Maybe I can find out something from Amelia without her suspecting anything."

"Why don't you go ahead. We're only a house away and I've got things I need to do. I'll be all right."

"Okay, but don't leave and don't answer the door or phone. I'll be back shortly."

"I know, I know," she said, waving him off. She walked him to the front door and noticed the mail truck at the boxes. He's early, she thought, glancing at her watch that read eleven o'clock.

She noticed Hawkman running to the store in a zigzag pattern. At least he practiced what he preached,she thought, remembering how he'd reminded her many times about how hard it is to hit it to shoot a moving target.

⸰⟨·⟩⸰⟨·⟩⸰⟨·⟩⸰⟨·⟩⸰

When Hawkman went into the store, he found Amelia sitting behind the counter reading. She closed her book and pulled off her glasses connected to a decorative chain around her neck. Letting them fall against her chest, she smiled.

"Good morning. How are you?"

"I'm fine, thanks. Say, I've been expecting a buddy of mine to come up for a little fishing. I haven't heard from him in a couple of days and wondered if by some chance a tall, red headed guy showed up here looking for me or a place to stay?"

Amelia looked thoughtfully at the ceiling, tapping her chin with her forefinger. "No, only one guy came in last night, but he'd already reserved a cabin. Gosh, I hardly remember what he looked like. Let me think a second." She snapped her fingers. "Got his picture now. He was definitely very tall, but he had long gray hair and a beard. You know, that half white and half dark color. What do they call that?"

"Salt and pepper."

"Yes, of course. Sort of an eccentric looking guy with real blue eyes. In fact, I thought it odd when he reserved the cabin for just one. That's a rarity up here."

Hawkman raised a brow. "Which cabin did he rent?"

She stood up and pointed out the window. "That two story one, behind the fire station. He'd requested this side of the lake when he called and luckily I had one left."

"Thanks, Amelia." Hawkman dashed toward the door as she let out a long sigh, slipped on her glasses and opened her book.

Running back toward the house, Hawkman spotted Jennifer jogging to the mailbox. "Damn, I told her not to go out of the house."

When he caught up with her, she glanced up with a guilty expression. They zig-zagged back to the house. Since nothing happened, he decided not to scold her.

Once they were safely inside, Jennifer silently dropped her mail on the counter then crossed over to the sliding glass door where she stood for several minutes staring out over the water. "This whole thing is really getting to me. It's pretty bad when you don't even feel safe going to the mailbox. And not only that." She turned and looked at Hawkman. "I have this weird feeling about this being the calm before the storm."

His thumbs hooked in his front jeans' pockets, he joined her at the door. "I'm afraid you're right."

"What if Dirk makes his move before Bill gets here?"

"We'll handle it."

She glanced up at him. "You said the Agency men were here. Where are they? And if they are, what will Dirk do if he spots them?"

"Well, to answer your first question. Amelia thinks her business boom is due to a good deer season. But, the men she described renting cabins with their unusual guns and dress are from the Agency. Unless Dirk recognizes an agent, I doubt he's too concerned at this moment. His mind is preoccupied with how to get me."

Jennifer fired a look at him. "You mean us."

Hawkman pulled her toward him. "Correct, he won't care who gets in his way."

Turning away from him, she walked to the center of the room with her hands gripped behind her. "What else did you find out from Amelia?"

"She told me she'd just rented a cabin to a lone, tall man with a beard. I figure it's Dirk incognito."

Her heart lurched and she swung around to face him, "Which cabin?"

He pointed out the kitchen window. "That one behind the fire station."

Her eyes filled with terror. "He's within rifle range."

"You learn fast, my dear lady. And more than likely, he's watching the house right now." Hawkman gently put a hand on her back and moved her to the side. "So don't stand directly in front of any window facing that direction."

She hugged herself and closed her eyes. "Shouldn't Bill be here by now?"

He nodded. "Yes. I can't figure what's happened."

⊹»⊱«⊹»⊱«⊹»⊱«⊹»⊱⊹

Dirk watched Hawkman take off for the store in a zig-zag pattern and threw back his head and laughed. "What's the matter, Hawk Man, you scared?"

After he disappeared into the store, Dirk turned the binoculars back on the house. I better not go near that house, he thought, remembering the night she'd thrown on the flood lights leaving him without a place to hide.

Suddenly, his stomach grumbled and he realized it was lunch time. He laid the field glasses aside and bounced down the stairs to the kitchen where he'd placed his ice chest filled with food. After fixing a sandwich, he grabbed a cold beer from the refrigerator and hastened back upstairs to his look-out spot.

Just as he started to take a bite, he noticed movement at the house and raised the glasses to his eyes. "Ah, our little lady is heading for the mailbox. He checked his watch. "Hmm, she's early today."

⊹×⊹×⊹×⊹×⊹

Co-pilot, Buck Cobert, shook Bill's shoulder. "Mr. Broadwell, wake up. We're landing at Tinker Air Force Base to refuel, but we'll be running into some weather ahead so you'd better put on your seat belt"

Grumbling, Bill struggled with the strap while the plane bucked and pitched. After a rough landing, he disembarked, only to be socked in the face by strong winds and rain. He dashed inside the base operation's building and brushed the water from his clothes. "Good Lord, what a storm." Glancing around the meager hall, he wished he'd snagged a sandwich at Dulles to bring along. It looked like his only hope would be a candy bar and a soft drink from the two vending machines.

While munching the candy, he paced, waiting for word to board. Just as he drained the last of the soda, the pilot, Fisk Hanes, entered, droplets of water dripping from his flight suit.

"What's the delay?" Bill asked.

Hanes shook his head. "Can't take off until this freak storm passes."

Bill wadded the candy wrapper into a ball and threw it into the waste basket. "Damn! How long? We need to get out of here."

"Not sure. They're saying it's a big one. Full of rain, wind and possible tornadoes."

Bill frowned. "Damn! You better radio ahead to the Medford Airport and explain our situation. Tell them we've changed our plans. Once we get out of here, we'll fly directly to Siskiyou County Airport. Have them send the helicopter waiting at Medford over there. He can fly me into the Folger Ranch where a couple of agents will pick me up."

Hanes stuck his note pad into his pocket and turned to leave.

"Wait. Before you go. Do you know if there's a private phone around here?"

The pilot pointed down the hall. "Try that first office."

"Thanks." Bill hurried toward the open door and poked his head inside.

A young secretary glanced up from her typing. "Can I help you?"

He flashed his badge. "Can you take a break? I need to use your office for a few minutes."

"Sure."

Bill closed the door and sat down at the small desk. He dialed Steve and drummed his fingers on the wood surface. "Steve, we're stuck at Tinker Field. Big storm rolled in and only God knows how long we'll be stuck here. Get hold of the team at the Lake and find out if Dirk's arrived."

Steve interrupted. "Got a call from Bob Raines. Dirk's there and he's rented a cabin within rifle range of Jennifer's house."

Bill hit his fist on the desk. "Shit! Get a twenty-four hour surveillance team on him immediately. But repeat my orders not to take him until I get there. Unless, of course, it's absolutely necessary. By the way, did Casey mention anything about Dirk?"

"No."

"Doesn't mean a damn thing. He could have him by the neck shaking his brains out, yet deny he'd seen him. Just pray he hasn't spotted him yet."

Bill stared at the phone after hanging up and wondered if he should call Casey? Or take the chance he'd get there before things came down? He chose the latter and left the office. He walked the hall from one end to the other. A large wall clock reminded him of the precious minutes ticking away.

Running his hand over his forehead, he stared out the window at the churning clouds. The rain pounded so hard on the tin roofs of the hangers that it sounded like hail the size of golf balls. Lightning streaks periodically lit up the sky and gave the runway an eerie appearance. When the thunder cracked, the whole building shook.

Hanes and Cobert ran in from outside, flipping water in all directions. Bill glanced at them with anticipation. But Hanes only shook his head. "Looks like it could be hours before we get out of here. They've even got tornado warnings out."

Bill threw up his hands in despair. "Dear God, why now? It isn't even the season for that type of storm."

Cobert shrugged. "Guess that's why they're calling it a freak one."

He dropped his arms to his side and took a deep breath. "Check with the Visiting Officer's Quarters and see if they could put us up for a while. We better try and get a few hours shut-eye."

After the two men left, Bill sat down in a lone chair and dropped his head into his hands. "Damn. What a time to be stuck in Oklahoma."

CHAPTER NINETEEN

Early the next morning, Cobert pounded on Bill's door at the V.O.Q.
"Broadwell, got a break in the weather. Hanes has the plane fired up and filed the flight plan with base operations. We're ready to go."

Within a matter of seconds, Bill raced down the hall with the co-pilot and they dashed across the tarmac toward the jet. They charged up the ramp and into the plane.

Bill secured the door and yelled. "Make this baby haul."

Hanes wasted no time in getting airborne and Bill watched the clouds slip behind them as they climbed above the storm. He settled back in his seat and thought about the last report he'd received from Steve. Dirk hadn't left his cabin since he'd arrived. This bothered him. Why?

One reason might be that Dirk hadn't discovered the Agency's presence and didn't feel pressured. Bill rubbed the stubble on his chin, praying that things would hold off until he got there. But he feared once Dirk spotted the Agency's men, all hell would break loose.

Pushing back his sleeve, he checked his watch. If there were no more delays, he calculated they'd arrive at the lake within five hours.

⟨⊹⟩⟨⊹⟩⟨⊹⟩⟨⊹⟩⟨⊹⟩

Dirk's eyes closed and his chin slumped to his chest. The night-vision binoculars attached by a strap around his neck, rested on his chest, moving up and down with his heavy breathing. Suddenly, his head jerked up and he glanced around the room. Cocking his ear toward the window, he sat perfectly still for several seconds.

Fumbling for the binoculars, he crossed the room to the opposite window. He stared through the glasses, but the moon's rays danced through the shadows, playing tricks on his vision. He blinked a few times and rubbed his eyes, then tried again.

This time he spotted a deer which shied away from the house, then leaped across the yard to the open lot next door. Dirk focused on the spot where the deer had been. A glowing figure emerged from the back corner of the house. "You stupid son-of-a-bitch, someone washed your camouflage suit in regular detergent," Dirk mumbled. "No wonder you scared that deer. You shine like a falling star."

Suddenly, focusing on the man's face, Dirk stiffened. What the hell is Bob Raines from the Agency doing here? He slowly lowered the binoculars when the grim realization hit him. Stepping back from the window, he opened the attache case and his hand closed over the T-shaped push knife. He dropped the binoculars onto the couch and made his way silently down the stairs. Slipping out the back door, he waited in the shadows close to the side of the house.

⊹❊⊹❊⊹❊⊹❊⊹

The early morning light trickled through the horizontal drapes and Jennifer groaned, pulling the cover over her head. Her nerves were raw with tension, for her sleep had been continuously interrupted throughout the night by the eerie sounds of breezes rustling through the lilac bushes and the nocturnal animals stumbling across the deck next to her bedroom.

She buried her head in her pillow and gritted her teeth. "I pray this will end soon." Finally, she gave up, threw the pillow aside and pushed back the covers. Swinging her feet to the floor, she worked her toes into the soft carpet and took several deep breaths.

Then with a sigh, she ambled over to the sliding glass door. Hawkman had made a point of warning her not to present herself as an easy target, so she just peeked through the slits of the drapes and looked out over the lake. The sun's rays danced across the shimmering water like diamonds bobbing up and down on the surface. A pair of pelicans paddled across her view immersing their large fish-net beaks down into the water, then throwing their heads up high in the air, letting the captured morsel of food slip down their long slender necks. The peaceful scene calmed her shattered nerves for a few moments, before she unwillingly turned from the window.

After her shower, she reluctantly put on her holster, hoping the day would soon come when it wouldn't be a part of her everyday attire. She pulled a loose fitting sweatshirt over her head then wiggled into her tight Levi's. Picking up the alarm card on the dressing table, she slipped it into her hip pocket then brushed her hair back into a pony tail and dabbed on some lipstick.

On the way to the kitchen, she could hear Hawkman's audible snores filtering through the door of his bedroom. With the disturbing things happening, it amazed her that he could sleep. But she knew that all she'd have to do was knock on that door or call out his name and he'd be wide awake in a flash. Well, I'll get him up my own way, she grinned. The aroma of bacon, eggs and coffee always did the trick.

Sure enough, after the fragrance of cooked food drifted through the house, Hawkman staggered into the kitchen. "Food, I smell food."

Jennifer laughed. "I've certainly learned how to get you out of bed."

They ate in silence for a few moments before she glanced up. "I'm getting stir crazy. Let's take the falcon hunting."

Hawkman shook his head. "Can't. It's too dangerous to be out in the open."

"But the guys from the Agency are watching Dirk. We'd be safe."

"Remember, Dirk's an agent. He went through the same school with the rest of us and knows all the tricks."

Jennifer let out a long sigh, finished her breakfast and went to her computer.

Hawkman tried reading the paper, but finally threw it on the floor with a disgusted groan. He meandered over to the kitchen window and stared out while drumming his fingers on the counter. Then he wheeled around and headed back toward the living room, stopping to stare at the phone for a second. He rubbed the back of his neck, then strolled back into the kitchen.

Jennifer threw up her hands in despair. "I can't concentrate with you running back and forth. You're making me dizzy."

Hawkman sat down on a bar stool and leaned across the counter on his elbows. "It won't be long now before it's all over. I figure this time next week, we'll be able to get on with our lives."

She stared at him over the top of the monitor. "You mean if we're still alive." Turning off the computer, she sauntered over to the falcon's perch and stroked his feathers. "Pretty Boy, we'll take you hunting soon, I promise."

At that moment, the fire station siren went off. Jennifer jerked around and dashed to the kitchen window, not realizing her hand had caught in the falcon's tether and yanked it loose from the perch.

Hawkman joined her at the window and they watched the volunteers arrive from all directions.

She stood on her tiptoes, arching her neck to see out. "I wonder what's happened?"

Hawkman hurried back to the small study that housed the two-way radio. "I'll find out in a second." The dispatcher's voice echoed over the wave. "Man over cliff, we need all available, over."

Jennifer followed and stood in the doorway listening.

Hawkman glanced up. "Doesn't sound like anything to do with us. It reads more like a hiking accident." He flipped off the radio and they walked back toward the living room. "People shouldn't hike on terrain they're not familiar with, especially this area where there's decaying and sloughing rock. It's too easy to slip and fall." Going back to the kitchen window, he studied the men and women gathering in front of the fire station. "I'm sure they could use my help, but I'm not going to leave you. It might be a ploy to get me out of here."

Jennifer shuttered and clutched her arms around her waist. "Thanks."

They watched the volunteers climb into the rescue trucks, while some doubled up in 4X4's. Several of the vehicles were left parked in front of the fire station.

Hawkman took the binoculars into the front yard and watched the vehicles until they disappeared over the hill. Then he slowly turned the glasses toward the log cabin beyond the fire station and focused on the blue Buick.

Jennifer viewed the group from the dining room window. When the last truck vanished from her view, her eyes lit up at the sight of the mail truck bouncing across the bridge. Her spirits rose for a moment, maybe she'd get something interesting in the mail.

Hawkman strolled into the house and placed the binoculars on the kitchen bar. "Okay, I saw him, so come on, let's get this mail run out of the way."

Jennifer ducked her head. "I'm sorry, Hawkman, but my mail is awfully important to me."

"I know, so let's jog together."

They zigzagged down the half block to the mail boxes and returned without incident.

⊹≺⊹≺⊹≺⊹≺⊹≺⊹⊹

Over two hours passed before the rescue volunteers returned. Hawkman ambled directly across the road to the fire station and stood inside the large garage area with Jennifer's house in full view of his scanning gaze. He heard Chief Ruskin make a call to the coroner. Then a few minutes later, the emergency truck containing the body pulled up out front.

Ruskin nodded at Hawkman as he met the truck. "A male. We found him on a ledge over one of the steeper grades. None of us recognize him. Want to take a look and see if you know who he is?"

"Sure." He waited for the stretcher to be carried in and placed on the floor before he knelt down and pulled back the sheet covering the bundled body. His throat tightened as he stared at the dead man's face. He slowly replaced the sheet.

Ruskin spoke gruffly. "You know him?"

Hawkman nodded, his taut jaw quivering. "Bob Raines. He's married, with two little kids."

The fire chief shuffled his feet and lowered his head. "We thought we were responding to an accident, but once the men got him up, they discovered the knife wounds."

Hawkman clenched his fist and hissed. "Murdered."

"Looks that way, but we'll have to wait for the coroner's report to know the exact cause of death. Do you know if he was staying around here?:

"Check with Amelia. It's conceivable he rented one of the cabins." Not wanting to answer any more questions, Hawkman quickly left the fire station. When he entered the house, he went straight to the phone.

"Steve, Tom Casey. Where the hell is Broadwell?"

"Stuck in Oklahoma at Tinker Air Force Base. Big storm moved in and grounded them. They're still there as far as I know."

Hawkman let out a ragged breath. "Bob Raines has been killed."

Silence reigned for several seconds before Steve spoke. "Now that he knows the Agency people are there, he'll be even more dangerous."

"He's a madman," Hawkman spat, gripping the phone until his knuckles turned white.

"Hang tight, Casey. We want him alive."

"I'll kill him if he comes near us," Hawkman said through gritted teeth.

"He's got a lot of questions to answer. We can't find out anything if he's dead"

"I'm not promising anything."

(·⫯·)¤(·⫯·)¤(·⫯·)¤(·⫯·)

Dirk stood at the second story window observing the two men with rifles guarding the front of the log cabin. He'd also spotted two other men out back. He couldn't understand why they weren't coming in after him. He knew how the Agency worked. And something wasn't right.

CHAPTER TWENTY

Pilot Hanes called ahead to the Siskiyou Airport and got confirmation on the helicopter's arrival. He gave Bill the thumbs up sign from the pilot's seat.

Bill checked his watch. Almost noon. He wiped the sweat beads from his brow. Would they make it in time?

The Lear jet touched down on the long runway and taxied to the ramp. He glanced out the window and spotted the Agency helicopter, sitting on the landing strip, trembling under its whirling rotary blades. A car raced out to the jet and transferred him to the chopper within minutes. Bill climbed aboard and signaled for the pilot to haul ass.

⚓•⚓•⚓•⚓•⚓

This waiting game played havoc on Hawkman's nerves. He needed to keep his mind occupied and yet stay out of Jennifer's way so she could work and keep her mind off the impending dangers. Pulling the 4X4 into the new garage to protect himself from Dirk's rifle, he tuned the engine, put in new spark plugs and changed the oil. After he'd finished, he went inside. "I'm taking a shower," he called over his shoulder. Jennifer glanced up from the computer and nodded.

⚓•⚓•⚓•⚓•⚓

She'd seen the mail truck come across the bridge and decided this would be a good time to get her mail. She'd be safe since the Agency had Dirk under twenty-four hour surveillance. And she'd be back long before Hawkman got out of the shower.

Jennifer waited until she heard the water go on, then deactivated the alarm and ducked out the front door. She shoved the card into her hip pocket after activating it on the outside. Remembering Hawkman's warnings, she ran a zig zag pattern down the road, but felt a pang of guilt, since she'd knowingly had disobeyed his orders. Her gaze darted up to the log cabin more than once before she reached the mailboxes. By the time she reached hers, she could hear the pounding beat of her heart.

⟨┅×┅×┅×┅×┅⟩

Dirk grinned, set the binoculars on the table and tucked the .45 automatic into his belt, covering it with his shirt. "Right on time, my pretty one." Things were working out beautifully. He'd watched the two agents guarding the back take off in a car, which left only two at the front. They were so preoccupied with their own conversation, they wouldn't even notice him.

He bolted down the stairs and headed for the back. Opening the door just a crack, he made sure the coast was clear before slipping out. He hurried toward the shallow gully behind the house and climbed down into the weed filled crevice lined with large oak trees. Hidden by the foliage, he followed the curve of the ditch to the end which put him only a few yards from the fire station.

Scooting up the incline on his belly, he peeked through the overgrowth only to spot a woman to his left walking her dog and heading straight toward him. He slid back down the embankment into the higher weeds. "She could ruin this moment," he cursed under his breath.

When the woman got just a few feet away, the dog whimpered and strained against his leash toward where Dirk lay hidden. He wanted to grab and strangle the mutt but didn't dare breathe or make a movement. She finally pulled the animal away and headed down the road.

He exhaled a sigh of relief, but waited until the beast had

trotted several yards past him before climbing from his hiding place and racing across the open field to the fire station. No windows graced the back side of the building so he didn't worry about being seen by anyone inside. Also, the structure not only hid him from Jennifer's view, but the trees lining the lot blocked him from sight of the two agents in front of his cabin.

He peered around the corner, afraid he'd missed Jennifer, but the top of her head was visible over the parked vehicles. He wondered what had detained her, until he heard the dog bark and a young excited voice.

"Damn, it's that kid and his dog," he whispered. The threesome had started down the road toward Jennifer's house. He inched around the side, keeping them in sight.

Suddenly, the boy jumped up and threw his arms around her, knocking the mail to the ground. Dirk stopped and shifted from one foot to the other, wondering how long this would take. After returning the kid's hug, she wiped her eyes and they picked up the scattered envelopes. This complicates things, Dirk thought, clenching his fist. "I don't need the boy and his damned dog," he hissed, ducking behind a large truck.

※◦※◦※◦※◦※◦※

Jennifer struggled with the slippery catalogs and envelopes while trying to concentrate on Sam's excited conversation about the prospect of being her son. Herman, trailing behind them, suddenly let out a low menacing growl. She whirled around only to face a tall red-headed man glaring down at her with piercing blue eyes. Her breath caught in her throat.

Herman's low rumbling continued and the bristles on his back stood erect. Sam reached down and grabbed his collar. "Stop that, Herman." He glanced up at the man, frowning. "Sorry sir, but I've never heard him growl like that."

When Dirk stepped closer, Herman bared his teeth and snapped at his ankle. Dirk jumped back and glared at Sam. "Call that damn dog off."

A chill slithered down Jennifer's spine when the man leaned his body into hers. Her heart all but stopped as the cold steel of a gun muzzle nudged her ribs. "Get rid of the kid and dog," he hissed into her ear.

His hot breath curled around the nape of her neck making her insides quiver and her stomach tie into a knot. She squeaked out a cough, then turned her attention to Sam. "I've got some business with this man. Will you run down and tell Amelia I'll pick up my order later."

Herman's threatening stance hadn't wavered from Dirk's ankle, even though Sam held a tight rein on his collar. The dog's upper lip curled backward, showing his sharp canine teeth, while the fur on his back remained rigid.

Sam tugged again and again on the dog's collar, but the canine held stubbornly to his place. "I don't think Herman likes you." Finally, Sam managed to pull the animal back and the dog snorted and shook his head. "Come on Herman, let's go."

The dog fought relentlessly against Sam's grip, but finally gave in to his master's order, letting out several warning barks before leaving Jennifer's side. Sam ran toward the store, holding on to the dog but glancing back each time Herman stopped and lifted his head in a warning howl.

Jennifer swallowed hard. Fear gripped her soul as she watched the two run down the road. Her sweaty hands stuck to the bundle of mail she held tight against her chest. Keeping her eyes straight ahead, she asked, "Who are you?"

Dirk snickered. "We've never met formally, but I've left you lots of messages."

Jennifer increased her pace. "Sorry, I don't know what you're talking about."

He grabbed her arm in a tight squeeze and yanked her close. "Slow down. I want you to walk normally and smile." He shoved the barrel hard into her ribs causing her to wince. "I said, look happy to see me."

She forced a quivering smile.

"Where's your body guard, Hawk Man? It's a shame he doesn't accompany you to the mailbox anymore. He's missing out on all the fun."

Jennifer remained silent and clutched the mail tighter. He knows every move we've made, she thought. By the time they reached the driveway, her mouth had turned so dry that her tongue stuck to the roof of her mouth.

She knew making any sudden movement would mean instant death. What could she do? Her mind raced. Hawkman had cautioned her that in a time of crisis one must stay calm. More than likely something will present itself. She glanced around and wondered, how? Her only hope would be Hawkman looking out the window. She now deeply regretted disobeying his orders.

⊹❈⊹❈⊹❈⊹❈⊹

Sam commanded Herman to sit on the porch while he dashed into the store. He almost ran into a man standing at the counter. "I've got an urgent message from Jennifer."

Amelia pointed a scolding finger. "Sam, hold it down and walk when you come into the store. You almost knocked this man down."

Sam ducked his head and stared at the floor. "Sorry."

"Now, what's this important message?"

He took a deep breath and leaned on the counter. "She'll be down later for her order. Right now she's taking care of some business."

Amelia frowned. "What order?"

Sam shrugged. "I don't know, but that's what she told me to tell you after that man walked up behind us. I don't know where he came from, but Herman sure didn't like him."

The man standing at the counter grabbed Sam's shoulder. "What'd he look like?"

Sam glanced up at him. "Real tall with red hair."

The man dropped his two sodas onto the counter and raced out of the store.

Amelia raised a hand full of coins. "Sir, don't forget your change." She dropped her arm with a sigh, then turned back to Sam. "Is that all she said?"

Sam fingered the new selection of candy bars. "Yep. I sure had a hard time holding Herman back or he would have taken a chunk out of that guy's leg."

⊹❈⊹❈⊹❈⊹❈⊹

Dirk held a tight grip on Jennifer's arm until they reached the front stoop. "Okay, open the door."

She started to reach for the knob, but he jerked her back sharply. "Oh no, pretty lady. Aren't you forgetting something?"

Jennifer glanced at him innocently. "What?"

He roughly whirled her around and caressed her buttocks with his hand. "Nice." Then he pushed his fingers into the opening of her jeans pocket and pulled out the access card.

Jennifer's stomach churned and the taste of bile bubbled in her throat.

Twirling the card in front of her nose, he sneered. "Hawk Man worked awfully hard installing that system, but we're not going to set it off."

Her heart dropped when she watched his hand move to the slot.

After deactivating the alarm, he pushed her forward with the barrel of the gun. "Now, you can open the door without a lot of noise."

She turned the knob and he gave her a hard shove, causing her to stumble and fall into the entry. Envelopes sailed through the air and scattered across the room. He quickly closed the door and grabbed both her arms, pinning them behind her. Planting a knee in the middle of her back, he held her wrists together with one of his hands while pressing the gun against her temple with the other. He bent close to her ear and whispered harshly. "Keep your mouth shut."

She thought of the defense exercises she and Hawkman had practiced, but they'd never mentioned what to do if you had a weapon pointed at your head. If he found out she had a gun, he'd kill her for sure. The pressure of his weight was making it hard for her to breathe and she began to feel light headed. Don't panic. Keep calm, she kept telling herself.

Straining against his power, she tried to pull upward so she could see his face. Finally, twisting her neck around, she managed to see his penetrating eyes darting to and fro, searching the room. Then it dawned on her as she lay on the floor, that she could hear water running. Dear God, she thought, Hawkman is still in the shower. Panic surged through her.

Suddenly, Dirk yanked her up by the arm. She screamed with all her might. "Hawkman! Help!"

He slapped her hard across the face and pushed the gun into the side of her neck, forcing her into the living room. His mouth brushed against her ear. "One more scream out of you and you're dead meat."

Her whole insides shook. Even though her hands fell free, the muzzle of his gun bore so hard into her flesh that she didn't dare make a move for hers. She glanced up at his face and saw his eyes transform from blue to a wicked turquoise as his glare locked on the bathroom door. When the shower water shut off, an evil grin seared his lips.

Adrenalin rushed through Jennifer's veins. She must distract him before Hawkman opened that door.

CHAPTER TWENTY ONE

Jennifer considered the idea of going for her gun, but felt it was too risky. So she searched the room for some way to distract Dirk. Her gaze fell on the falcon's empty perch. Where is he? How'd he get loose? An idea formed in her mind as she scanned the room for the hawk. She spotted him in a far corner, half hidden by the wine rack, pecking the floor. Taking a chance, she began pulling fiercely at Dirk's hand covering her mouth.

The harder she pulled, the deeper he dug his fingers into her flesh. She struggled until she managed to get her mouth open just wide enough to clamp her teeth deep into the fleshy part of his fingers.

He yanked his hand away, but then locked his arm solidly around her throat, almost choking off her breath. "Be still, woman," he hissed. "You want me to kill you first." He moved the gun from her back and pressed it firmly into her temple.

Jennifer again pulled on his arm and pointed. "The falcon's going to attack us."

Dirk jerked his head around just as the hawk moved toward them, flapping his large wings. He yanked Jennifer around so that she stood between him and the hawk. She tried to tear away but his arm held her tight. The barrel of the gun left her temple and he leveled it at the falcon.

"No! No!" she screamed, squirming and contorting with all her might. Then, she hit his arm with an upward motion just as he pulled the trigger, causing the bullet to penetrate the ceiling.

At that moment, Hawkman, clad only in jeans, opened the bathroom door. When the shot rang out, he hit the floor and spun into his room.

Dirk belted Jennifer hard across the face with the back of his hand. "You bitch!" he yelled.

The blow landed so hard that she fell against the couch and rolled to the floor. She winced from the sharp pain that radiated from her mouth and felt the warm trickle of blood flowing onto her chin. Her eyes narrowed into angry slits. She reached under her blouse and wrenched out her gun. Grasping it with both hands, she aimed and fired.

Dirk's jerked around and grabbed his shoulder, glaring at Jennifer with unbelieving eyes. Blood oozed between his fingers and ran down the front of his shirt. He brought up his gun and aimed at her head.

Jennifer froze in horror.

Suddenly, a sound like a cannon exploded through the room, and Dirk's gun flew from his hand. Jennifer screamed and scampered behind the couch on her hands and knees. Dirk twisted around and pulled a blossom from his belt. He flipped it open with a flick of his wrist and hurled it across the room.

Hawkman ducked. It whirled past his head and stuck in the wall. Rotating his body, he jumped and threw a quick kick into Dirk's groin sending the bleeding man to his knees.

Jennifer crawled behind the big chair and peeked around the side, watching with wide eyes.

Hawkman leaped toward Dirk, who, even though injured, managed to knock Hawkman's gun from his hand and jumped back onto his feet like a flash of light. He stood in front of Hawkman, waving the glistening blade of a Clipitt knife. Hawkman crouched, on guard, his hands in front of him, his eye on the knife. He stepped back when Dirk lunged forward, avoiding each swipe by jumping from side to side.

Hawkman yelled out. "Jennifer, shoot."

Trembling, she licked at the blood on the corner of her mouth and brought her gun up over the top of the chair, but Hawkman was in the line of fire. He finally placed a kick sending Dirk against the wall. Jennifer aimed and fired.

Dirk clutched his side and slithered to the floor, the knife dropping from his hand. Hawkman grabbed it and straddled Dirk, gripping him by the throat as he brought up the knife. "Your time has come, you bastard."

Jennifer screamed, "No, Hawkman. No!"

Behind her, three men crashed through the front door with their guns drawn. They stopped short when they saw Hawkman ready to kill Dirk.

Bill hurried toward him. "Good job, Casey. We'll take care of him now."

Jennifer held her breath and waited.

Hawkman's hand trembled and the muscles in his back quivered. He stood slowly, sweat running down his back. His face guant, he stepped away from Dirk's fallen body and handed Bill the knife.

The other two agents, their guns poised, moved in on Dirk. They grabbed him under the arm pits and lifted him into a standing position. Yanking his blood soaked shirt from his waistband, the agents patted him down for any hidden weapons before clamping on the handcuffs.

Bill crossed over to the slider and pulled the pole so the other two agents standing on the deck could enter. Just as they stepped inside, the sound of a loud squawk filled the room. All heads turned toward the falcon, who flapped his wings a couple of times, then strolled over to Dirk's feet and pecked at the bright buttons decorating his boots.

"Get that goddamned bird away from me," Dirk yelled, kicking at the hawk.

Pretty Boy quickly retreated to the other side of the room.

Dirk's turquoise eyes flashed as he stared at Hawkman. "I'll kill you yet. You've got the best of everything: the assignments, the promotions, the women. But you blew it when you let Sylvia drive your car that day. You were suppose to die, you stupid son-of-a-bitch, not her."

Hawkman whirled around and grabbed Dirk's shirt. His eye narrowed, festering with hate and anger as the muscles in his jaw twitched. He brought his gun up to Dirk's chin. "You fumbling bastard, you aren't worth the pot to boil you in."

Bill quickly stepped forward and laid his hand on Hawkman's arm. He motioned to the agents. "Get Henderson out of here."

After two agents went out the door with Dirk between them, the other two followed leaving Bill inside. Hawkman put his gun on the kitchen counter, moistened a tea towel and hurried to Jennifer who'd collapsed on the couch. Removing the gun from her hand, he placed it on the coffee table and gently wiped the blood from her mouth. "Are you all right?"

She nodded, tears rolling down her cheeks. "It's finally over."

"Yes, sweetheart. It's over. " He hugged her close and stroked her hair as she trembled with sobs of relief.

After a few moments, she raised her head, a big smile on her face. Hawkman looked down at her with surprise. "What is it?"

She pointed toward his feet. "Look."

He glanced down and grinned. "Okay, Pretty Boy," who busily pecked at some strings hanging from the hem of Hawkman's Levis. "Time for you to back upon your perch." He picked up the bird with his bare hands and placed him on his throne. "You've had an exciting day," he said, retying the tether. Hawkman glanced at Bill who stood quietly watching.

Bill cleared his throat and started toward the door. "Well, I guess I better be going."

"Oh, no, you don't," Hawkman chuckled. "You've got some explaining to do."

Jennifer went to Bill and extended her hand. "Hi Bill, I'm Jennifer Morgan."

He held her hand for a moment and looked deep into her eyes. "It's a real pleasure to finally meet you, Jennifer." He furrowed his brow and put a finger under her chin as he studied her injury. "You need some ice on that lip to keep the swelling down."

Hawkman threw some ice cubes into a plastic baggy and handed them to her. She put the pack to her lip and motioned for Bill to have a seat at the kitchen bar.

Hawkman raised an empty glass in Bill's direction. "Scotch and water?"

Bill nodded.

"What the hell took you so long getting here?" Hawkman asked, clunking ice into the glasses.

Bill slapped the palm of his hand to his forehead and laughed. "I've never been so frustrated in all my life. Can you imagine being stranded in Oklahoma?"

Jennifer held the ice away from her mouth. "What happened?" .

Bill described the freak storm. Then turned toward Jennifer, raising his glass to her. "I wouldn't have been quite so worried if I'd known Casey had you at his side. You handle a firearm quite well."

"Thank you." She grinned at Hawkman. "I have a good teacher."

Hawkman patted her hand. "I might not be alive today if it hadn't been for her.

A slight blush tinted her cheeks. "We have to give Pretty Boy some credit. He did a darn good job of distracting Dirk."

They all laughed.

Bill looked around at the falcon. "By the way, where'd you get that bird?"

"I found him up in the hills, injured and near death. I brought him home and nursed him back to health. He's been with me ever since."

Bill snickered. "Boy, Henderson sure didn't want anything to do with him.

Hawkman and Jennifer glanced at each other grinning. "Someday we'll tell you why."

Jennifer raised a brow. "How in the heck did he escape from his tether?"

Hawkman shrugged. "He occasionally pecks at that leather. More than likely he worried it enough to come untied."

"Well, I'm glad he persisted." She tried to smile but grimaced in pain from her busted lip.

Hawkman sat down on one of the stools. "Now, getting back to the business at hand. Why didn't you tell me in the beginning that it was Henderson?"

Bill rubbed the back of his neck. "Well, I knew you'd worked with him years ago and it wouldn't take you long to put it all together if I gave you his name."

"Well, you've got that right." Hawkman scratched his chin. "Because, I'd pretty well narrowed it down myself, but wanted your confirmation. So, how long have you known?"

"About a week. Things pointed at Dirk as soon as we discovered those charred pieces from the garage explosion had been stolen from the Agency's warehouse several years ago. At that time, Henderson was attending classes on bombs and explosives. His instructor felt a bit unnerved about his over-active interest in the subject, so he took time to write up a report and inserted it into Dirk's file. This information started the ball rolling."

Hawkman took a gulp of his drink. "Thank God for an alert professor."

"Then I started tracing those phone numbers. One of them happened to be a phone booth in front of Dirk's office building. The other number happened to be an answering service he'd subscribed to. Took us awhile to zero in on that one."

"Find out anything on that helicopter that shot at Jennifer and me?"

"Dirk."

Hawkman looked puzzled. "When did he learn to fly a chopper? And how'd he shoot at us and pilot it at the same time?"

"Two, maybe three years ago. He took a helicopter course in flight school and passed with high marks. From that course, he learned lots of manuevers and how to rig a gun in the cockpit. We found a hole he'd bored into the outer shell where he was able to rest a gun, shoot and pilot all at the same time. The man was brilliant, but also stupid. We also discovered he'd taken up one of the Agency's choppers regularly, which is definitely against regulations without specific orders. But for some odd reason no one questioned his authority."

"Where'd he get the one he came in after us? I didn't recognize any of the markings."

"He stole if from a rancher's field. But, he got careless. After wiping the whole inside prints away, he failed to hit the outer edge of the door when he left the chopper. The technician found a clear full four fingered print. Once we made the positive identification, I dug deeper into his file and sure didn't like what I found."

Jennifer leaned forward. "Who shot at me on my dock?"

"That happened to be a flunky Dirk hired. Guess he figured a motorcycle could make a quick getaway in this area. You were supposed to get hit, so that Hawkman would take you out of this area. Dirk didn't like dealing around Copco Lake. Too remote and he figured a small community would get suspicious of strangers.

Detective Williams finally located and busted the punk, plus the guy who vandalized Hawkman's place. They're in jail waiting trial." Bill shook his head and smiled. "Williams gladly handed them over to us." He shifted in his seat and took a drink before he continued. "Once we thoroughly go through everything in Dirk's apartment and office, we'll probably find a large list of those types."

Jennifer sat quietly, staring at her glass.

Bill noticed her silence. "Something bothering you, Jennifer?"

She glanced at him. "You haven't mentioned who tried to break into my house."

Bill twirled his glass and hesitated before speaking. "There's evidence that points to Dirk."

"What evidence?"

He took a deep breath. "We found a personal calendar in his apartment. He had that night circled in red with 'J's house' written in the square. Also the car you spotted on the road, we traced it to a rental agency where we discovered it had been rented in his name."

Jennifer took a ragged breath, closed her eyes and leaned back in the chair. "He planned on raping me."

Bill reached over and touched her arm. "Don't think about it. You scared him off before anything happened. That's all that matters."

He then quickly turned his attention back to Hawkman. "Dirk left an amazing paper trail. After all those years of criminal activity and not getting caught, must have made him think he was invincible."

"Yeah, he's a cocky bastard. What else have you found out?"

"Well, for one thing, he's the one who exposed your cover on the last mission. We got you out of that country in the nick of time."

Hawkman brought his fist down on the counter. "That son-of-a-bitch."

"That isn't all. We found large bank accounts in his name, not only in foreign countries, but also in the states. Many of the deposits were made by foreigners. He had more money stashed than he's ever made with the Agency."

Hawkman let out a long breath, "I can see why you needed him alive. He's got lots of explaining to do."

"We also found a notebook in his apartment listing names of people who owed him substantial amounts of money for getting them out of trouble, like those two Iranian assassins. They owed Dirk a lot. He must have offered them the job to knock down their debt. What's strange is that we found nothing that warranted his taking you out other than a personal vendetta." Bill shook his head. "Boy, he must have really hated you."

Hawkman stared into space, then glanced at Bill, his expression serious. "How long do you think he's been a double agent?"

"Not sure at this point, but we'll find out eventually." Bill lowered his voice. "Unfortunately, we found evidence verifying he'd hired two men to plant the bomb in your car that killed Sylvia."

Jennifer sucked in her breath.

Hawkman's hands clenched into fists before he abruptly changed the subject. "Did you find anything mentioning John Alexander Jr?"

Bill raised an eyebrow. "Now that's a puzzle we haven't solved. We know Dirk made contact with John, but we don't know why. We figured it must have had something to do with John's dad's formulae. Can you shed any light on that subject?"

"Maybe," Hawkman said, glancing at Jennifer.

"We know Dirk got involved with this house after Mr. Alexander's death. But there's no evidence that he ever found the formulae. So we figure Alexander Sr either destroyed, hid them, or his son has them. But we haven't been able to locate John for verification. Can you spread any light on this?"

Hawkman ambled over to the window overlooking the lake. "John and his family had been threatened with bodily harm. But he didn't know by whom as he knew nothing about Dirk. But, John innocently exposed my whereabouts, not realizing the danger he put me in. At the time I talked with him, even I didn't realize I would be dealing with just one man. So, as far as any wrong doing on John's part, I don't think so." He turned and sauntered back to the kitchen bar. "Now, tell us more about Dirk."

"Well, I think you're absolutely right when you say the vendetta grew through the years. We found a journal hidden behind a filing cabinets at his apartment. It contained entries like a personal diary where he'd written down all the missions that he'd applied for, but had been passed over. Research showed they were given to you instead. Several times in the margin, we found some lewd remark on how he hated you and that one day he'd get even."

Hawkman scratched his head. "Boy, lots can go down in just a couple of years."

Bill shook his head. "His anamosity grew into a disease. It appears when he blundered and killed Sylvia instead of you, he went over the edge. He feared you'd never rest until you found him, so he kept track of your whereabouts. Then he panicked when you suddenly dropped out of sight. We found memos in his office files searching for you right after the identity change."

Hawkman frowned. "Didn't anyone get suspicious?"

"No one questioned questioned him, so he must have made up some damn good excuses. Otherwise, he'd never have gotten this far without our catching on." Bill lowered his head. "And, we owe you a deep apology for that, Casey."

Jennifer put the ice pack on the counter. "What's going to happen to Dirk?"

"He'll be put away for life, possibly put to death for treason, several murders in the past and the one committed here."

Jennifer's mouth flew open. "What murder here?"

Hawkman raised a hand. "I didn't tell her because she had enough to worry about at the time."

Bill faced her. "Dirk spotted and killed one of our men and threw his body over a cliff."

Jennifer covered her mouth with her hand. "So that's what that emergency was all about?"

Hawkman patted her arm. "I'd noticed Dirk's car parked in a different spot the next morning from the night before. So when they brought in Raines' body, I knew what had happened."

Bill checked his watch. "Well, I think that pretty well tells the story. I've got a helicopter waiting so I better get going. You two can relax now."

Hawkman held out his hand, "Thanks for getting here."

Bill turned to Jennifer and pointed to her mouth. "You take care of that lip, you hear?"

She grimaced. "I will."

He then took both her hands in his. "It's been a pleasure meeting such a brave woman."

❖❖❖❖❖❖❖

Jennifer watched Hawkman accompany Bill to the waiting car. What would Hawkman do now that she didn't need a body guard? Would he leave and go on with his life? Did he mean those things he'd said during their close moments? Her heart heavy, she stepped back inside and closed the door.

CHAPTER TWENTY TWO

Jennifer opened her eyes to a room filled with morning light. She couldn't believe she'd actually slept through the night without some sort of a horrid nightmare. Shocked at the late hour, she jumped out of bed.

In the bathroom, she checked her lip, relieved it hadn't turned into an ugly discolored bruise, even though it still felt tender to the touch. She carefully rinsed her face with cold water and brushed her hair. Tightening her robe sash, she headed for the kitchen to get a cup of coffee before her shower.

When she passed Hawkman's room, she noticed the door stood ajar. She stepped back and glanced inside. He'd made his bed, but the closet door stood open, empty of his clothes. Her heart skipped a beat. She wandered deeper into the room and hesitated a moment before opening one of the dresser drawers. Empty. A lump formed in her throat and tears stung her eyes.

She fled the lonely room and hurried into the kitchen where the aroma of coffee hung in the air. Hawkman's alarm access card lay on the kitchen counter along with the extra house key. She halfheartedly fondled them before reaching for a cup. Her hand brushed against a piece of paper taped to the cabinet door. She watched it float lazily to the floor. When she picked it up, she immediately recognized his handwriting. "I figure it's time you had your space. Hawkman."

She brushed the tears from her cheek. What did you expect?

He did his job and protected you. Be thankful you're alive and safe. She laid the note on the counter and poured herself some coffee, then headed for the sliding glass door, but stopped abruptly in the middle of the room. Pretty Boy and his perch had disappeared. She sucked in her breath and stared at the vacant spot for a few moments. It seemed those few weeks of her life had vanished into thin air.

When she slid open the door, a cool brisk breeze whipped around her body. causing her to wrap her robe tighter around herself before stepping onto the deck. Running her hand along the wrought iron railing, she walked to the end and leaned against the post. Her gaze drifted across the lake toward Hawkman's place.

She really felt alone now. And she didn't like the feeling at all. The unrestrained tears rolled down her cheeks. Hawkman had stayed at her house for the sole purpose of protecting her and for no other reason. He'd carried the guilt of Sylvia's death on his shoulders for so long that he couldn't have borne the burden of something happening to her also.

"But he could have warned me before he left," she said aloud. She set her cup down on the small table and took inventory of her own feelings. Her arms folded, she paced the deck. Why am I so upset? True, she'd taken him for granted, never thinking the day would come when he'd actually leave. She stopped and ran her fingers through her hair. They'd been through so much together. And he seemed genuinely interested in Sam. Why now, had he chosen to give her back her space? Did I give him the impression that I wanted it back?

What did she want? Did she really know? What if he'd decided to leave the area and go someplace else to start over? Where would he go? Maybe back to the Agency? He could just disappear. Her head jerked up in realization. The thought shocked her. No, she thought frantically. I might never find him again.

She dashed back into the house and quickly dressed. Throwing her purse straps over her shoulder, she hurried toward the front entry. But just as she reached for the knob, someone knocked. She gasped, grabbing her throat and stepped back. Could this be another gunman? "Whose there?"

"It's me, Sam."

She breathed a sigh of relief and opened the door. Her anxiety disappeared when her gaze met those big sparkling blue eyes. He stood there with a huge suitcase on one side and Herman, his head tilted and ears perked high, on the other. What a picture, she thought.

"I'd like to move in today."

Jennifer pushed her personal emotions aside and laughed. "Heck, why not. Come on in and we'll get your room ready." She helped Sam drag the big brown suitcase to the guest room. Herman followed close at their heels.

⊹)⊷⊹⊷⊹⊷⊹⊷⊹⊷⊹⊷

Hawkman stood looking out his kitchen window, drumming his fingers on the counter. His clothes hung over the back of a chair and the falcon, cocking his head back and forth, sat on his perch in the middle of the floor.

Now that I'm back home, why do I feel so strange and void? The falcon turned his head and followed Hawkman's movements as he paced the kitchen floor. I'll get my things put away, then go see her. But talking to himself didn't work. He kept glancing out the window toward her house and strolled from room to room, getting nothing done. This is crazy. I'll go over there now. He grabbed his hat off the table and dashed out the door.

When he pulled into Jennifer's driveway, Herman lay on the stoop and eyed him until he recognized the familiar 4X4, then sat up, barked a friendly greeting and beat his tail furiously against the cement.

Sam must be here, Hawkman reasoned, climbing out of the truck. Herman bounded off the stoop, wagging his whole body. He received the dog with hearty pats then threw a stick for him to fetch.

At that moment, Sam opened the door. "Jennifer it's Hawkman." He ran out and grabbed Hawkman's hand, pulling him inside. "Come and see my room."

Hawkman grinned as Sam dragged him past Jennifer in the hallway. "Guess I moved out in the nick of time."

Herman's friendly barks heralded another visitor and Hawkman glanced out the bedroom window. "Looks like the Jordans."

Sam dashed out the front door and ushered them inside. Even Herman managed to sneak in without anyone's notice. They all congregated in Sam's new room.

Mrs. Jordan put her arm around Jennifer's shoulder. "We apologize for that young man's intrusion this morning." Smiling, she pointed a finger at Sam. "But after he found out from Father O'Brien what was going on and then your conversation with him at the mailbox yesterday, he couldn't contain himself." She dropped her arm and dabbed her eyes with her hanky. "I'm so happy he's going to be nearby."

Jennifer smiled and squeezed Mrs. Jordan's arm. "There's no problem. It's a great feeling to know he's so eager to move in."

Mr. Jordan reached down and patted the dog. "Herman's really mine, but I don't think he'll leave Sam now, so I'll be happy to supply his dog food."

Jennifer waved off his offer. "Please don't worry about that, Bob. A boy and his dog belong together. Herman is more than welcome to be a part of the family."

Hawkman stood silently against the wall, listening. He decided this wasn't the time to have a personal talk with Jennifer, so he slipped from the room and left in his truck.

⊹»⊹«⊹»⊹«⊹»⊹«⊹»⊹

The next day Hawkman received a surprise call from Bill.

"Don't tell me Dirk escaped."

Bill laughed. "No way. He's under tight security recovering from his wounds. I'm calling with a proposition."

"Oh?"

"The Agency wants you back. You're invaluable to us."

"I appreciate the offer, Bill, but you know I can't come back to a desk job."

"I figured you'd say that, but you can't blame me for trying. You know you'll always have a place with us."

"Thanks Bill, but I'm going to try my hand at being a private investigator."

"Well, if you run into a snag and need us, give a call."

"I'll remember that." He took a deep breath and replaced the phone on the cradle. His life would never be the same without the Agency.

That afternoon, Hawkman drove into Yreka. The time had come for him to find an office for his new profession. His research had led him to the conclusion that a private investigator's office should be located inconspicuously.

He'd also made an appointment with Detective Williams, the type of man he'd like to have on his side in the future, to thank him for his help on the Henderson case. He pulled up at the police station and went directly to the detective's office. When Hawkman poked his head around the door, Williams glanced up and broke into a big grin. "Come in. Hope this visit isn't about another guy after you."

He chuckled. "No, this isn't a business call. Just wanted to come by and thank you for your work on the Henderson case."

"Thanks. Appreciate that. Glad I could help."

"I know you're busy so I won't take up anymore of your time." Hawkman turned to leave.

"You had lunch yet?" the detective asked, stepping out from behind his desk and shrugging on his jacket.

"No."

"I'm getting ready to run out and grab a bite. Want to join me?"

"Sure."

The two men lunched at a local restaurant and Hawkman told Williams about his future plans. The detective informed him of an office vacancy he'd seen in Medford at one of the small shopping centers, which might be just the ticket for a private investigator's office.

After they finished, Hawkman headed for Oregon. Being familiar with the locale he went straight to the mall and found the donut shop Williams had described. Hawkman jogged up the outside enclosed staircase, but found the door locked. When he asked at the donut shop where he could locate the person in charge of leasing the office, it surprised him when the girl pointed to a man purchasing donuts.

The office consisted of one large room with windows overlooking the parking lot, a half-bath in one corner, plenty of electrical outlets plus air-conditioning. Hawkman haggled over the lease for only a few minutes before he followed the man downstairs and signed the contract.

Driving home, he felt as giddy as a little boy with a new toy and anxious to get home so he could tell Jennifer. In his excitement over the new office, it occurred to him, that maybe she really didn't care. The realization shocked him to his senses. He definitely couldn't go home empty handed, especially after not contacting her for several days. So, he turned off the freeway, made a u-turn and headed back to Medford.

CHAPTER TWENTY THREE

Hawkman returned home early that evening and found Pretty Boy in a state of agitation. He'd neglected the hawk lately, so he put on the glove and approached the perch. The bird cocked his head, let out a squawk and hesitated to step onto his arm.

"Hey, come on fella. I know I look different, but it's me, your ole' buddy."

Reluctantly, the hawk obeyed and Hawkman carried him outside. The falcon circled above his head for a few seconds before taking off toward a heavily treed area.

Hawkman finished unloading his purchases from the truck and had just put away the last item when he heard the familiar squawk of the returning falcon. He walked outside and found the bird setting on the porch railing, cleaning his beak. He shook his head and smiled. "That sure didn't take you long, you old home body." He brought the bird inside and tethered him to his perch. It was too late to visit Jennifer. He'd wait until tomorrow and prayed she'd be receptive to his plan.

Mid-morning of the next day, he drove over to Jennifer's. He sat in the truck for a moment, staring at the house and thinking about what he wanted to say. Taking a deep breath, he removed his hat and ran his fingers through his newly cropped hair. He picked up the small package from the seat and slipped it into his pocket.

Just as he got out of the truck, Herman charged around the

corner of the house, wagging his tail and barking greetings. He threw a stick several times for the dog to retrieve until the animal finally tired then Hawkman stepped up to the front door and knocked.

⊰·⊱·⊰·⊱·⊰·⊱

Jennifer couldn't get Hawkman off her mind. She knew he'd wanted to talk the day Sam moved in. But finding the household in chaos, he'd left. She couldn't blame him, but it bothered her that he hadn't come back or called. When she heard someone drive up, her heart leaped. She glanced out the kitchen window and her spirits soared when she saw his truck. She dashed to the bathroom, smoothed down her hair and applied some lipstick.

She stood behind the front door praying for him to knock. It seemed like an eternity. Finally, she pulled open the door and gasped. "Hawkman, is that really you?"

He chuckled. "You know, you're as bad as Pretty Boy. Do I really look that different? I just got a shave and haircut."

"Y...Yes, you look very different," she stuttered.

He reached up and rubbed his bare chin. "I feel naked, not having that long beard."

Trying to gather her composure, but mesmerized by his handsome face, she took his arm and guided him inside. "Well, it certainly changed your looks and I really like it. I guess I just never imagined how you'd look without a beard and long hair. It's nice."

Hawkman embarrassed, glanced around. "Hey, where's Sam?"

"In school. But he won't be home until late. The Jordan's are taking him shopping. They insisted he needed new jeans and shoes before he settled in here with me." She kept staring at Hawkman's face and found herself searching for conversation. "Uh...Sam will really be surprised when he sees you."

He tossed his hat on the kitchen bar. "Do you think he'll still like me?"

She laughed. "Of course."

"I'm glad we're alone, because I want to talk to you about something personal."

Jennifer put a hand on her hip. "Well, I want a word with you, too."

He raised his brows. "Oh? What about?"

"I didn't appreciate the way you packed up and left without a word. Even taking Pretty Boy."

Frowning, he ducked his head. "I apologize. I realize now, I shouldn't have done that. But I just felt I'd been here long enough and the sooner I got out of here the better for you."

Jennifer's gaze softened. "I accept your apology but what took you so long to come back."

He sat down at the kitchen bar and rubbed his chin. "Took a while getting all this shaved and cut off."

She eyed him suspiciously. "I don't buy that."

His eye twinkled and he smiled. "A lot of things have happened these past few weeks. Our lives certainly weren't normal and I've been doing a lot of thinking and hope you have too."

Jennifer raised her hand to say something but the phone rang. She dropped her hand. "You might as well answer that. It's probably for you."

Hawkman reached over and pushed the speaker button.

"Hello."

"Jim, this is John Alexander." His voice vibrated with agitation. "What's gone down? When can I go home? I'm tired of this hiding out."

Hawkman glanced at Jennifer and smiled.

"Good news John. You can go home right now. It's all over."

"Thank God."

He heard John's heavy sigh and even felt the man's relief. "The culprit's behind bars. Same guy screwed us both."

"Who the hell?"

"Name's Dirk Henderson."

A moment of silence elapsed, then John spoke in a puzzled voice. "Never heard of him."

"Doubt you would have. He'd turned double agent, knew about the formulae and wanted to sell them to other countries. Glad you stood strong on your dad's principles."

"I don't think I'd have weakened, but he sure applied the pressure."

"Speaking of your dad's work, I know someone in the Agency you can trust with the secret. But we'll talk about that later when you get your family home and settled."

"Thanks, Jim. How can I ever thank you?"

"Forgive your dad. He was a good man."

Another long sigh came over the wire, "I will. I promise."

"Oh, by the way, John, my name's Tom Casey now."

"Uh, oh yeah. Okay, Casey."

Hawkman hung up and looked at Jennifer. "Glad he called. I didn't have the vaguest idea how to reach him."

"I'm sure he's relieved and anxious to get back to a normal life."

Hawkman nodded. "Now, back to what I wanted to discuss with you. First of all, I found a perfect office in Medford to hang out my shingle." He raised his hands in mock interpretation, outlining a small sign. "Tom Casey, Private Investigator."

Jennifer's eyes lit up. "That's great. I'm eager to see it."

Then Hawkman's drummed his fingers on the kitchen bar, his gaze downcast.

"You don't seem too happy about the prospect of being an investigator."

"I guess I'm anticipating a let down after spending so many exciting years with the Agency."

She moved close to him and put an arms around his shoulders. "Perk up, it may turn out more challenging than you think. At least you'll be your own boss and be able to work in the field."

He smiled and turned toward her, putting his arms around her waist. "What I really need is your help in decorating my office. I'm not good at that type of thing."

"I'd love to. Now, tell me more about it. Where's it located?"

"It's in the Rogue Valley Mall in Medford, over a donut shop."

She shot a mischievous look at him and patted his stomach. "Uh oh, that could be dangerous to your figure."

"You're probably right." He rubbed the back of his neck. "Maybe I'll need someone to fix me good healthy lunches so I won't be tempted to pig out on donuts. You interested in that job?"

Jennifer laughed and looked into his face. "Are you asking me to be your chief cook and bottle washer?"

He stood and put a finger under her chin, lifting her face toward him. "No, I'm asking you to be my wife." He leaned forward and kissed her gently. "I love you, Jennifer. And have for a long time. I hope you care for me a little."

She started to say something, but Hawkman held up his hand. "And another thing. I've thought a lot about Sam. If you'll marry me, we'll be able to cinch the adoption plus I'd like trying my hand at being a dad." He stepped back. "Well, what do you say?"

Happy tears welled in her eyes and spilled down her cheeks. "You make a very convincing argument. Yes, I'll marry you."

He held her for several moments before pulling the small package from his pocket. "I have something for you."

She stepped back and wiped the moisture from her cheeks. Her eyes glistened when she snapped open the box. "Oh, Hawkman, it's beautiful."

He slipped the engagement ring onto her finger and kissed her. "I love you Jennifer. More than you'll ever know."

She couldn't stop crying.

⋅⟨⊹⟩⋅⟨⊹⟩⋅⟨⊹⟩⋅⟨⊹⟩⋅⟨⊹⟩⋅

Shortly thereafter, the Jordan's returned with Sam. His eyes sparkled with excitement as he bounded out of the truck and ran into the house. "Jennifer! Jennifer!" He grabbed her hand and pulled her outside. "Just wait till you see all the new things the Jordan's bought me."

He stopped abruptly and stared. "Is that really you, Hawkman?"

"Yep."

"Wow! Do you look different."

Mr. and Mrs. Jordan walked in the door, their arms laden with boxes.

Sam grabbed Hawkman's hand, without taking his eyes off his face "There's more stuff to carry in. You wanna help?"

"Sure."

Jennifer walked out with them and pulled the boy aside, putting her arm around his shoulders. "I've got some good news I want to share. Hawkman and I are going to get married. I think he'll make a great new dad for you."

Sam's face broke into a wide grin as he beamed with approval.

⋅⟨⊹⟩⋅⟨⊹⟩⋅⟨⊹⟩⋅⟨⊹⟩⋅⟨⊹⟩⋅

After the cold winter months passed, the trees unfolded with new growth glistening in the sunshine and bird songs filled the air. Ossy flew to his favorite perch and whistled his greeting, cocking his head back and forth.

He stared down at the dock where his favorite human sat fishing, but now a big black furry animal lay at her feet. She glanced up and waved, the sun's rays glinted off the finger of her left hand.

While he waited for her whistle, the big furry animal stood, stretched and gave a friendly bark. Ossy watched him trot up the ramp and run across the open lot to the road. Shortly the big yellow school bus appeared and the animal's constant companion jumped out. The two came running home.

Soon the familiar 4X4 bumped across the bridge and drove into the driveway. Within a few minutes, the big human with the eye-patch came out the back door carrying a hawk on his arm. Ossy puffed out his white chest and let forth a barrage of whistles. The big man, strolled down the ramp with the boy and the furry animal close behind.

Suddenly, Ossy jerked his head around when he heard the familiar whistle. He leaned forward, waiting until she threw the fish high in the air. Then he lifted from the branch.

THE END